CUPID'S MATCH

LAUREN PALPHREYMAN

PENGUIN BOOKS

PENGUIN BOOKS

UK | USA | Canada | Ireland | Australia
India | New Zealand | South Africa

Penguin Books is part of the Penguin Random House group of companies
whose addresses can be found at global.penguinrandomhouse.com.

www.penguin.co.uk   www.puffin.co.uk   www.ladybird.co.uk

Published in Great Britain by Penguin Books in association
with Wattpad Books, a division of Wattpad Corp., 2019

001

wattpad books

www.wattpad.com

Printed and bound in Great Britain by Clays Ltd, Elcograf S.p.A.

A CIP catalogue record for this book is available from the British Library

ISBN: 978–0–241–43889–3

All correspondence to:
Penguin Books
Penguin Random House Children's
80 Strand, London WC2R 0RL

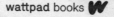

MIX
Paper from
responsible sources
FSC® C018179

Penguin Random House is committed to a
sustainable future for our business, our readers
and our planet. This book is made from Forest
Stewardship Council® certified paper.

Dear Lila,

I am contacting you on behalf of the Cupids
Matchmaking Service.
 You will not have heard of us but we are an organiza-
tion that works behind the scenes of society, identifying
each person's perfect match.
 Usually, we do not contact our clients. We prefer to
work in secrecy—setting up ideal environments for our
matches to have a chance encounter.
 Recently, however, we ran your details through our
system and . . . well . . . in your case. . . .
 We think you'd better come in.
 Please respond at your earliest convenience.

Yours Urgently,
The Cupids Matchmaking Service

1

The Cupids Matchmaking Service is written in elegant calligraphy above the glass shop front. A sign reading "Not Taking New Clients at This Time" is taped to the door.

"That place never takes anyone new on," a girl remarks to her friend as they pass by with shopping bags.

I frown as I look up at the towering building, shielding my eyes from the sun with the stack of letters in my hand. *I can't believe I'm actually here.*

When I couldn't find information online, I'd assumed the dating agency would be small. I didn't expect a skyscraper with gilt window frames and cherubs carved into the white stone walls. I feel out of place. I can't imagine anyone in battered Converse, skinny jeans, and a leather jacket has passed through its doors before.

But then, it's not like I wanted to spend the last day of summer break on the bus to Los Angeles. And, if anyone in this huge building had bothered to answer the phone, I wouldn't have had to.

I push open the glass door. A bell tinkles as I step inside.

Shiny white tiles cover the floor and several stylish neon-colored armchairs surround a large coffee table boasting a range of fanned-out fashion magazines. On the opposite side of the room stands a high, stone reception desk where a blond in a crisp white suit chatters into a headset. Above her, hanging by wires from the ceiling, is a long, golden arrow.

Something glinting on the wall catches my eye. It's a plaque that says *Making Matches for 3,000 Years.*

Shaking my head incredulously, I march over and dump the stack of letters onto the desk. The blond looks up, startled. A name badge reading *Crystal* is pinned to the pocket of her white suit jacket.

"Can I call you back?" she says into her headset. "Something's just come up."

Her blue eyes look me up and down. Suddenly, I am aware of how I must look; she is immaculate, not a hair out of place, and here I am, having spent an hour and a half on the ripe-smelling bus from Forever Falls. I catch sight of my dark, tangled hair in the reflective surface of a glass door. I could be her polar opposite.

"I'm sorry," she chimes, "we're not taking on any new clients at this time."

She fiddles with her headset and I realize she is about to continue her conversation. A wave of irritation washes over me.

"I'm not here to become a client, I'm here to tell you to *stop bugging me.*"

She looks back at me, confused. "Excuse me?"

I gesture toward the five letters scattered across the reception desk.

"All summer you've been spamming me with letters, text messages, emails," I say. "I am *not* interested in your services. I don't know how you have my personal details, but you need to remove me from your mailing lists. I *have* a boyfriend already, thanks very much."

I turn on my heel and march toward the exit.

"Wait."

Her voice is lower, more assertive than before. Urgent, even.

I spin back around.

"You say we have been trying to contact you?"

I nod slowly.

She frowns. "Well, that is most . . . irregular." With a manicured hand she picks up one of the letters I've dumped unceremoniously on her desk. "We don't contact our clients, ever. It's against our—"

"Privacy laws?" I shrug. "Whatever. Just don't contact me again. Okay?"

I'm about to turn and leave again when she stands up abruptly.

"No!" she says, her voice higher pitched now. "Please!" As if suddenly realizing the weirdness of her behavior, she sits back down with a robotic smile. "Just let me run your name through the computer, find out what has occurred here. Then we can remove you from our database. Yes?"

I sigh. "Fine."

Relief washes over her face as I walk back to the imposing reception desk.

"Name?"

"Lila Black."

Her long nails click on the keyboard as she enters my name. She waits a few moments. Then she frowns and hurriedly types something else. As she stares at the screen, all the blood drains from her face. A mask of surprise replaces her faux smile. There's another emotion there too.

Fear?

"Miss Black, we have a *big* problem. You have been matched with"—she stops and bites her lip—"I think . . . I think one of our agents is best suited to fill you in on the situation. Please take a seat. *I will send someone out right away.*"

"I really—"

The receptionist raises one hand, signaling me to be quiet, while pressing a white button on the intercom beside her. A few moments later a muffled male voice sounds through the small speaker.

"What is it, Crystal?" He sounds disgruntled.

"Cal," she chimes, "I need you to come through to reception right away."

"You know the line, Crystal," he snaps. "We're not taking on any new clients at this time."

She coughs, a little embarrassed, then quickly slips off her headset and picks up the receiver. "It's not that," she whispers. "Look, you just really need to come out here."

There's more muttering on the other end before Crystal places the phone back down. The robotic smile reappears.

"One of our agents will be with you momentarily."

I'm about to argue that I don't want to see an agent, I just want them to stop contacting me, when the frosted-glass door beside reception swings open to reveal a young man I can only presume is Cal.

He is as beautiful as Crystal, with well-groomed blond hair and sharp silver eyes. He wears a crisp white suit even though he looks like he could be around my age, seventeen. He's definitely attractive, if you like that sort of thing; he's a bit too clean cut for my taste.

His eyes sweep over Crystal, irritated, before settling on me. "I'm sorry," he says, his voice laced with disdain, "we're not taking on any new clients at this time."

"Yes, I get the picture," I say through gritted teeth, "but I'm not here to become a client. I'm here to tell you to stop contacting me."

"You *do* need to see this, Cal," Crystal says.

He exhales sharply through his nose then makes his way over to the desk, leaning over Crystal to read whatever is on the screen. His eyes darken. Shock flickers across his angular features. Then he regains his cold composure.

"So, you're the girl," he says. "Of all the girls in the world, *you're* his Match. I must admit, you're not what I expected. Now, please come with me. We have something very important to discuss. Your very life could be at—"

Crystal coughs and gives him a warning look.

He sighs. "Please come with me, Miss Black. I'll explain everything." He spins back around and heads through the glass door.

For a moment I consider just walking out, despite Crystal's encouraging nod. But my best friend, Charlie, isn't back from her journalism camp yet, and James, my boyfriend, has a shift at the diner all day. So it's either this or sit at home with no promises that the Cupids Matchmaking Service will stop contacting me.

Plus, I hate to admit it, but I am kind of curious about who exactly they think I've been "matched" with.

"Fine," I say. "But for the record, this is seriously weird."

I walk to the door, swing it open, and step inside.

2

Beyond the door is an immensely hectic, open-plan office.

It's predominantly white—like the reception area—but with black classical columns that reach up to the high ceiling and a left wall that has been turned into a collage of faces, names, and places linked together with pieces of pink string. Through an arched door in the far wall, I can just make out a weathered stone statue of a woman draped in a toga in the room beyond.

People in white suits rush around babbling into headsets. I can't help but notice that everyone who works here is stunningly attractive, as though they made being good looking a job requirement.

Cal strides through them, looking over his shoulder only once as I follow him between the rows of computers, maneuvering around people who don't seem to care whether we knock shoulders. *It looks more like a stock-trading floor than a dating service.*

As we walk forward, I notice a number of wall monitors looping through a stream of different images. "Top Ten Undesirables" suddenly flashes across one of the screens, followed by a mug shot of a guy with penetrating eyes. But before I can focus properly on the rest, the image fades into darkness.

Cal opens the door to a glass-walled office and gestures that I go inside. "Take a seat, Miss Black," he says, his tone of voice still cold.

I glare at him as I sit down in a quaint red armchair.

He closes the door, grabs a black envelope from a filing cabinet against the wall, then takes a seat behind the desk. He sighs heavily, making him seem older than on first impression. In fact, his whole demeanor makes him seem more grown up; there's a cool confidence in the way he maintains eye contact, and I don't think I've ever seen a teenager sit so upright in a chair before.

"You're not what I was expecting," he says while opening the envelope.

"Yes, you said. Now are you going to tell me what I'm doing here?"

Cal slides a piece of paper out of the black packet and scans it. "We recently ran your details through our system," he says, "and you were matched with someone we did not expect to see matched with anyone."

I shake my head. "Why would you run my details through your system? Why do you even *have* my details?"

Cal smiles coolly. "We have *everyone's* details, but that is not the issue here."

"Well, can you tell me what the issue *is*?"

His eyes flash an icy silver. "It's a difficult situation. I risk breaking our . . . our laws by telling you what I'm about to tell you."

"Have a lot of dating-club laws, do you?"

Cal ignores me and takes a deep breath. "We are . . . cupids," he says, running a hand through his perfect blond hair. "We match people. We have done so for many centuries. But we do not dabble with love ourselves. It is too dangerous. Many years ago, one of our own went off the rails. Dabbled with human affairs, human hearts. Obsessed over human women and made them obsess over him. He became very dangerous. His power grew, his ideology became extreme. And we banished him from our organization. Forever."

I stare at him. "Is this some kind of joke?"

Cal shakes his head slowly. "Unfortunately not, Miss Black."

I sit a little straighter in the armchair, my gaze sliding to the busy open-plan space outside Cal's office as I calculate how long it would take me to get back to the exit.

"Okay, *Cal,* that's great." I keep my voice as even as possible and force my lips into what I hope is a reassuring smile. Charlie's going to love this when I tell her. She'll probably want to put it in her blog: "Dating Service Thinks It's Run by Cupids!"

From the way Cal's brow furrows, my acting may not be as good as I thought.

"So, what has this got to do with me?" I ask, continuing to play along.

Cal stares at me, then takes another deep breath. "Recently, for the first time in cupid history, he was matched with someone." He shakes his head. "He shouldn't even be in the system. He *definitely* shouldn't have a match. It's dangerous. And if he finds out . . ." Cal pauses but doesn't remove his gaze from my face. "Miss Black, he will do anything to get what he wants. He is the original. The most powerful of us all. He is Cupid himself. And he has been matched . . . with you."

Neither of us speaks for a moment. Then I laugh—I can't help myself. Cal merely stares at me, his cold eyes unreadable.

"You're telling me that my match is Cupid?" I say. "Cupid?! As in the little guy with wings and a bow and arrow?"

For a moment I wonder if I've been brought onto a reality TV show. I risk another glance at the busy office, half expecting a camera crew, but all I see is a stream of white suits and another glimpse of the stone statue beyond the archway.

Cal slowly slides the piece of paper he's been holding across the desk. "No," he says. "*This* is Cupid."

I take the glossy sheet. It's a black-and-white head shot of a guy with ruffled hair and eyes that seem to pierce my own, even from the page. Although he could be the same age as Cal, there is something more mature about his features; his jawline is squarer and his shoulders broader. His lips are curled into a mischievous smirk and he has a cute chin dimple that softens his ruggedness with boyish charm.

There is no denying he is good looking—the page could have been ripped from a menswear magazine—but there's also something familiar about him.

"You're telling me *this* is Cupid?"

I return my gaze to Cal, who looks disappointed.

"Your pupils dilated," he says, staring at my face in unnerving fashion. "You find him attractive."

"That's a pretty weird thing to say."

A flicker of confusion crosses his face, as though usually people love it when he tells them about their dilated pupils. I throw the photograph back onto the desk and look him directly in the eye.

"I have a boyfriend. I've already told you that."

I wonder momentarily what James would think about me coming here in the first place. I didn't tell him. He's been so busy working over summer that we've not had time to hang out much lately.

Cal looks exasperated. "Yes, but your boyfriend is not your match. His match is . . ."—he stops himself—". . . someone else," he finishes, ignoring my dirty look. "*You* have been matched with Cupid."

I look back at the head shot. Then suddenly it clicks where I've seen "Cupid's" face before. "This is the picture I saw on the screen out there. One of the Top Ten Undesirables." *Whatever that means.*

Cal nods darkly. "The number one undesirable."

I blink. Then I bring back my weird smile.

"Riiight, okay. Well, thank you, Cal. This has been very . . . informative." Hands on the chair's red armrests, I slowly lift myself out of the seat. "Now, I'm just gonna . . . you know . . . *go.*"

"Please sit down, Lila Black," says Cal. "And stop smiling like that. It's quite unnerving."

"*I'm* unnerving *you*? Seriously, what is this? Are you trying to con me out of money or something?"

Cal exhales and pinches the bridge of his nose.

"You don't believe me. You don't believe anything I'm saying."

"Of course I don't!"

He stares at me. "But you *need* to. You are in danger. He *will* come after you."

Suddenly he reaches out to his computer monitor and switches it on with a long slender finger. He has musician's hands, I observe, then shake the random thought off as he hurriedly types something on his keyboard. And after a few moments of silence, a look of satisfaction creeps onto his face.

"I have something to show you, something that will make you believe in cupids."

He grabs a scrap of paper and scribbles down a sequence of numbers. Then he abruptly stands, triumph glinting in his cool eyes.

"Follow me, Miss Black. You're going to want to see this."

3

I don't move. Cal pauses, eyes holding mine.

"If you still don't believe me after what I'm about to show you, we'll stop sending the letters," he says.

"And emails. And Messages."

"I will see to it myself. Personally."

I exhale. "You'd better . . ."

He inclines his head sharply, then spins on his heel to lead me through the chaotic office and into the indoor courtyard beyond the arch, where the statue I noticed earlier overlooks a stone-rimmed pond. The water is so clear that it reflects a perfect mirror image of the summer sky shining in through a skylight. Ivy creeps up the high walls and trails over the three other archways. The scent permeating the air is a strange mixture of old and sweet, like flowers in a museum.

It's beautiful and still—a stark contrast to the bustling office we have just left behind.

Cal pauses to give the stone statue an odd look I can't quite read before quickly striding across the courtyard to one of the arches on the other side. It might just be my imagination, but he seems to put as much space between himself and the toga-wearing woman as possible.

The statue is clearly ancient, its face worn and its body chipped. Any recognizable features have been eroded. There's something unnerving about her blank eyes, so I let my gaze wander down to her podium, where something's been carved—a list, although the only line I can make out is: "No cupid must ever be matched."

"Miss Black," Cal says sharply. "I haven't got all day."

I look at him as seriously as I can. "Yes, being a cupid must be very busy work."

He looks at me coldly. Then, as he disappears beneath the ivy-covered arch, I hear him mutter, "Should have known *his* match would have an attitude problem."

We enter a long corridor that employs the same chiaroscuro color scheme as the office. Dimly lit by faux candle lamps, it's lined by closed doors and wallpaper with jet-black swirls. Cal heads to the door at the very end, his footsteps echoing against the white linoleum. I walk behind him and we enter the room.

I blink a couple of times as my eyes adjust to my surroundings.

We're in a huge, dark space. Artificial beams of light cut through the darkness, causing pools of white to collect on the black floor tiles. A vast screen surrounded by hundreds of smaller monitors dominates the opposite wall. On each small screen I can see a variety of different people going about their daily busi-ness—having coffee at a street cafe, eating ice cream in the park, waiting at the checkout line in Walmart, and some even sleeping in their beds.

The whole place smells like warm electricity—that overheating-computer smell that reminds me of Dad's old office before he was let go.

Cal walks over to a black control desk in the center of the room that has a joystick, a keyboard, and a range of red and amber buttons. He clicks something and the screens fade into darkness.

"Who *are* all these people?" I ask. "Do they know you're watching them? You're a *dating service*, not the freaking CIA."

Cal doesn't look at me. He types something into the keyboard and a serial number appears in the middle of the central screen.

"Hey," I say, frowning. "You haven't answered my questions."

"We're *not* a dating service. We're cupids. How many times must I tell you?" He looks at me, and even in the near-darkness his eyes blaze silver. "Monitoring our clients is necessary when setting up a match. We use advanced statistical algorithms to ensure our clients end up in the right place, at the right time. But unfortunately, statistics cannot always predict human behavior. Manual interference is sometimes required. Now," he says, looking at the screen once more, "I'm about to show you something a little shocking. Something that you may not be prepared to see. But I have little choice."

Before I can protest, he clicks Enter and a crowded scene materializes on the largest monitor. When he clicks another button, the screen zooms in on a person who's halfway through a laugh. I inhale sharply and feel a sudden jolt in my heart.

Bright eyes, dimpled cheeks; I'd recognize that face anywhere.

It's my mother.

But how?

My mother died two years ago.

Cal presses a button and the image pauses. I can't stop staring at the woman. It's my mother, there's no question, though on closer inspection she's younger than she was when she died. A teenager.

I glare at Cal. "*What is this*?" I'm no longer finding this situation remotely amusing.

Cal's gaze moves away from the monitor, his cold eyes softening momentarily before he becomes stone faced once more. "I'm sorry for your loss."

I don't say anything, my attention fixed to the image of my mother. She looks beautiful and carefree, with her strawberry blond hair long and her green eyes sparkling. This was before the cancer diagnosis—before the battle she was forced to fight, before her hair thinned and her eyes lost their brightness. This was before I was born, before I loved her, before she was gone forever.

I feel a tightening in my throat.

"Do you know how your parents met?" asks Cal.

Part of me wants to leave. Part of me wants to grab Cal and slam him into the wall until he feels a fraction of the pain he's just forced upon me. I feel the buildup of violence inside of me that I've been trying to suppress ever since she left us on our own. I grasp for the breathing exercise the school counselor made me learn after I shoved someone who made a comment about my mom into a locker.

Breathe in. Count to four. Breathe out. Count to eight.

I can't just walk away from this recording of my mother.

I need to know why he has this.

I swallow my anger and calm my nerves. "They met at a bowling alley. The person behind the counter got their shoes mixed up."

He nods, then presses another button on the control desk. The image zooms out and the recording begins to play.

It's a bowling alley.

I watch as my mother gracefully approaches the counter, then gently slips off her bowling shoes and places them on the surface. An attendant in a striped uniform and baseball cap marked *Castle Tenpin Bowling* takes them from her and swaps them with a pair of shoes in one of the cubbyholes behind him. I can't see his face as he places a pair of men's shoes on the countertop.

She looks confused for a moment then throws her head back in laughter. Farther down the counter, a dorky-looking man with dark hair and gray eyes is clasping a pair of stilettos.

It's my father.

He approaches her. The sound is muted, so I can't hear what is being said, but I can tell my dad has just told one of his lame jokes; my mom's face lights up the way it always did when he tried to be funny.

They swap shoes.

Cal pauses the screen.

I look up at him weakly, not wanting the recording to stop. "How do you have this?" I ask. "Why are you showing it to me?"

He doesn't say anything, only turns back to the control desk and moves the joystick to the left. After the recording rewinds, he pushes the stick forward so the monitor zooms in on the bowling alley attendant as he bends over the cubbyholes. I start as I see him swap the shoes around.

"Wait, did he do that on purpose?"

Cal fast-forwards the recording and I watch my parents meet again in triple time. Then he again pauses and zooms back in on the attendant. I take a step backward in cold shock.

I can now see the face below the striped baseball cap.

This video must have been taken thirty years ago, but he looks the same as he does now—around seventeen years old, with sharp eyes, blond hair, and smooth skin.

It's Cal.

4

Five minutes later we're back in Cal's office. Neither of us has spoken. I sit in the red armchair, clasping my hands together so tightly that my fingers have started to turn white.

"You matched my parents," I say after a while.

Cal nods, then looks at me curiously. "You're upset."

I shrug. I don't really know how to feel.

"Tea?"

He abruptly stands and makes his way to the corner of the room, where he fiddles about with an old plastic kettle on top of the file cabinet. I watch as it clicks and he pours the steaming water into a chipped mug.

He carries it over. *World's Best Boyfriend* is written across the front.

"Who gave you this?" I ask, distracted, as I take it from his hands. "I thought cupids didn't fall in love. You didn't buy it for yourself, did you?"

Cal looks bashful for a moment before shaking his head and taking a seat in his swivel chair. "Long story."

I bring the mug to my lips; the warm liquid smells sweet, like my grandmother's herb garden in the summer.

"Chamomile and lavender," says Cal. "Soothes the nerves."

I take a sip and it does actually make me feel a little better.

"Do you believe me now?" he asks.

I set the mug down on the desk beside the photograph of Cupid. "Say I do believe you. Say that I take the video you just showed me as the real thing. . . . What does that even mean?" I glance at the ruggedly handsome portrait. "Even if it *is* true that this *superbad paranormal being* is my match, I have no interest in being with him. I *have* a boyfriend. His name is James—we've been together for almost a year now. And—"

The office door opens to reveal a tall guy with curly black hair standing in the doorway.

"What is it, Curtis?" Cal asks pointedly. "We're in the middle of something here."

"You told me to report to you immediately with anything regarding the"—he darts a sideways look at me then lowers his voice—"*assignment*."

Cal leans forward in his chair and clasps his slender hands together. "Well? Did you find it?"

"Not yet. But the archives are huge." Curtis steps into the office and closes the door behind him. "If I could have more resources . . ."

"I've told you—I don't want anyone else knowing I'm looking for it."

Curtis places a palm flat on the desk, seriously invading my personal space, and leans closer to Cal. He glances at me again.

I roll my eyes as I grab the mug of tea and shift back in the armchair. Like I care what they're being so sneaky about. They've already told me about Cupid. Maybe they're looking for the Easter Bunny too.

"Right," he says, voice low. "Because you think people might question your . . . loyalties."

Cal's expression hardens. "Need I remind you who you're speaking to?"

Curtis stares at him a moment longer. Then he exhales and takes a step back in clear submission. "Sorry. Of course. I'll let you know when we find its location." His eyes slide over me one more time as he moves to the exit. "Is this the girl?"

"Yes."

"She's not what I expected."

I glare at him as the door swings shut behind him, and accidentally slosh a bit of hot tea onto my jeans. I curse under my breath.

"Curtis is . . . he's undertaking a . . . a task for me," Cal says in rare ineloquence.

I put the chipped mug down on the desk, and Cal stiffens. His eyes flit to the glass wall of his office.

"Yeah, I don't care." I glance at the picture of "Cupid" on the desk between us. "I was telling you that this whole thing is ridiculous. Because I have no interest in this guy. I'm perfectly happy in my relationship, thank you very much. And even if I was interested, I've never met this guy before. He could be anywhere in the world. How likely is it that our paths would even cross?"

Cal rubs the back of his neck awkwardly. "Yes," he says, "that is where we have a problem, Miss Black. In usual circumstances, we would have deleted your records from our database to ensure he would never find out about this. And we did. But that was not before a slight, er, administrative error was made."

I stare at him. "What administrative error?"

Cal fidgets in his swivel chair. "The path to the match was put into motion." He clasps his hands together on top of his desk. "Your high school?"

"Forever Falls High."

Cal nods and lets out a heavy sigh. "Yes, I thought so," he says. "Cupid starts there . . . tomorrow."

5

The sky is burnt orange when I get off the bus at the Forever Falls town square.

This place couldn't be more different than downtown L.A. There's hardly anything here other than a small convenience store, a florist, a thrift shop, and the town's only two hangout spots. My eyes drift over the dark alley that leads to the Love Shack—the "cooler" of the two—and focus instead on the run-down diner, Romeo's.

James will still be working.

Turning off the travel podcast that kept me company on the hour-and-a-half ride, I pull out my earphones and start to walk toward the restaurant.

I hadn't planned on seeing James today, but all the talk of cupids, banished love gods, and my boyfriend being matched with someone else has rattled me. Even if it *is* all ridiculous.

As I enter Romeo's I wave at Martha, one of the older waitresses, before slipping into my usual booth by the window, where

a half-drunk chocolate and peanut butter milk shake is still waiting to be bussed. It's Charlie's favorite.

"Not seen you in a while, honey," Martha says.

"Huh? Oh. Yeah . . ."

She leans over to clear the table and I'm hit by the abrasive
scent of floral perfume and disinfectant. "Usual?"

I smile. "Please. Is James—"

"I'll let him know you're here."

Her heels click against the chipped black and white floor tiles
as she heads past the booths to the kitchen. I glance at the security camera in the corner as she disappears from view.

After Cal told me about the "administrative error," he walked
me back to reception and told me he would be "monitoring
the situation." I think back to the room full of screens at the
Matchmaking Service.

"If you're watching me, Cal, cut it out," I whisper. Then I sigh
and lean back against the tattered red leather seat. "And now I'm
talking to myself. I'm clearly going mad."

"Lila!" James's voice makes me jump as he slides into the other
side of the booth. "Hey!"

I smile. James might not be model good looking like Cupid,
but he's definitely attractive—slightly taller than me, he's athletic
and lightly tanned, not to mention confident enough to pull off
wearing his pink and black Forever Falls soccer jersey beneath his
apron. He pushes a strawberry milk shake across the table.

"What are you doing here?" he asks. "You just missed Charlie."

I frown. "Charlie was here?"

"Yeah. She just got back from her journalist camp thing.
Marcus dropped her off while he went to the store. Her family's
having a welcome back meal, apparently." He runs a hand through

his light-brown hair and his forehead crumples at my expression. "She probably messaged you. The signal sucks in here, and the Wi-Fi's down again. You'll probably get it later."

"Yeah . . . probably."

I'm not quite sure why it bothers me to have not heard from her yet. The three of us have been friends since kindergarten—it's not weird she would stop by the diner without me.

I force a smile and James leans across the table and brushes his lips against mine. Something tenses in my stomach.

Your boyfriend is not your match.

He is matched with . . . someone else.

I pull away, shaking Cal's stupid words out of my head.

Maybe there was no big firework display when James and I got together, but he was there for me when I lost Mom, and we built something based on friendship and trust. *That's* realistic. *That's* the way it's supposed to be.

The idea of matching is ridiculous. There's more to relationships than compatibility statistics—or whatever Cal was talking about. And I certainly don't believe in soul mates.

"So—what you doing here? Missing me?" asks James. He grins. "Or you just here for the free drinks?"

I take a slurp of my milk shake. "Can't a girl can't come and visit her boyfriend at work without arousing suspicion?!"

"Of course! Just surprised. You haven't stopped by in a while. Your dad doing okay?"

I shrug. "Oh, you know. Ups and downs."

He gives me a sympathetic smile but doesn't push. Dad was let go from his accounting job a few months ago. He wasn't doing well after what happened to Mom. He hated that job, but being stuck at home hasn't been good for him.

"He said he'd make us pancakes for breakfast tomorrow, though," I say, brightening.

"That was you and your mom's thing, right? Pancakes on the first day of school?"

"Yeah. He forgot last year, but I think him bringing it up again means he's trying."

"Remember fifth grade, when Charlie and I stayed over the night before? We were almost late to school but your mom insisted we get our fill before dropping us off."

"You ate so many you had a stomachache all day."

"Yeah! And Charlie spilled syrup all down her new top."

I laugh even though it hurts a little to remember. "Yeah. Charlie was *not* pleased about that."

"So, what you been up to?" asks James.

Oh, you know—visited a supernatural dating agency, met the guy who matched my parents, and learned that Cupid is looking for me. My day has been way too weird to talk about so I shrug. "Nothing much."

The door to the diner opens and a noisy group of sophomores from the debate team come in.

"Jack's in luurrrrve!" one of them yells, slapping a short guy with black hair on the back as the five of them pile into a booth.

"James?" Martha calls from across the room as she precariously balances a pot of coffee and a pile of plates on her arms.

"On it!" He gets up and gives me an apologetic grin. "Duty calls. Stick around for a while?"

I glance at the security camera again and imagine Cal watching me. "I think I'll head back," I say, getting up.

James kisses me again before I go. This time I sink into his body as he wraps his arms around my waist. For a moment I allow myself to bask in his warmth and familiar light cologne, which is somehow only made more comforting by the notes of burger grease and peanut butter.

James is my boyfriend. I'm happy. And I don't need some weird dating agency to tell me otherwise.

I smile at him when I pull away, and this time it doesn't feel forced.

"See you at school tomorrow," I say.

On my way out I glare at the security camera in the corner of the room, imagining Cal watching me on the other side. I don't care if this mysterious Cupid guy is starting at school tomorrow.

I am *not* interested.

6

I get up early the next morning, ready for pancakes with Dad, and head downstairs to an empty kitchen. I call him, put the dirty plates littering the counter into the sink, and line up the batter ingredients.

Then I make myself an instant coffee in the chipped *You BOWL Me Over* mug Mom got Dad, before sitting at the table. As I sip the black liquid my disappointment grows.

Dad's not coming down. He's forgotten. Again.

I glance at the time on the microwave.

I consider waking him—there's still time. But then I exhale, gulp down the rest of my coffee, and get to my feet.

Whatever. It's no big deal. I wanted to catch up with Charlie before class anyway.

I grab my leather jacket from the coat stand in the hallway then head out to wait for the bus to school.

When I get there, I head straight to the IT classroom that doubles as the school's online newspaper office. Charlie's not here yet, and the space is empty except for a petite junior named Laura, who's huddled with two of her friends around one of the computers.

They're talking in hushed tones as I wheel a chair to Charlie's usual spot. It's facing a window overlooking the school courtyard, which is filled with flowers and picnic benches. She told me once that she can see *everything* that's going on from here—who's getting kissed, who's getting ignored, and who's worn the same outfit three days in a row. Her bright-pink notepad and an empty paper cup are already on the table by her keyboard. She must have gone to one of the vending machines.

"He's hardly even spoken to me before," Laura says, adjusting her mousey brown ponytail. "Not since he called me a nerd in fourth grade. And now he's leaving cards, flowers, chocolates . . . it makes no sense."

"I think it's sweet!" says her friend Lisa, eyes glinting beneath her dark bangs.

"Creepy, more like . . ." Rachel, her other friend, disagrees as she picks at a loose thread on her sleeve.

I pull out my phone and fiddle with it, realizing I'm oddly nervous at the prospect of Cupid starting at my school, even though I'm still not entirely convinced that this isn't part of some weird reality show.

I have a boyfriend anyway, I remind myself. *So who cares if he does start?*

Suddenly, the door bursts open. I turn to see Charlie hurtling past the computers, her jet-black hair flying behind her.

"Hot . . . there's . . . a . . . hot . . ." She stops to pant, bending over slightly with her hands on her knees as she composes herself. "Hot guy . . . starts today," she finally gasps before collapsing into the chair beside me. "I saw him . . . in the registration office . . . when I was getting . . . a breakfast bar . . ." She looks exceedingly pleased with herself for passing on this knowledge.

My stomach plummets. Cupid? It must be.

I feign a smile. "And you ran all the way from the vending machine to tell me this?"

She grins while switching on the computer monitor, and the school's student-run blog materializes. There's a tapping sound as her fingers dance across the keyboard. The words *Hot Guy Starts Today!* appear at the top of the blank article.

"To tell *everyone* about this!" she corrects.

I roll my eyes. "Yeah, Mr. Butler's going to love that . . ."

"Just giving the people what they want, Lila," she says.

I laugh. "How long do you think before he deletes this one? More or less time than your exposé on the teachers' night out at the Love Shack?!"

"Hey! He's just lucky I didn't write about how I saw him flirting with Ms. Green!" she says.

"Oh yes, you're very restrained!"

She grins. "Anyway, how was—" She stops talking abruptly, her dark-brown eyes widening on something above the screen. "Make that *two* new hot guys."

Frowning, I follow her gaze. My stomach jolts as I catch a flash of pale-blond hair pass by the window in front of us. I only see the back of his head, and he's traded his white suit for a pair of jeans and a blue and white checkered shirt, but I recognize him instantly.

It's Cal.

I watch as he strides past the picnic benches to the school entrance, a brown leather satchel over his shoulder.

What is he doing here?

". . . summer? Lila? Helloooooo?" Charlie says, waving her hand in front of my face.

"Huh?"

She raises her eyebrows. "What's wrong with you this morning? I asked how you managed to pass the dull, Charlie-less hours while I was at journalism camp."

"You wouldn't believe me if I told you. Just give me a second."

I stand up—ignoring Charlie's startled look—and make my way to the door. Cal's about thirty feet down the corridor, opening one of the lockers on the other side of a group of football players in black and pink Forever Falls jerseys. I stride out of the computer room and come to a halt just beside him.

"What are *you* doing here?" I ask in a low voice.

Cal doesn't look at me, eyes fixed on the inside of his locker. "It's best if you're not seen speaking with me."

"Yeah, that would be easier if you were back at your dating agency instead of here at my high school!"

Cal turns and looks straight at me. "I'm here to monitor the situation. I told you I would be doing that yesterday."

"Yes, but I didn't think you'd be *coming to my school!*"

Cal pulls up his bag and unpacks what seems to be the entire Back to School section of Walmart into his locker. "When Cupid arrives, you'll need my help."

I watch as he neatly arranges a calculator next to a brightly colored Avengers binder. It seems an odd choice for a stern, immortal matchmaker.

"You're a Marvel fan?" I ask.

He looks at me like I'm speaking another language. "What?"

I shake my head. "Never mind. Look, I'm *not* going to be interested in this Cupid guy, I've told you that!"

Cal looks at me stonily from beneath his thick eyelashes. "So you have," he says dismissively. "But if he finds out you're his Match, he will be *very* interested in you, and that's why I have a plan to keep his attention from you for as long as possible. Part of that involves you not speaking to me."

I swallow my growing irritation. "Fine. But do you think you might tell me what your plan is, exactly?"

Cal smiles coolly, tilting his head to the side. "I intend to befriend another female student here so that Cupid thinks I have been sent to protect *her*."

"Okaaay, but say this incredibly well-thought-out plan does work . . . aren't you just passing the danger on to one of my classmates?"

An unreadable expression flickers across Cal's angular features. "That's not how it works. *You* are his Match. You, alone, are in danger. No one else."

The bell rings for first class and more people begin to spill into the corridor. I turn my head, catching sight of Charlie in the doorway. She's talking to Laura but her eyes are on me.

Cal's not the only one who doesn't want to draw attention to this conversation. Charlie's going to have a million questions.

"Look, fine. But does Cupid even know that you work for the Matchmaking Service?" I hiss. "Because if he doesn't, this whole charade seems incredibly pointless."

A dark look crosses Cal's face. "Oh, me and Cupid go way back."

Before I can say anything else, he hands me a folded slip of paper, spins around, and shuts his locker.

I glare at the back of his head as he walks down the corridor. Then I quickly flatten out the note and read it, aware that I only have five seconds before Charlie swoops in with questions.

Meet me after school by the gym. If you are to resist his charms, you will need to undergo some serious training in the arts of the cupids. Don't be late. Cal.

I groan. I just wanted a nice, simple, drama-free semester. Instead, I seem to have acquired an irritating paranormal match-making agent, a match, and . . . training in the arts of the cupids?

7

"So," Charlie says as we head toward history, our first class of the day, "are you going to tell me what *that* was all about? Do you know that guy?"

I shrug, feeling the cryptic message through my jeans pocket. "Not really."

I don't want to tell her about yesterday. Charlie loves relationship drama, and she'll be unbearable if she thinks there's even the slightest chance it's true I've been supernaturally matched with someone other than James—especially if that someone else is hot enough for her to sprint across the school to spread news of his arrival.

She just looks at me expectantly.

"Nice dress," I say, attempting an innocent smile. The dress does look good on her; it's a flowing pastel-pink number that complements her dark skin.

She rolls her eyes but I can tell she is pleased; I'm sure she bought it especially for first day back at school.

"Don't change the subject! You haven't, like, *made out* with him or something, have you?" she asks sternly, but her eyes are twinkling.

I can't help but laugh. *Make out with Cal? I don't think so!*

"No!" I say. "What were you and Laura talking about, anyway?"

It's another attempt to change the subject, but this time it works. Her dark eyes brighten the way they always do when she has a bit of gossip.

"Apparently Jack—you know that guy from the debate team?—has been seriously crushing on her for the last few weeks," she says. "Like, out of nowhere. They've never hung out at all. But *anyway*, about this new mystery guy . . ."

As we approach the history classroom, I spot James through the window. He waves at us from a desk in the middle of the classroom.

"Leave it now," I say. "I don't want James getting the wrong idea."

"Fine," Charlie says. "But this is *not* over!"

James gestures at the two spare desks behind him and I smile as we make our way over. He stands up and gives me a light kiss on the lips, wrapping his arms around my waist, before I settle down at the desk.

"Hey, I've been thinking," he says. "It's been almost a year since we started dating. We should do something. Remember that time we went surfing at Venice Beach?"

Cal's words suddenly wash over me again. *Your boyfriend is not your match.* I shake it off. "Yeah. Sounds fun—even though you're terrible at it."

"Pfft. I only fell off because I didn't want to show you up with my mad skills."

"Fell off? Funny, I don't seem to remember you actually man-
aging to get *on* the board!" I tease.

"You'll see! I'll make you eat your words, Lila Black!"

He grins then turns back to continue a conversation with one
of his friends. Charlie leans toward me and gestures at Cal.

"Your lover boy is *all over* Chloe."

"Shh!" I hiss, but I follow her gaze. Cal is talking animatedly
to one of the girls from the hockey team. This must be step one of
his ingenious plan to distract Cupid.

I feel an unbidden stab of annoyance when I recall Cal's surprise that *I* could possibly be the match for the original cupid.
Cal's been nothing but rude to me, but apparently Chloe's *believ-
able* match material.

I'm uncertain why Cal's actions have bothered me. I don't
want to be thought of as Cupid's Match—not by Cupid, not by
Cal, not by anyone. *Get a grip, Lila,* I think, tearing my gaze away
just in time to see the classroom door open.

My breath catches in my throat. The whole room goes quiet.

He's wearing a black leather jacket over a gray cotton T-shirt
that clings to his hard stomach. He has an arm slung around
Kelly, one of Charlie's friends from the party-planning committee, and she's laughing hysterically at something he's said. He is
tall and broad, with dark-blond just-got-out-of-bed hair. His eyes
glint with mischief.

The black-and-white photograph didn't even come close to
capturing his beauty.

His gaze falls on me. A dangerous half smile curls onto his
face and my stomach clenches. But then his gaze slides to Cal.
An immediate flicker of recognition sparks in his eyes, but not
surprise.

Cal's shoulders have tensed, his posture even more rigid now than it was when I first met him. They tense farther when Cupid's eyes move to Chloe.

Cupid grins wickedly, and I exhale, not even aware that I'd been holding my breath. *Has Cal's plan worked? Does he think she's his Match?*

Charlie leans over to my desk. "Told you he was hot! I heard he was expelled from his old school. Moved to Forever Falls halfway through summer and he's already dated half of our year."

"Sounds like an ass."

"A hot ass," she agrees seriously.

Cupid throws himself into a seat near the front and Kelly skips off to sit with her friends. I have to fight to keep from staring—my eyes feel helplessly drawn to him.

You're just curious because of what Cal's told you. You have a boyfriend, I remind myself. *And Cupid's not your match, because there's no such thing as matching. The whole thing is ludicrous.*

I pull out a notebook as Ms. Green walks into the room, high heels clicking against the linoleum.

"Welcome, class. Hope you all had a good summer and are ready to *study* this year." Her tone is pointed as she meets my eyes over her thick-rimmed spectacles. She had me for geography last year and became increasingly frustrated that I wasn't reaching my potential in what was once my favorite subject.

As she smooths her short, graying hair and sits behind her desk, Cupid glances over his shoulder to see who she looked at. The corner of his lip tugs up. I look resolutely down at my notebook as Ms. Green calls roll. She arches an eyebrow when she reaches Cal's name.

"Cal Smith. You're new?" she says.

"Yes, ma'am."

She inclines her head and looks back at her screen, continuing to reel off names in a monotone. Both her eyebrows lift above her spectacles when she calls Cupid's.

"Cupid? Cupid Bellator?"

"Here," he says, giving her a half wave before leaning back in his seat and stretching his legs out in front of him.

A number of people laugh, while James leans over and murmurs, "Is this guy for real?"

Unfortunately.

Ms. Green looks momentarily confused. "Very well . . . um, Cupid," she says. "Two new students joining us this year. How exciting. Well, class, I hope you will make them both feel very welcome."

When she's done, she smooths her pencil skirt and approaches the blackboard to write *Classics and Ancient History* across it.

"This semester we will be exploring the ancient world—the gods and goddesses, the wars, the art, and the people. To start, let's get inspired by our friend Cupid, here." She beams at him. "Can anyone tell me the name of the ancient Roman goddess of love?"

Charlie leans over to my desk again. "She's totally crushing on him."

I roll my eyes. "Gross."

"I've heard he's called Cupid because of his reputation with the ladies."

If only she knew the truth—well, the truth according to Cal, anyway.

"You said he got expelled from his old school?" I ask, wondering whether that was just a cover story. It must be; it seems unlikely that an age-old paranormal being would attend high school under normal circumstances. Charlie is about to respond when Ms. Green makes her standard "I'm annoyed at being interrupted" throat-clearing sound.

"I was going to ask for volunteers to act as mentors for our new students, to make sure they know where everything is," she says, staring at us. "But as you two are already such chatterboxes today, I don't need to. Charlie, you will look after Cal," she says, then turns to me.

Cupid swivels around to look me in the eye once more, clearly amused. I breathe in sharply. I already know what Ms. Green is going to say.

"Lila, you will be matched with Cupid."

8

Charlie doesn't seem too bothered about her new job as mentor; as soon as the bell rings, she skips over to Cal, who, incidentally, spent the rest of the lesson firing dirty looks my way. He now looks bored as my friend tries to engage him in conversation about the Welcome Back dance she's helping plan for next Friday.

I hurriedly pack up my things, hoping to sneak off without having to deal with Cupid. "I'll see you at lunch," I whisper to James.

"Not wanting to escort the 'love god' around school?"

"You know me too well."

I dodge swiftly around my classmates, trying not to catch Ms. Green's attention as she concentrates on lesson planning. Finally, I reach the exit and look back. Cupid is still watching me with that same amused smile, which turns into a wicked grin when I give him my best innocent eyes. He coughs loudly.

Ms. Green looks up from her desk.

"Lila," she says sharply, "make sure you take Cupid to his next lesson. English, I believe."

"I'm sure we can both find our own way around," Cal protests.

"Speak for yourself," Cupid says. "I think I'd prefer *Lila* to take me."

His accent is different—American with a slight British edge that makes me think he's spent some time in England. He says my name as though he likes the feel of it on his tongue, and it makes me uncomfortable. It feels too familiar, too personal. His blue-green eyes are twinkling violently.

"Come on, then," I say, making my way out of the door. I don't look back to see if he's following, but I know that he is.

"So, *Lila*," he says as we step outside.

He pauses and I stop to look up at him. There's something almost angelic about his features. The artificial light in the corridor—harsh and unflattering on everyone else—gives his fair skin a faint glow. He smells like summer—like grass stains and honey and a light floral fabric softener. I can feel the heat radiating from his body as he stands closer to me than appropriate.

But, weirdly, I don't step away. It is intoxicating. I want to be closer to him, to drink him in, to reach out and touch him despite myself. He makes me feel tiny—the top of my head barely reaches his shoulder—and I remember what Cal said back in the Cupids Matchmaking Service. *He dabbled with human affairs, human hearts. Obsessed over women and made them obsess over him.* I shiver involuntarily.

He grins. "Your teacher seems to think you should give me *everything* I need."

For a second I feel the way a fly must feel when it's caught in a spider's web. *What the hell is wrong with me?* Then I blink and pull myself together and set off down the corridor.

"Sure. As long as what you *want* is to get to English class without severely annoying me."

Cupid shrugs, falling into step beside me. "I suppose I could do that," he says. "You have English too?"

I shake my head, not really wanting to continue the conversation. He takes long strides and I have to pick up my pace as we walk outside to cut through the small square courtyard at the heart of the school. The fall sun coats the picnic benches with warm light.

"You were talking all the way through history," he goes on. "Legends not your thing, huh?"

"No," I say, looking him in the face. "Not really. I'm not one for fairy tales. I prefer the present, not relics from the past."

He grins again. "I think you should give myths a chance. There may be more to them than you think."

"I highly doubt that."

As we approach the doorway on the other side of the courtyard, Cupid stops. "That other new guy didn't seem to want me to have a mentor. I wonder why that is."

He shoots me a sly look, and I wonder if Cal has unintentionally given away that I'm Cupid's Match. Wouldn't it be ironic if the thing that alerted Cupid he was on the right path to the Match was Cal being here in the first place? I knew from the start it was a dumb plan.

"Didn't notice. Do *you* know the other new guy?" I ask, deciding to play his game. "It seemed like you did."

Cupid smirks but doesn't say anything as we reenter the school. As we walk through into another locker-lined corridor, a couple of the females shoot not-so-subtle admiring looks at him, which Cupid not-so-subtly notices.

"The girl he was talking to," he says, ignoring my question. "What's her name?"

"Chloe."

His eyes darken as we stop outside his classroom. "Chloe. I should probably get to know her a bit better." He looks at me, eyes slightly narrowed, as though trying to gauge a reaction. *He's not going to get one.*

I smile. "Sounds like you've been *getting to know* quite a few girls from here already."

He laughs a low, musical laugh that attracts a few more admiring glances. "What can I say? I'm a friendly guy." He opens his leather jacket and pulls a scrap of paper from an inside pocket. "Got a pen?"

I raise an eyebrow. "You came to school without a pen?"

His eyes glint. "I'm not on a quest for knowledge. I'm here for something much more interesting."

The way he says it makes my heart thud hard against my chest; for a moment I am sure he can hear it.

He's here for me.

Then I roll my eyes and swing my backpack in front of me so I can pull out a blue pen from the side pocket. "Here."

His fingers brush mine as he takes it, and I feel my stomach clench. *Seriously, what is wrong with me?* To my surprise, he seems caught off guard too. He's staring at his hand.

"Do you believe in soul mates, Lila?" he asks suddenly, and I can see the storm behind his eyes. *He's trying to figure me out; trying to work out if I'm the girl he came here to find.*

I hold his gaze. "No. Love comes from friendship, and trust, and work. It's not some magical force." I think of my parents: my dad, lost in his memories, and my mom, gone from this world. "And it doesn't always have a happy ending."

An emotion I can't interpret flits across his face. His expression is serious, watchful. Then the grin is back.

"Bad breakup?" he says.

"I'm in a perfectly happy relationship, thanks very much."

"Sure you are." Cupid holds my gaze a moment longer then scribbles something down and passes it to me.

"What's this?"

"My address. My mother is . . . out of town and I'm having a party this Friday. You should come. Your friend too."

I don't miss the emphasis on his mother being out of town. *Do cupids even have mothers?* I make a mental note to ask Cal later.

Cupid turns and walks into the classroom, but before he disappears he looks over his shoulder. "By the way, I'm no longer so interested in getting to know Chloe," he says. "It's you I want to get to know better, Lila Black."

9

At the end of the day I tell myself I'm not going to go to the gym to meet Cal for "training in the arts of the cupids," whatever that means. I tell myself I'm going to go home and see how my father is doing and suggest that, hey, maybe we can have pancakes for dinner. However, when I pass by the dark gym on my way out the door, curiosity gets the better of me and I step inside.

It seems empty. Rays of sun slip in through the high windows and cause elongated shadows to stretch out from the climbing frame stacked against the wall.

"Cal?" I say tentatively, feeling stupid as my voice echoes back. "You here?"

There's silence for a moment, then the sound of footsteps.

"Here."

My eyes dart toward the basketball hoop at the far end of the gym. When Cal emerges from the shadows, I take an involuntary step back. He has a bow slung across his body, and a sleek black case filled with arrows over one shoulder.

"Jesus Christ! You've not been carrying that around school all day have you?"

Cal scowls. "'Course not. They were in my car."

"You're not going to . . . shoot me are you?"

Cal looks insulted. "I told you before, I'm going to train you in the arts of the cupids."

"Does *that* involve shooting me?"

Cal shrugs. "Not for the time being."

"For the time being?!" I take another step backward. *This is insane.*

"They're not ordinary arrows," he says. "Each cupid has access to them. Our branch of the Cupids Matchmaking Service no longer uses them—we believe them old fashioned. But if you are to understand the ways of the cupids, and to understand Cupid himself, they are a good starting place. They were very common-place up until the beginning of this century, when we started to rely on our advancing technology."

Taking another step closer, he pulls an arrow from its case. It is smaller than a normal arrow, and bright silver with indecipher-able markings around the base of the shaft. The tip is pastel pink.

"There are three types of cupid arrow, all extremely danger-ous," he says. "Arrow one: the Capax—or 'Fool's Love,' as it has been nicknamed."

Before I can move or react, he swings the bow in front of him, looks right at me, aims, and then fires.

I gasp as Cal's arrow speeds past my face. I feel it happen in slow motion—the whoosh of cool air, the feather fletching brush-ing against my cheek, and the surge of adrenaline that makes my heart pound and my entire body feel cold.

There's a *thunk* as the projectile hits the wall behind me. The arrow quivers where it's now embedded in the Forever Falls Lobsters team mural painted above one of the exits, adding an obstacle for one of the spirited crustaceans as it dribbles a basket-ball toward the hoop. I turn back around, dismayed to find my hands shaking.

"What the hell?!"

Cal clearly doesn't think he's done anything remotely odd. He pulls out a second arrow. This one is a deep gold, with a dark, blood-red tip. "Arrow two," he states matter-of-factly as he holds it up. "The Ardor—or the 'Burning Flame.'"

He shoots again. I flinch as the second arrow pierces the air beside me and embeds itself next to the first.

"Hey—"

"And lastly," Cal says, ignoring my protest and pulling out a sleek black arrow. "The Cupids' Arrow."

As arrow three hurtles past me, Cal's expression turns dark. I stand frozen to the spot, my heart racing.

"Was there any need for that?" I ask weakly, attempting to regain my composure.

"Look behind you."

I look at him curiously then turn around. The three arrows, all lined up, simultaneously turn into ash that crumbles to the ground.

"I wanted you to see," he says.

He walks toward a large blue gym mat that has been dragged out onto the floor. Gracefully, he sits cross-legged, placing his bow and three more arrows in front of him. I shake my head as I join him. I think the weirdest thing about all this is that I'm start-ing to believe what I'm seeing.

I lower myself onto the mat, instantly engulfed in the scent of bare feet and antiperspirant that seems to linger in all school gyms.

"I remember when my life was normal," I say.

Cal looks at me curiously. "Do you?"

I realize it's the first time that Cal's wanted to know anything about me. I shrug, not really wanting to answer. My life hasn't been normal for a while now, not really. Not since my mom left us. It's been more of a pretend normal, a life with dulled edges—with my dad acting like everything's okay while he becomes part of the sofa, and me following a script that was written before she died but not really feeling it anymore. But that's an entirely different type of abnormal than this utter descent into madness.

"You said there are three types," I say, changing the subject as I look down at the weapons between us. If Cal is disappointed that I didn't answer his question, he doesn't show it.

"The first one, the Capax, is the mildest. It lasts a couple of hours—longer if the person hit is pierced in the heart. Someone who gets hit by that becomes more susceptible to love or suggestion. It was used before we had access to technology to speed up our matches."

"Like mind control?"

Cal shrugs. "More like hypnosis. There has to be a feeling there in the first place for it to work."

I gently run my finger along the body of the silver arrow, realizing it's almost a perfect match for Cal's eyes. It's cool to the touch and there are ridges where runic symbols have been carved into it.

"Does it hurt—to get hit?"

Cal shakes his head. "Humans can't feel it. In fact, it is known to give a certain feeling of euphoria. It leaves no mark and humans immediately forget they have been hit."

I study the second arrow—deep red and gold.

"What does this one do?"

Cal looks at me seriously. "The Ardor is more severe than the Capax. It fills its victim with a fiery obsession. It was meant to be dealt out only in punishment. It consumes a person—some will stalk people they believe to be their match, others will die of longing."

I frown. "What about the last?"

The dark look reappears on Cal's face as he turns his attention to the black arrow. "The last one is arguably the worst of them all." He pauses. "It turns a human into someone like me: a cupid—strong, fast, powerful, immortal . . ."

He flicks his gaze up to mine, his silvery eyes deep and sad. "Alone."

10

Cal abruptly stands and gathers the three arrows, slipping them back into the case over his shoulder. When he heads toward one of the doors, I get up and follow. The mood's clearly shifted.

"Everything okay?" I ask as we walk down the dimly lit school corridor, which is decorated with flyers for team tryouts, auditions for the drama club's production of *Romeo and Juliet*, and a couple of pink posters for the Forever Falls school dance, which I'm pretty sure Charlie stuck up.

Cal keeps his eyes fixed straight ahead. "Yes."

He doesn't speak for a moment and I find myself staring at the bow and arrows slung across his shoulder.

"You need to be more careful," Cal says suddenly, as we walk outside. He makes his way around the angular building toward the parking lot and I fall into step beside him.

"What do you mean?"

He glares at me, exasperated. "With Cupid. Day one of meeting him and you're already his mentor." He shakes his head. "As

I said, the path of your match has already been put into motion. You will be drawn to each other. And Cupid, if he realizes who you are, will create reasons be alone with you. But you must fight it. You mustn't create more opportunities."

"*I* wasn't the one who put the path of the match into motion."

Cal looks a little sheepish for a moment, then pulls out a key from his jeans pocket and points it straight ahead. A double beep sounds and the two side doors of a bright red Lamborghini slide upward.

"*That*'s your car? Way to fit in with the students, Cal. I take it being a cupid pays well, then?"

The corner of his lip briefly quirks. "It has its perks." He slides into the driver's seat. "Want a ride anywhere?"

I was planning on walking across town to the Love Shack, one of Forever Falls's only places to hang out. I said I'd meet James and Charlie, and there's usually a good crowd out on the first day back at school.

"Sure," I say, making my way to the passenger side. "You know the Love Shack?"

Cal nods as he smoothly reverses and pulls out of the parking lot. We pass the houses dotting the quiet roads, and I look out the window, suddenly feeling awkward at the close quarters. Soon we approach the cobblestone town square and Cal pulls up beside the alley between the florist and the diner. The Love Shack sits at the end of it.

As he presses a button that opens my car door, I look at him tentatively.

"Do you want to—"

He holds up a finger, silencing me, as he puts his cell phone to his ear.

"Curtis?" he says urgently.

I roll my eyes. Cal seems to act like everything is an end-of-the-world situation and I wonder whether I should just leave him to his call.

His eyes narrow. "If the *Records of the Finis* isn't in our archives, then maybe it's in one of the other Matchmaking Service branches." He lowers his voice. "No, do not involve anyone else. Let me know when you find it."

He clicks off the call and puts the phone back in the pocket of his jeans. He looks at me, confused. "Well? We're here," he says.

I suck in an irritated breath. "I know, Cal. I was asking if you wanted to come? You can get to know some new people. James, Charlie . . . it could be fun."

A fearful look passes over his face at the mention of my best friend, and I recall her chattering to him in class earlier. I can hardly think of a more unlikely pair; him stern and silent, her dizzy and loud.

"She's not so bad if you give her a chance," I say.

He frowns. "Will a lot of people from school be there?"

"Yeah, a whole crowd of us. There's nowhere else to go."

Cal pulls his keys out of the ignition and unfastens his seat belt. "Then Cupid will be there, so I had better come along"—he gives me a pointed look—"and make sure you don't get into any trouble."

With an electronic beep, Cal locks his car and we head down the cobbled alleyway.

"So. . . . what's this Records of the Furnace thing you were talking about?" I ask in an attempt to make conversation.

"*Finis.* Nothing." His eyes remain fixed ahead.

I roll my eyes. Fine. I tried.

The afternoon air is scented with petunias and lavender as we pass the florist on our way to the Love Shack. I dare a glance at Cal, who is making no effort to hide his distaste at the flashing pink letters above the door. The sound of nineties pop music drifts toward us as we approach.

Eric, the bouncer and a friend of my father's, blocks our way.

"All right, Lila!" he says, giving me a quick bear hug. "How's your dad doing? Any better?"

"Yeah, he's doing okay," I lie, sticking my hand out for him to brand me with the under-twenty-one stamp. Eric glances suspiciously at Cal. We don't get a lot of new people in Forever Falls.

"This is Cal. He just moved here from L.A."

Eric shrugs then stamps the matchmaking agent, who instantaneously looks horrified at the palm tree now staining his pale skin.

"Third new guy I've admitted today," says Eric. "Well, in you go. Say hey to your dad from me. He's always got a space on our bowling team if he ever wants to get back into it."

I tell Eric I'll pass on his message but silently think it's unlikely. Bowling was Dad's thing with Mom, even if she thought it was kind of silly. I try not to think about the video Cal showed me of the ten-pin bowling alley.

There are other things on my mind.

"Third guy?" I whisper to Cal as we walk down the long hallway to the main area of the club. "I guess Cupid was the first, but who is the other?"

Cal is too preoccupied with rubbing at the stamp to pay attention. "I *am* over twenty-one, you know."

I open another door and we enter the noisy main room of the Love Shack. It is familiar and homey to me, but I feel a flash of amusement at what Cal may think. It doesn't seem like his sort of scene. The crowded room is washed in unnatural pink

light, straw litters the sticky floor, and high tables sit below worn
sunbed umbrellas. Neon signs reading *Beach Party* hang about
the room and the staff all wear brightly colored leis.

"It's meant to be a luau beach party theme," I say to Cal.

He surveys the room coldly. "It's even tackier than I remember."

"You've been here before?" I ask as I see Charlie wave us over.
We weave our way through the crowd.

"Not by choice."

Charlie sits with James at one of the high tables, nursing a
lavish pink drink with a paper umbrella. Her face lights up as she
realizes I'm not alone. Cal inclines his head in greeting, but his
expression is a little hostile.

"Where have you two been?" James asks. As if sensing Cal's
dark mood, his face hardens.

"Lila was just helping me out with some registration tasks,"
says Cal.

Charlie gives me a coy look. "Me and James were just discuss-
ing Cupid's party. James thinks the guy is an ass, but I think it'll
be fun. *And* it's on Friday, so it's just logic really . . . I mean, why
wouldn't we go? Right, Lila?"

Cal shoots me a warning glare and I feel the burn of Cupid's
address still folded in the pocket of my jeans. I think of the flutter
in my stomach when his fingers brushed mine and those stormy
ocean-colored eyes.

"I don't know," I say tersely. "I'm not sure about that guy."

A brief flicker of approval passes over Cal's face.

"You don't have to *like* him. You don't even have to talk to
him," Charlie says. "It's a party. Everyone's going. *And* I heard he
has a pool. James?"

James gives me an apologetic smile. "Well . . . when you put it like that." He reaches for my hand. "What do you think, Lila?"

I feel my resolve weaken as his warmth encloses my fingers. As long as I go with James and Charlie, there's no harm in attending. And it could be fun, as long as I avoid Cupid. Plus, he may be a jerk, but he doesn't exactly seem dangerous.

We chat for an hour or so about school, summer, and how Charlie's going to write a blog post about Cupid's party, while Cal, looking increasingly uncomfortable, perches on one of the stools.

"So where are you from, Cal?" asks Charlie in an attempt to rope him into the conversation.

He's just about to reply when I see him tense up. I look behind me to see that Jason, one of the football players, is holding Jack against the wall by the scruff of his blue hoodie.

"What's he doing to Jack?" Charlie asks over the music.

"You stay away from Laura!" Jason shouts.

Jack struggles against him, his eyes wide as he jerks his head back and forth. Jason is raising his fist to punch him in the face when suddenly Cupid appears out of nowhere. He is no longer wearing his leather jacket, and his arm muscles bulge through his gray T-shirt. He intercepts the blow, grabbing the jock's fist and pushing him backward. The two square up for a moment before Jason is pulled away by two other guys from the football team.

Cupid turns back to Jack, who is looking stricken, still flattened against the wall.

I'm about to spin back toward my group when Cupid makes a swift movement toward Jack. When he pulls his arm away, he is holding something sickeningly familiar.

A gold arrow, tipped with dark red.

As I watch, it crumbles into ash.

Cupid looks right at me and smiles.

11

Did Cupid just use the Ardor arrow on Jack?

Cal's words from earlier creep back into my mind. *The Ardor is much more severe than the Capax. It consumes a person—some will stalk people they believe to be their match, others will die of longing.*

I think of Jack's friends teasing him at Romeo's last night about his crush. I think of Laura's statement that he'd been leaving her gifts. And I think of Charlie's surprise at this development, considering Jack didn't used to like Laura at all.

Had Cupid been shooting Jack with Ardor arrows during the summer?

Across the crowded dance floor, Cupid dusts his hands together as though brushing ash from his fingers. He doesn't take his eyes off me; they glitter pink under the Love Shack's neon lights.

For a moment, I feel like we're the only two people in the room. His expression taunts me, draws me in. There is a dangerous curl in his lip, and as he arches one of his thick, fair eyebrows, I know he's daring me to confront him, to tell him that I saw what he just did. No one else seems to have noticed the arrow or its disappearing act.

I tear my gaze away, spinning back around on my stool to talk to Cal. He is no longer beside me. He's powering through our classmates toward the exit.

"Oh. My. God," says Charlie, her eyes bright with excitement. "Can you believe it? Jason and Jack? I'm definitely writing about this in the school blog. And did you see Cupid?"

"What about him?" For a moment, I'm hoping that she saw the arrow too.

Charlie's eyes widen. "What about him?! He's been here for one day and he just squared off with the quarterback of the football team . . . and Jason backed down! That was so hot!"

I roll my eyes as an odd expression flashes across James's face—his jaw clenching—before the smile is back. He has no way of knowing what's really going on with Cal and Cupid, but maybe he feels subconsciously threatened.

"What's up with Cal?" asks Charlie. "Where did he go? And where's Cupid gone?"

I do a quick sweep of the room. Neither of them are here. And Jack has disappeared too. I wonder if I should catch up with Cal—if Jack has been hit by another arrow, we should be keeping an eye on him.

Anger spreads through my body as I think of Cupid. I'm angry at Cal, too, for leaving me here.

"Listen," I say, rising from the tall stool, "I think I'm going to head out. I'll think about the party. Okay?"

James begins to stand. "Want me to walk you out?"

I shake my head. "No, it's okay. You stay, keep Charlie company." I force a smile then make my way across the sticky floor and out of the club.

I step into the alley, the cobbled stones tainted pink by the buzzing Love Shack sign behind me. Ahead, the late-afternoon sunlight shines over the square. I head toward it, keen to get out of the shadows after what I've just seen. Suddenly, my phone buzzes.

It's a text from an unknown number.

Meet me in the square. I'll drive you home. It's not safe. Cal.

The town square is deserted when I reach it. I head to the middle and perch on the edge of the tired-looking fountain, listening to the water dribbling into the basin. A few minutes later, Cal pulls up in his red Lamborghini and opens the passenger door.

"Where did you go?!" I ask as I fasten my seat belt.

Cal smoothly turns the car around and drives out of the small square. "I had to check something out."

"Because Jack was hit by the Ardor?"

Cal looks uncharacteristically surprised. "Humans don't usually notice," he says, his eyes focused on the road.

"So what do we do? The Ardor is serious, right? Jack could be in danger."

"There's no *we*," he says, "this is Matchmaking Service business. But yes, Jack is in danger. At least he was hit in the leg, which is not as severe as being hit in the heart. Getting hit in the heart can be deadly, but this will wear off within a couple of days." He pauses. "But that doesn't mean he won't cause any trouble, especially for that girl they were fighting over. I'll get someone from the Matchmaking Service to make sure she's safe."

"I've been hearing things all day about Jack and Laura. People are saying Jack's been practically stalking her," I say as we pull up outside my house. I don't even bother asking how Cal knows where I live—or how he got my phone number.

"That is to be expected with the Ardor," he says.

I shake my head. "No, you don't understand. They said that *before* what happened at the Love Shack. Apparently, he's been leaving gifts for her for a week at least."

Cal's fair eyebrows dip as he turns his head to look at me. "Oh," he responds darkly. "In that case, we could be in more trouble than I thought."

He ushers me out of the car—barking that he has work to do—and I walk up the driveway to my house. As I'm fumbling for my keys, I turn to wave good-bye to Cal. He has already driven off.

That guy has the social skills of a potato.

I open the door and go inside. It's quiet in the hallway; I hear only the ticking of the antique wall clock and gentle snores coming from the living room. Gently, I close the door behind me and head toward the flickering light.

In the living room, the curtains are drawn and a muted home video of our last trip to the beach plays on the screen. Dad is asleep on the battered leather sofa. I look down at him. Graying stubble on his jaw, black hair unkempt, drawn face—he's a different person than the bright-eyed figure on the screen lifting my mom in his arms.

I sniff. There's no glass, but the scent of bourbon hangs heavy in the air, weighing down the memories. What is the point in love when all it does is break you?

I switch off the TV.

I cover him up with the patchwork quilt hung over mom's old armchair, head into the kitchen, and stick a ready meal into the microwave. I take it up to my room to eat, and push my clothes off the white wooden chair so I can sit at my dresser.

I glance at the large map tacked to the wall as I fork spaghetti into my mouth. It's covered in black and pink pins marking the places I've been and the places I told Mom I wanted to visit someday.

Mom always wanted to travel but she married my dad straight after high school. She never got around to doing it. Now she never will.

I wonder if love is to blame for that as well.

I spend the rest of the evening trying to distract myself from strange thoughts about cupids by texting Charlie, who keeps me updated on the goings on at the Love Shack, and watching travel vlogs on YouTube.

Later, though, as I slip between the sheets and turn off the lamp, the darkness provokes unbidden thoughts of Cupid, the supposed god of love, with his broad shoulders and wicked grin. I feel a surge of rage mixed with something else as I recall his wild, challenging eyes.

I clench my sheets and force him away. *I shouldn't be thinking of him. Especially after what he did.* And then my thoughts are brought to Jack. What will happen to him? Why would Cupid have used the arrow on him? It doesn't make any sense.

My phone buzzes on the bedside table. It's Cal.

I've been thinking. If Cupid has been dosing your classmate with the Ardor, then he's got something planned. Something bad. You should NOT attend the party on Friday.

I sigh and put the phone back on my bedside table. Two days of knowing him, and I'm already fed up with Cal telling me what to do. He's right, though. I know that I shouldn't go to the party.

But I think of the way Cupid's lip curled when he saw me watching him in the Love Shack. I think of the thick arch of his eyebrow as the arrow's ash fell from his fingers.

He knows I saw him hit Jack with the Ardor. I think he *wanted* me to see.

And I want to know why.

12

All anyone can talk about at school during the next few days is Cupid's party, Jack's weird crush on Laura, and Cupid squaring up to Jason in the Love Shack.

It means Cupid is constantly surrounded by people. Girls, mostly. And he basks in the attention. He struts around the school, his dark blond hair messy like someone's just run their fingers through it, his jeans, rolled-up shirt sleeves, and black leather jacket looking professionally rumpled. Yet every time he sees me—passing through the corridor or hanging with Charlie and James by the picnic benches between class—his blue-green eyes lock onto mine. And every time they do, the force of his gaze knocks something loose in my stomach and heats the blood in my veins.

It's anger, I tell myself. Anger that he's been dosing Jack with Ardor arrows. Anger that even though Cal is ignoring me and following Chloe around like an irritating shadow, he's really at school to babysit me. Anger that I've been unable to confront Cupid about what he did.

What am I supposed to do? March up to him in the middle of his new entourage and start yelling about cupid arrows and love gods? Everyone'll think I've gone mad. Plus, with Cal hanging around it's clearly a terrible idea.

So why do I want to do it so much?

On Thursday, the day before Cupid's party, I catch sight of him in the corridor as I prepare to help Charlie put up more flyers for the Forever Falls dance. I grit my teeth. He's chatting with Chloe, and they seem to be getting along well, which will probably please Cal. He says something and she throws her head back in laughter, red hair shimmering down her back. His eyes slide past her and meet mine, though, the corner of his lip quirking.

I fold my arms across my chest.

"Flyer," Charlie says.

"Huh?"

"Pass me a flyer!"

"Oh . . . right. Sorry."

She gives me a hard look as I hand her a slip of pink paper.

"What's up with you?" she says. She looks over her shoulder. "Oh. I see." She wiggles her eyebrow. "I don't blame you, girl. He is pretty fine."

"Charlie!" I hiss, my eyes darting to where James is counting coins by the vending machine.

She shrugs and turns to pin the flyer to the notice board. "You're allowed to look, Lila," she says, lowering her voice. "You're allowed *some* element of excitement in your love life from time to time."

I frown. "What do you mean?"

Before she can answer a shadow washes over us.

"Aren't you supposed to be my mentor, *Lila*?"

Slowly I turn and find myself facing Cupid's chest. Heart thudding against my rib cage, my gaze travels up his denim shirt to meet his eyes.

"Is there something you need help with?" I ask, tone even. Because I can't say what I want to say—not with Charlie here. I can't mention the obsession arrow or what I saw him do to Jack.

He runs a hand across his mouth. "I saw you at the Love Shack the other night," he says.

My eyes hold his. "I saw you too."

A smile spreads slowly across his face, as though I have confirmed something he already knew. Charlie looks between us, confused.

James approaches, Coke in hand. "Hey, dude," he says. "Everything okay?" His tone is light but there's a hint of something harder behind it.

"This your boyfriend?" asks Cupid without looking at him.

"Yes."

His gaze slides lazily to James, then Charlie, then back again, and the smile on his face broadens, like he knows the punch line to a joke yet to be told. Raising his eyebrows, he starts to back away.

"I'll see you at my party tomorrow," he says. "I've a feeling something pretty *legendary* is going to happen. You won't want to miss it, Lila."

He turns and heads down the corridor.

For the rest of the day I try not to think about him. I fail miserably. He knows I saw what he did to Jack, and he knew that I wouldn't say anything in front of James and Charlie about it. *I should have said something.*

It makes my blood boil that he thinks he can antagonize me;

that he assumes I'll let him get away with manipulating my class-mates. And it sets my mind reeling as to why he'd do something like that in the first place.

If soul mates are real and I'm matched with someone callous and cold and reckless, what does that say about my soul?

By the next morning I'm so worked up that I decide to play my mentor card and speak to him properly, even if it is dangerous, or irrational, or totally going against Cal's wishes. I need answers. And I need to wipe that smug, irritating smile off his face.

My plan is thwarted when he doesn't show up for history class.

"I heard he always skips school the day of his parties," Charlie says at lunch as she takes a bite of her sandwich. "To set up."

I try to act nonchalant, but I'm disappointed, frustrated even, that I didn't get to confront him.

I gaze across the cafeteria as Charlie reels off the list of people going to Cupid's party tonight, and I spot Cal sitting in the corner by himself trying to poke a straw into a juice box. He looks mis-erable and I feel a pang of pity. I catch his eye and gesture that he should come over. He merely shakes his head in response.

Charlie is throwing out ideas for her next school blog post when a sudden screech sounds from the courtyard. Cal jerks up, his expression alert, as a freshman bursts through the double doors.

"He's going to jump!"

Cal and I lock gazes before he races out of the room. I jump up alongside Charlie and we get swept outside with the mass of stu-dents eager to see what is going on. Behind us, a lunch monitor barks at us all to settle down as she tries to figure out what's going on. No one listens; her voice is drowned by the chaos. When we're packed together on the dry grass among the picnic tables, Kelly points up at the school roof and screams.

It's Jack.

He's teetering on the edge.

"Laura!" he shouts. "Laura, I love you!"

As I scan the crowd for Cal, Laura gets pushed forward through the group.

"Jack," shouts Laura, her voice shaking, "this is insane. Get down. You're going to hurt yourself."

"Laura!" he shouts again, grinning too widely. "I love you, Laura!"

He takes a step closer to the roof's edge and spreads out his arms. Charlie's hand grips my arm tightly. My heart is racing.

"I LOVE YOU, LAURA!"

He takes another step. Then, closing his eyes, he leans forward. Silence reigns as everyone holds their breath. It seems to happen in slow motion—Jack falling through the sky, his arms outspread like a manic angel. There is a sickening thud.

And then the screaming starts.

♡

School closes early. Charlie and I go to her house, which is only a block away. Now, as we lie on her bed, the sound of sirens drifts through her open window. *They're probably putting up police tape now.*

It is rumored that when the ambulance arrived Jack was still breathing. After it happened, the courtyard was so full of screaming panic that I couldn't see for myself. Nor could I find Cal among the crowd.

I glance at Charlie. She lies on her stomach staring at the phone on her pillow, waiting for any news about Jack. I stare at the ceiling, where the glow-in-the-dark stars Charlie stuck up there as a kid still interrupt the perfect white.

I find myself clenching my fists as I think of Cupid holding up the red-tipped arrow at the Love Shack. He did this. He hit Jack with an arrow, and now the poor kid might die.

Suddenly Charlie's phone buzzes. She swipes it up and reads, staring intensely at the small screen for a few moments before sighing.

"Relief sigh?" I ask cautiously.

She nods. "He's broken both of his arms and his neck, and his condition isn't great, but . . . he's stable." Charlie smiles. "They think he's going to make it."

I feel the tension inside of me release slightly. Quickly I glance at my own phone. Two missed calls from Dad, an *R U OK?* from James, and a text from Cal.

"I don't know how he survived it," Charlie says, pushing herself up and leaning back against her pink pillows. "He must have put his hands out at the last minute to cushion the fall. He's lucky he didn't hit his head too hard. If the roof had been any higher . . ."

I read the message from Cal:

Lila, whatever Cupid is planning will come to a head at the party. If Jack wasn't the grand finale, then I dread to think what is. May I again remind you: HE IS DANGEROUS. DO NOT ENTERTAIN THE IDEA OF GOING TO HIS PARTY. This is my responsibility. Cal.

I stuff the phone back into my jeans pocket then sit up. As I shuffle up to the headboard to sit beside Charlie, I take a look at the room I've come to know so well: deep-pink walls covered with movie posters, cushioned window seat, and white desk with her laptop open in the center. Scribbled Post-it notes with ideas for the school blog are stuck around the screen. I smile. Charlie will make an excellent journalist. She always knows everything before everyone else.

"I wonder what possessed him to do it," she says, looking at me with wide brown eyes. "Before Laura mentioned him on Monday, I never would have guessed he even liked her."

I debate whether to tell Charlie what I know—about Cupid and Cal and the arrows and the secret paranormal race of match-makers. No. She'll think I'm going crazy.

"I guess you never know what's going on inside someone's mind," I say instead.

Charlie shrugs then suddenly beams—transformed back to her old self.

"Well, it's good news the party's still on, at least. I think we need to cut loose after today. I'll get Marcus to drop us off. What do you think?"

My memory flashes back to Cupid's ocean-colored eyes chal-lenging me across the sticky dance floor. I think of Cal's text, warning me that Cupid is dangerous. Then I think of Jack hur-tling through the air, arms outstretched like a falling angel.

I need to know why he did this.

If I go, I'm like a lamb walking into a lion's den. But if I don't, I know Cupid will find me anyway. So I'm going to make sure it's on my terms, not his.

I smile tightly, my brain screaming at me for what I'm about to say.

"Sure," I say. "Just let me call my dad to tell him. I'm in."

13

Twilight paints the dusty road as Marcus, Charlie's older brother, drops us off at the outskirts of Forever Falls. We get out of the car at the foot of Juliet Hill and he leans out of the open window.

"Be good," Marcus says, giving us a wink.

Charlie rolls her eyes as Marcus drives away. We set off along the footpath lined by palm trees and dominated by the scent of dry grass.

Charlie chatters and stops every few seconds to pull down her short black dress. I look down at my own outfit—Charlie said that I could borrow some of her clothes, but I'd settled on the dark skinny jeans, boots, and black tank top I had worn to school beneath my shirt. Charlie has about a million dresses, but they're not really my style.

As we reach the top of the hill, I suppress a grin as Charlie attempts to gracefully navigate over dry twigs in her heels. Her mouth drops open when she reaches the summit. I hurry to see why.

Below us is a clearing surrounded by blossoming plants and trees, all lit by white fairy lights that wink from the branches. The grounds are already full of people. Many have congregated around the pool to the side of the house, while others sit on decorative garden benches or linger around the stone statues dotting the grounds.

"Oh my God!" whispers Charlie. "It's amazing."

Silently I agree as I look past the crowds at the large house in the center. It is modern and cube shaped, with a huge glass entrance that offers a glimpse of the party going on inside. It must have cost a fortune.

So this is where the god of love lives.

There's a large second-floor terrace that looks down on the pool. A solitary male figure stands there, leaning against the decorative terrace railings as though surveying the scene below. Even though his face is partly hidden in shadow, I know immediately who it is.

As I watch, he slowly turns his gaze to the top of the hill and jerks his head backward—it's subtle, but I know what he is silently communicating.

He wants me to come to the terrace.

He wants to speak with me.

Something clenches in my stomach as Charlie turns to me with a wicked grin. "Well, let's get going then!"

My eyes are still fixed on Cupid as she makes her way down the hill. I'm frozen with indecision. This is a bad idea. I should go back. So why do I want to go forward? I close my eyes, the scent of beer and grilled burgers wafting toward me. Then I start to move.

"Did you say James was meeting us here?" Charlie calls as I follow her.

"Yeah. He should be here already. He was heading down with Tom after soccer practice."

We stop at an elegant black gate, thrown wide open. Music blares from the poolside speakers and I can see a number of kegs dotting the lawn. Charlie smooths down her dress again. There is a buzz of anticipation in the air. A small town like Forever Falls doesn't usually have much excitement, and in the space of five days, we've had two new guys join the school, a student jump off a roof, and a huge party.

And they don't even know about the paranormal race of cupids.

We walk toward the glass front of the house. The path is lined with marble statues that remind me of the one I saw back at the Cupids Matchmaking Service. The one Cal seemed to want to avoid.

"Bit extravagant," I say, staring up at a stone woman with snakes for hair.

Charlie laughs. "His parents must be loaded."

I recall Cupid's strange comment about his mother being out of town and wonder if it is just a cover story. Even if cupids have mothers, one clearly doesn't live here. This is Cupid's house, no question.

As we reach the crowd by the barbecue, a couple of girls from the party planning committee catch sight of Charlie and wave us over—probably to talk more about next Friday's dance.

"You go ahead. I'm going to go find James," I say, unsure whether I mean it. *James is waiting for me. But so is Cupid. He is on the terrace. He is waiting too.*

"Okay," says Charlie. "I'll come find you both in a bit—but first stop, burgerville." She grins and bounds off to her friends, grabbing a cheeseburger en route.

I take another deep breath and head into the house, weaving through the crowds milling about the large granite island in the open-plan kitchen. It has fancy undercupboard lighting and large glass windows that let in the light shining from the pool area outside.

I say hi to a couple of girls from the cheerleading squad as I pass by, but my thoughts are elsewhere. I recall the storm behind Cupid's eyes when our fingers touched and his words: *It's you I want to get to know better, Lila Black.* And I think of Cal's terrible plan to lead him away from me.

He knows. I'm sure of it. Cupid knows.

I keep an eye out for James and Cal as I edge into a white-tiled hallway leading off from the kitchen, peeking in doorways as I make my way to the winding black staircase at its end. As I place my foot on the first step, I tell myself that James is upstairs and that's why I'm heading in this direction, but part of me knows who I am really looking for. *The terrace has to be up here somewhere too.*

At the top of the stairs I find myself in another hallway from which a number of open archways lead into other rooms. Modern prints hang on the walls between them. I take a closer look at one; in it a man with the head of a bull stands in front of hundreds of colorful intersecting lines that make my eyes feel funny. It's silent up here, the noise of the party seeming far away.

At the end of the hallway is a large glass door that leads to a dark terrace; that leads out to Cupid. I halt, my breath catching in my throat.

What am I doing here? He's dangerous. He's come here for me. And I am walking straight into his trap.

Then suddenly, the sound of angry voices coming from one of the rooms breaks me out of my daze.

"Yes, well, *your* assignment directly conflicts with *mine*."

It's Cal. I frown and creep to the doorway to listen.

"I'm just doing my job," comes the irritated female reply. "I have a match to make and I'm going to make it." The voice is familiar.

"Like you did your job looking after Jack?"

There is an angry splutter. "That assignment was to make sure no harm came to the girl," says the female, "and last time I checked, Laura was absolutely fine."

"Try telling the poor soul who jumped off the roof."

I'm just about to peer inside when someone grabs my shoulders. "Hey!" a voice says from behind. "I've been looking for you."

It's James. The two figures arguing in the room spin around toward us. Cal's angular face is etched with rage. I see immediately who the female figure is. Beautiful, blond, and immaculate in a glittering blue evening dress, it's Crystal, the receptionist from the Cupids Matchmaking Service.

She looks straight past me to my boyfriend standing behind me.

"Hi, James," she says, smiling sweetly.

"Hey, Crystal," he says.

14

How could James have met the Cupids Matchmaking Service's receptionist?

An unreadable expression passes over Cal's stony face, but he merely stands by the elegant four-poster bed that dominates the room. My eyes are drawn to its carved oak posts and red and gold bedspread. *This is Cupid's bedroom.*

James takes a step closer and wraps an arm around my waist.

"This is Crystal," he says. "She got a part time job at Romeo's at the start of summer."

My forehead crumples. Why would Crystal, a matchmaking cupid receptionist, be working at the diner? Cal gives nothing away; he only casts a frosty look in Crystal's direction. I think back to my time at the Matchmaking Service and recall the video image of Cal in a bowling attendant's uniform, matching my parents.

Sometimes manual interference is required.

A fire flares up inside me as I recall the conversation we just interrupted.

Is she trying to match my boyfriend?!

I'm suddenly furious; with her, with Cal, and, somewhat irrationally, with James too. Crystal ignores the sudden tension in the room and takes a step forward, engulfing me in a cloud of cotton candy–scented perfume.

"You must be Lila," she chimes. "I've heard *so much* about you."

Her blue eyes glitter, and I know she is daring me to tell James who she really is.

"Nice to meet you," I say through gritted teeth.

"Cal and I were just heading downstairs for a drink," she says. "Care to join us?"

James looks at me and raises an eyebrow in question.

"You go on without me," I say, forcing my voice to sound even. "I'm going to use the bathroom."

Every fiber of my being says I should follow them downstairs, but I'm shaking with anger. I can't be around them right now. *They're trying to match my boyfriend.*

Cal doesn't look happy but says nothing. The three of them head out of the room. As the matchmaking agent passes me, he shoots me a warning look.

"Don't do anything stupid, Lila. I'm going to go find *him* once I've sorted things out with Crystal," he says, face contorted as though tasting something sour. "Something weird is going on. I'll check on you later."

Cal doesn't know that Cupid is on the terrace, I realize in relief.

The thought that I've been left alone in Cupid's bedroom makes me slightly exhilarated. This is his personal space; it's private, not meant for my eyes. I move toward the large, four-poster bed—the place where he sleeps, where he dreams. Tentatively, I sit down on the mattress, taking a deep breath to steady the emotions bubbling inside of me. The sheets are silky beneath my fingers and I can smell the faint lingering scent of summer, sweat, and cologne.

Don't go to the terrace, I tell myself. *Don't do it.*

I peer around, trying to distract myself. On Cupid's bedside table rests a pile of well-thumbed books. I trace my finger along their battered spines, picking out *Wuthering Heights, Jane Eyre,* and *Pride and Prejudice* among many others. I'm surprised. *The dangerous, banished Cupid—the guy who made a young guy hurl himself off a rooftop this very afternoon—likes to read romance novels?*

My curiosity deepens. It doesn't make sense. None of this makes sense. There has to be a reason for what Cupid did. There has to be a reason he is my match.

I have to confront him. I have to know why he did it.

I head out to the hallway and move toward the terrace entrance, taking a deep breath before I open the door and step out onto the large balcony. Cupid's silhouette is backlit against the dusky sky by the pool lights below.

"Cupid," I say softly.

Slowly, he turns. His eyes lock on mine.

For a moment he looks almost surprised. "Lila," he says, "you came."

My heartbeat accelerates as he takes a step toward me. He is wearing a long-sleeved light-blue shirt over dark jeans. His feet are bare, and his dirty blond hair is mussed, as though he just got out of bed. His expression looks softer than when I saw him at school—more vulnerable.

He could pass for an angel in the faint light of the moon.

But he's no angel, I remind myself.

"I know it's you," we both say at the same time.

A flicker of amusement crosses his face. Then he's serious once more, half hidden in shadow.

"I know what you did," I say.

"You're my Match," he says. "You're the one I came here to find."

He takes another step forward. I can smell his scent; it is no longer soft like summer, but intoxicating, like the edge of a storm. I should move back. I should turn away from him, but I don't.

"You saw the Ardor," he says. "The only way a human can see the arrows is if another cupid has shown them what they are. Cal?"

He stares at me, his expression open, beckoning; the green flecks in his eyes seem to dance against the dark blue, reminding me of sea waves splashing against the rocks. Our bodies are so close they are almost touching. I can feel energy racing between us, like warm crackles of electricity, pulling us closer.

What am I doing here? What about James?

"He was trying to protect you," Cupid says, and for a second he looks almost sad. "But he can't protect you," he says, his jaw hardening. "It is already too late."

His words jolt me out of my stupor. *It is already too late.*

I take a step backward. I don't think he will hurt me, but I can sense danger in the air, like an animal sensing an approaching storm.

"I am not your Match," I say quietly. "You nearly killed someone. I would never be matched with someone like you."

Cupid laughs, and there is a bitterness behind it that I do not understand.

"It doesn't work that way."

I try to keep my voice even. "Why did you do it? Why did you shoot Jack?"

He smiles and shakes his head. "Lila, that wasn't me."

I frown. *He's lying. He has to be. The Cupid that Cal told me about would lie. But the Cupid who reads romance novels and has sadness behind his eyes . . .*

"I saw you," I say. "I saw you holding the arrow."

He holds his arms up in surrender. "I just pulled the thing out. What would I have to gain from shooting a random kid?"

"Well, who was it then? Who shot him if it wasn't you?" Irritation itches beneath my skin. *I just want answers*, I tell myself. *I didn't come here to look into his wild eyes, or to feel a kind of energy I've never felt with James.*

The door closes softly behind me and I start.

"It was . . . someone else," comes Cal's tired voice.

I spin around to see the matchmaking agent standing in the shadows. He shoots me an I'll-deal-with-you-later look before bringing his gaze back to Cupid.

"Hello, Cupid," he says in cold greeting.

Cupid's mouth curls into a grin.

"Hello, Brother," he says.

15

A cold breeze whips through the terrace as I spin back around to face Cal. He stands rigidly, his silvery eyes unmoving from Cupid's face.

"He's your *brother*?" I say. "Is that just what you call other cupids? Or is he actually, like, your *brother* brother?"

A dark look crosses Cal's face. "Unfortunately, the latter."

Cupid forces out a laugh as Cal moves to stand protectively beside me. I size them both up; Cal, slender and clean cut with his serious eyes and angular face, and Cupid, broad and rugged with a boyish grin. They don't look alike, and I wonder momentarily whether they share two parents.

"You didn't tell her we were related?" Cupid asks, his ocean-like eyes twinkling in the moonlight. He drags his gaze back to me. "He always wants to keep me a secret."

"I can't imagine why," I say as the ghost of a smile flickers across Cal's face.

"So, Brother, what got me off the hook?" Cupid asks. "Crystal tell you?"

Cal gives a tense nod. "Yes, she was tracking your movements. I presume we've come to the same conclusion?"

Cupid nods. "You presume right."

"How long have you suspected that they were here?"

Cupid shrugs. "Since the Ardor in the Love Shack."

Cal sighs heavily, his whole body seeming to deflate.

"What are you talking about?" I cut in. "Who shot Jack if it wasn't Cupid?" Suddenly, something clicks into place. I look at Cal. "The bouncer said that you were the third new guy he'd admitted to the club that evening."

The matchmaking agent gives a half nod, his eyes unmoving from his brother's. "It's because of you, you know," he fires at Cupid. "You should never have come here."

Cupid raises an eyebrow. "And miss all this fun?"

Cal does not look amused. He steps closer until they are standing nose to nose. "*You need to leave*," he says, lacing each word with ice and threat. "You know what will happen if you don't."

I look from one brother to the other. Cupid is taller, more muscular, but Cal's face is etched with greater fury, and I know from sophomore year, when I shoved Jason after he made a comment about Mom, that anger alone can win a fight.

"Guys," I say sharply, "what's happening?" The tension between them isn't just about me, or Jack, or the match.

Cal shoots me a sideways look. "It's none of your concern."

Cupid gives an incredulous laugh. "I should think it is *now*!"

The two brothers stare at each other a moment longer before Cal takes a step back and sighs. He runs his hand through his fair hair. "She should never have been involved in any of this. Why did you come here?"

Cupid shrugs again. "She's my *Match*, Brother. You really expect me, of all people, not to show?" A look of disdain passes over his face. "Terrible job of hiding her from me, by the way."

Cupid catches my eye and I only just stop myself from nodding in agreement. *I said it was a dumb plan from the start.*

"Seriously, guys," I say, "what the hell is going on?"

Suddenly, there is a loud clatter from downstairs. The two brothers lock gazes as screams, along with an odd whooshing, fill the night air. Then silence falls once more. A chill travels through my body and my skin prickles.

I race to the balcony edge. One of the brothers reaches out to grab me as I pass, but I brush the rogue arm out of my path and lean over the black railing to see the pool below.

Everything looks normal—my classmates are still chatting, drinks in hand, by the water. No one seems as though they even noticed the disturbance. I look over my shoulder at the two brothers, who seem to be silently communicating.

This isn't right.

Suddenly, Cal pulls me back from the edge and down on top of him. I feel the hardness of his stomach muscles and the surprising strength in his arm across my torso as he holds me down.

"What the . . . ?" I begin, when a single arrow whizzes through the air where I was standing just moments before.

It embeds itself in the wall; silver and pink.

It's the Capax.

And there's a slip of paper pinned beneath its tip.

"A message," Cupid says, almost to himself.

He pulls the note free just moments before the arrow turns to ash. After reading it, he looks back at Cal, who still has his arm clamped around my middle.

"They're here," he says. "We were right. It's the Arrows."

I feel Cal's short intake of breath beneath me. Then he rolls me off him and gets to his feet and brushes himself down.

"We need to get Lila out of here. *Now.*"

PART 2
THE ARROWS

16

Dear Cupid,

*We have been notified about your potential Match.
We regret to inform you that we will have to terminate
said Match. We have not yet determined who she is,
but we advise you to turn her in to prevent further
repercussions.*

*Surely we need not remind you of the consequences if
you, or indeed any cupid, matches. **You know what is
stated in the company policy**. We cannot allow this to
happen.*

*You may now be aware that we have already dis-
tributed a number of Capax arrows in your town of
residence, and you will have already seen the results of
the Ardor. We wanted to be sure you understand how
difficult we can make life for you and the residents of
Forever Falls if our terms are not met.*

More complications will arise if the situation is not soon resolved.

If we cannot terminate the girl, we will come for you even if this requires locating the Finis.

We will give you twenty-four hours to consider our proposition. One of our agents will be waiting for you in the town square.

Drop the girl off at the fountain within the time period—or face the consequences.

Yours Severely,
The Arrows

ᐯ

Cupid folds the piece of paper and puts it quickly into his jeans pocket.

"What does it say?" I ask, pushing myself to my feet and brushing myself off. "Who are the Arrows?"

I look from one brother to the other. There's a different energy in the air now, one of urgency.

"Later," says Cupid. He looks at Cal. "They could still be here. It's too dangerous for Lila to be seen with me. Meet me in the garage. Can I depend on you for this, Brother?"

Cal gives a half nod, his jaw tense. "I will protect her."

I look between them both. *Protect me?*

I think of the screams by the pool just moments before, and the silver and pink arrow that almost hit me.

"Seriously," I say, "what's happening?"

Cupid looks at me. The storm behind his piercing eyes has reached its peak.

"There isn't time now. You need to trust us," he says carefully. "We have to get you out of here before it's too late."

He hurries through the glass door, leaving Cal and me alone on the terrace. The matchmaking agent waits a few moments after his brother disappears into the house before turning back to me.

"It is time to go," he says, not quite meeting my gaze.

"Go where?"

His eyes dart about the terrace, his slender fingers tapping restlessly against his leg. "It doesn't matter where, you're in danger. If you can't trust Cupid, then trust me. I'll explain in the car."

I stare at him. "You told me Cupid was dangerous and now you're saying we should just go along with him?" Even as I say it, though, I know it's the right thing to do. Cupid wasn't the one who shot Jack. He's not as bad as Cal has made him out to be—I know it. There's something else going on.

Cal runs his hand through his hair. "Cupid *is* dangerous, but the Arrows are worse. I trust him when he says they are here— and I believe him that you are in danger. Now please . . ."

He awkwardly extends his hand, beseeching me to take it. I look at the pained vulnerability on his face and my resolve softens. He's never really tried to make physical contact before.

I sigh. "I want an explanation as soon as we get in the car," I say. "And don't worry—we don't have to hold hands."

Relief washes over his face, but there's also embarrassment and . . . *hurt?*

"Come on, then," he says sharply, dropping his arm.

We rush back into the building and down the winding black staircase to the ground floor. Cal leads me down an unfamiliar hallway.

"The garage is down this way."

We're just reaching the end of the hall when Crystal steps out from a doorway to block us, her face marked with trepidation.

"Cal," she says, holding up her arms, "I know what it looks like but I swear it wasn't me. They were hit by the Capax—both of them. I think the Arrows are here."

Cal frowns then pushes past her into the room she emerged from. Before I can follow, the blond receptionist moves in front of me. Moments later, Cal comes out and grabs my arm.

"Come on, we need to go," he says, pulling me forward.

I look past, trying to get a view of what is inside. "What did you see in there?"

It's then that I hear a familiar male voice.

"I've always liked you," James murmurs softly. "You have to know that."

I tug my way out of Cal's grip and rush back to the doorway, pushing Crystal out of the way. It's dark inside, but as my eyes adjust, I make out two shadows clinging together.

"I like you too," says Charlie, "but what about Lila?"

A wave of nausea consumes me as James moves his face toward hers and his hand skims her cheek. They kiss.

Cal grabs my arm and swirls me around, taking my face in his musician-like hands until I'm forced to look at him. Another wave of screams suddenly sounds from the party along with the whoosh of another stream of arrows.

"It's the Capax, Lila, that's all. Just the Capax."

I can hear the faint sound of a car starting in the garage beyond.

"We need to go. *Now.*"

Then he drags me along the hallway, down some steps, and into the garage. I am too shocked to resist. *James and Charlie?*

In a blur, Cal bundles me into the back of a cream Aston Martin, then jumps into the passenger seat. Cupid looks once over his shoulder, hands on the steering wheel. He grins, seemingly not picking up on the tension.

"Shall we go, then?"

17

I sit in the back of the Aston Martin, my hands clasped tightly in my lap. Cal is tense in the front seat, his eyes fixed on the rolling landscape outside of the car.

I feel cold all over. *James and Charlie. My James. And my Charlie.*

My mind can't process it. I think of all the times we hung out together. I think of the looks they shared, and how Charlie always teased me about my boring relationship. I recall the way James smelled like peanut butter—Charlie's favorite milk shake—when I dropped in on him at Romeo's.

Was there always something there? How could they do this to me?

"What's up with you two?" asks Cupid, breaking the silence. "Did I miss something? This road trip is turning out to be as fun as a tour of the British quilt museum."

I stay silent—defiant—not wanting to say it out loud. Not in front of Cal, who brought Crystal and the Matchmakers into my life; and not in front of Cupid, the guy who made me doubt my relationship with James in the first place.

"And in case you're wondering, it's not fun. Believe me. I've been. Twice."

"It was the Capax, Lila," Cal mutters, still staring out of the window.

Cupid looks at his brother, then me. "Ah—the boyfriend got hit by an arrow, I take it. Although, you know, they only work when the person has feelings for—"

Cal shoots him a withering look, and thankfully, Cupid shuts up. He's right, though. That's what Cal said, back in the school gym. *There has to be feeling there in the first place for it to work.*

I feel numb. For a moment the only noise is the soothing sound of the purring engine. I lean back, feeling the cool leather against my skin. I try to lose myself in the rolling landscape, but the image of James kissing Charlie is burned into my mind. I think of what Crystal said in the bedroom about an assignment, and I remember what Cal said to me in the Matchmaking Service's office.

Your boyfriend is not your match. His match is . . .

I can finish the sentence now. *Charlie.*

Cupid looks at me in the rearview mirror. "If it makes you feel any better, you and your boyfriend were never meant to be. You're *my* Match, not his." In the passing light of the streetlamps, his eyes waver between different shades of blue.

"No, it doesn't make me feel any better," I say, holding his gaze. "James was my boyfriend. I cared about him. You are someone I met five days ago, and you've been nothing but trouble. I don't care what some *statistical algorithm* said. You are *not* my match."

His gaze flicks back to the road. "He was nothing but a place-holder, Lila. I saw it in your eyes when we first met. You don't love the boy—why else would you have come to meet me on the balcony?"

Rage ignites in the pit of my stomach. "Don't presume you know anything about me."

There is a heavy silence and I notice his jaw tense. I tear my gaze away to look out of the window, leaning my head against the cool glass and trying to force my anger to steady.

"Where are we going anyway?" I ask after a while, noticing we're taking the exit out of Forever Falls. "What was on that piece of paper?"

Cupid reaches into his pocket and pulls out the folded message. He gives it to Cal, one hand still on the steering wheel.

"We should go to the Matchmaking Service," Cal says as he skims the letter. "They would protect Lila."

Cupid shakes his head. "No. I don't trust them. There are too many people who don't want the match to be made—it would be easy for them to get rid of little miss cheerful back there." He gestures to me in the backseat. "We're going to see an old friend of mine," he says. "She should be able to provide us with some protection and some answers."

Cal passes the letter over his shoulder to me. "You don't mean . . . ?"

Cupid nods solemnly.

As I read the letter, a sense of dread grows inside of me. For a moment, I can only sit there staring at the paper before me. *Terminate said Match? Repercussions? Locate the Finis? The Arrows?*

"What does it mean they're going to *terminate* me?" I ask finally. "Like . . . *kill me*?!"

"Probably," says Cupid. "Or if you're lucky, you might get shot with a black arrow—it'll turn you into one of us."

"And this is all because you're here?"

Cupid shrugs. "Kinda."

"Well, can't you just . . . leave?"

The corner of his lip tugs upward. "Afraid it's not that simple."

"You're not going to take me to the fountain, are you?"

"Well, it would be simpler if we did . . ."

"No," says Cal.

Cupid laughs. "I was just kidding, Brother. You really think I'd turn in my Match?"

He looks over his shoulder, catching my eye. "I've been looking for you for a long time, Lila. You're safe for now . . ."

Unsurprisingly, I don't feel reassured.

"I would have thought *you* would be keen to turn her in, Brother," Cupid says, casting his brother a sideways glance. "You're the one flying the banner for Team No Match for Cupid. Didn't you come to Forever Falls specifically to stop us from getting together?"

"We wouldn't have got together anyway," I say, although I don't know if that is true. I think of my stomach fluttering when his fingers brushed against mine, and the way his eyes seem to reel me in. *And if James was always going to get together with Charlie . . .*

I force both Cupid and James out of my head, taking note of our surroundings. After a while, buildings and bright lights start to pop up around us as we drive through L.A. I look back at the letter.

"Who are the Arrows?"

Cal gives a disgusted huff. "They're a group of cupids, very hard core, very devoted to the old ways. They mostly come from the European branches. Some of their methods are a bit more . . . extreme."

"But why do they want to *kill* me?"

"Because a cupid cannot be matched."

All this time Cal's been insisting that we shouldn't be matched because Cupid's dangerous, but I remember the writing below the statue in the Matchmaking Service. *No cupid should ever be matched.* I wonder if that is a rule from the old days. *Does he agree with the Arrows? Does he think I should be terminated?*

Cupid smiles, revealing a gentleness I haven't seen before. "You'll be fine. If they can't get you, then they'll just go for me instead," he says, catching my eyes in the mirror. "And we won't let them get you."

I look back at the letter. "What's the Finis? I think I've heard that word before."

"No, you haven't," says Cal abruptly.

Cupid's face darkens—or maybe that's just the shadows. "The Finis is the last arrow."

"What does that mean?"

Cal turns around. "It was an arrow forged thousands of years ago. Other cupids can be killed by the black arrows, but we—my brother and I—are the original cupids. *Finis* means final—that arrow is the only one that can kill us. It looks like the Arrows intend to put an end to Cupid once and for all if he doesn't turn you over."

He shoots a sideways glance at his brother, and I wonder whether he would be pleased if Cupid was gone for good.

"It's been lost for centuries, though," says Cupid. "Supposedly."

Suddenly he pulls to a halt on the side of a busy boulevard. Palm trees loom over the road, and a number of noisy clubs line the sidewalks. In the distance I can see the lights from Santa

Monica Pier. Cupid clasps his hands together and stretches, cat-like, his forearms skimming the roof of the car. Then he turns to me and grins.

"We're here."

18

A steady flow of people in party clothes stream around Cupid and Cal, who are already standing on the pavement. I get out of the car. The air here is humid and smells like perfume and car exhaust.

"Where are we going, exactly?" I ask as the two brothers walk down the colorfully lit boulevard.

"Cupid knows someone who may be able to help us," says Cal, but a hint of distrust remains on his face.

A few hundred feet down the road, we stop outside a club bearing the word *Elysium* in glowing pink letters. A low beat vibrates from its open doorway, and the line to enter extends all the way down the street.

I look at Cal. "We'll be here all night. Can't he speak to his friend by, I don't know, phone or something?"

Cupid looks over his shoulder. "We're not going to the *human* part of the club. And Selena doesn't have a phone—cell reception is terrible at the bottom of the ocean."

I shake my head. "You know what? I'm not even going to ask."

Cupid's face breaks into a wide grin as he walks toward the two tall bouncers guarding the front. When we catch up to him, he's whispering to the suited female. I see her pass him something that he places in his pocket.

"They're with me."

She allows us to pass. As we step inside, she catches my eye with an amused expression. There's something not quite *human* about her—her pupils are too big, and her skin seems to shimmer. I breathe in sharply. Unreassuringly, Cal looks equally tense, and his posture is even more rigid than usual.

He's not happy to be here either.

Cupid leads the way down a dark corridor filled with flashing strobe lights and pounding music. Before we reach the main room, Cupid veers off to the left and stops at a small, unremarkable door. He leans against the wall as he waits for us to join him. As I reach it, I notice that music notes and the image of a three-headed animal have been carved into the rotting wood above it. *A dog, maybe?*

Cupid grins, the brightness of his smile catching me off guard. I wonder for a moment what it would feel like to run my fingers through his dark-blond hair. And then I blink hard, forcing the feelings away. James might not be enough to make me feel guilty—*Especially now that James has a reason to feel guilty himself*, I think darkly—but Cupid is clearly trouble. He's the one who has put me in danger.

He reaches into his pocket and brings out whatever the bouncer handed over to him.

"Stay close to me," he shouts over the deep thud of the bass, "and put these in."

He hands Cal and me two small, foamy shapes.

I look down at the palm of my hand. "Earplugs?"

Cupid nods. "You're going to need them," he says as he pushes open the door. "Welcome to Elysium."

Once we're inside the new room, the loud throbbing music from outside ceases, replaced by a woman singing a cappella. Her voice is strong, soothing, and peaceful, and for a moment, it's all I can focus on. Then I look around.

A vast space full of happy, reclining people stretches out before us. The green, grassy ground is peppered with checkered picnic blankets, and a paved walkway lit by small solar lights cuts through to a bar serving drinks in the center. Rope netting dotted with white fairy lights hangs over the transparent ceiling—every few seconds the lights twinkle and add to the stars in the night sky. The air smells sweet, like honey and sugared lemons.

I just want to lie down among the people and sleep. I feel like I'm in heaven, and Cupid knows it; he's watching me with a knowing twinkle.

"Earplugs, Lila," Cal says tiredly.

I turn to him, confused. He looks hazy and ethereal, his eyes dancing silver below his blond eyebrows. Still, he looks annoyed. "Earplugs."

Grinning, Cupid grabs the foam shapes from my hand and gently slips the two buds into my ears. I stare at him a moment, the reflection of the fairy lights dancing in his eyes like fireflies. And then I yelp and take a step back in horror.

The room has changed.

The walls and floors and ceilings are concrete, not grass and stars. The picnic blankets are dirty, worn rugs, and the people atop them look out of their minds—lolling into one another, drool stringing from their gaping mouths. I can smell the stench of stagnant seawater.

The singing still resounds around the room, but it's less beautiful than before— more *American Idol* auditions than Met stage.

"This is a siren-owned club," Cal says disapprovingly.

I'm about to ask what he means when a suited, dark-haired man approaches.

"Not here to indulge?" he asks, noticing our earplugs.

"Not tonight, friend," says Cupid. "Will she see us?"

The man nods. "She will make an exception for you, Cupid. Come with me."

"Are these people . . . *human*?" I ask as we follow the man through the dimly lit room.

"No," Cal says. "The people who run the club are sirens."

I frown. "As in women who sing songs and lure sailors into the rocks?"

"Well, that's the myth that humans tell. It's true, the sirens' power is in song, but it's not just women—men can be sirens too. And while they're powerful, not *all* are killers."

I don't feel reassured as we pass more groups of people gormlessly swaying to the music.

"What about *them*?"

"Cupids, mainly." His face contorts. "Djinn, too, sometimes, and the Oracles come from time to time, though they're usually smarter. The odd human sometimes slips through the cracks, but they don't last long under this kind of addiction."

We pass a tall dark-haired woman in a figure-hugging green dress singing on a podium. Her eyes follow us as we walk toward the far wall, and I can feel the power radiating from her.

"They're addicted to *song*?"

He nods solemnly. "The sirens who set up here give doses of their music in exchange for secrets," he says, looking uncomfortable. "It's corrupt, and the Matchmaking Service ought to shut it down."

"Why don't they?"

Cal's eyes warn me not to press the subject anymore.

"Because they have your secrets," I whisper, answering my own question.

Anger mixed with discomfort passes across Cal's angular features. I'd meant Matchmaking Service secrets, but from his reaction I wonder if they have something on Cal personally. *What could Cal's secrets be?*

As we approach a door Cupid turns to us, looking suddenly pained.

"By the way," he adds, "about the, er, friend we're about to meet. She may not be too pleased with me at present. Just a heads-up."

Cal turns to stare at him. "I thought you said it ended amicably."

Before he can continue, a suited man opens the door and we are confronted with a billow of hot, ocean-scented steam. For a moment I find it hard to breathe. Nevertheless, I push forward to ask Cal, "Wait. Tell me what we're doing here? Who are we going to see?"

Call looks at me, stone faced.

"Selena. Queen of the L.A. underworld, owner of Elysium, and"—he scowls—"Cupid's ex."

19

Cupid looks over his shoulder at me. "I know, I know. Past girl-friend meeting the future girlfriend—ever the uncomfortable situation."

"I'm *not* your future girlfriend." I direct an accusing glare at Cal. "You said cupids can't do the whole love thing."

"Cupids can't be matched. It is forbidden for us to fall in love—"

"Selena wasn't my Match," Cupid interrupts, "but being immortal can get a little tedious if you don't let yourself have a bit of fun every now and again." He throws a pointed look at Cal. "Though some of us choose not to."

"You said she won't be pleased to see you?" I ask as Cal studiously ignores Cupid's dig. "Are we in danger?"

Cupid pulls a face. "You saw the power of the sirens back in the other room, you felt it yourself. It made you see things that weren't really there, made you feel things that were out of your control. Well, Selena can do that, and more. Now, imagine you've upset her and she wants to wage full-scaled vengeance from hell against you . . ." He shudders and Cal looks marginally alarmed.

"Just how bad *was* the breakup?" Cal asks sharply. "Is it really a good idea for Lila to be here?"

Cupid looks at us thoughtfully. "Well, there was that time that Selena made that girl—" He stops talking then waves his hand dismissively. "She'll be fine. Maybe best not to mention Lila's my Match, though."

Cal looks exasperated. He touches my arm, clearly ready to take me back out, but Cupid gives a small shake of the head.

"The Arrows could be out there, Brother. We need Selena on our side if we're to protect Lila. She's safer here with us."

Our guide leads us along a walkway that arches over a steaming indoor pool. I feel a pang in my heart as I look down at the water. It makes me think of Charlie and James; we used to hang out together in James's parents' hot tub all the time. I long for those days again—the normal days: before the Arrows, before James's betrayal, before Cupid's wild ocean-like eyes. I long for James's stability, Charlie's laugh, mocktails in the Love Shack, and eating hot dogs by the beach.

But I push the feelings away. Those days are over. *Now I'm being hunted down by a group of crazed cupids, protected by two immortal brothers, and on my way to meet a siren crime lord who might be able to help save me.*

We turn a corner, and suddenly we're in a lagoon-slash-cabaret bar. Hazy figures in elaborate swimwear perch on stools at tables just above the water level, and dark rocks loom on each side. Up above I can see the moon through a skylight.

"This way," our guide says, leading us to a VIP area cordoned off by black rope. There is a picnic blanket laid out by the pool and covered with an array food. Whoever Selena is, she's not here yet.

The man who was leading us bows slightly and disappears.

"Well . . . sit down," Cupid says, dropping to the ground and grabbing a chunk of bread from a basket.

Hesitantly, I do as he says, then cast a glance at Cal, whose distaste is clearly etched on the angles on his face.

"I don't like this," he says.

Cupid rolls his eyes. "Of course you don't," he says, between mouthfuls. "You don't like anything. But just sit down, will you, Brother? You're making me nervous."

Instead of answering, Cal looks toward the lagoon. I see the flash of uncertainty cross Cupid's face.

"Oh God, there she is," he mutters.

A woman is watching us, half submerged in the water. The steam twists and turns around her torso as though she is wearing the mist itself. Cupid swallows, getting rid of both the bread and any hint of his previous joviality.

As the siren moves toward us, I realize she may be the most beautiful woman I have ever seen. Water cascades down her flawless black skin, though it doesn't seem to touch the dark, flowing dress that skims her legs as she walks up the stone steps of the lagoon. Her eyes flash with the brightness of stars.

Cupid jumps to his feet. "Look, Selena," he begins, raising his hands in surrender. "You have every reason to be upset . . ."

Selena arches a perfectly formed eyebrow.

"Cupid, honey? Get over yourself."

Then she casts her gaze at me and smiles.

"I'm Selena," she says. "You must be the Match."

20

So much for hiding that I'm Cupid's Match.

Selena takes a seat next to me and leans back on her hands, allowing her long hair to brush the gingham blanket.

"Hello, Cal," she says.

Cal is standing rigidly on the rocks. He nods sharply, his expression clearly indicating his discomfort. "Selena."

The siren's eyes twinkle. "Still a barrel of laughs, I see. You going to be joining us?"

She looks pointedly at the blanket and he finally sits down, although he keeps his back ramrod straight.

Selena grabs an apple from the spread before us and takes a bite. "I'm guessing you haven't had time to eat," she says to me. "Help yourself." Then she focuses her attention back on Cupid. "So, how can I help? You know I don't see just anyone at such short notice."

As she's talking, I grab a few sandwiches and try to work out how old she is. She looks around my age, but then so do Cupid and Cal.

"I think you know why we're here," Cupid says.

She nods. "I do. But I would rather hear it from you. As far as I see, there is a very simple solution to your predicament," she says, sliding her heavily lashed gaze over to me.

I look at her, then the brothers, my mouth full of bread and brie. "Huh?"

"We're not handing Lila over to the Arrows," Cal says sharply.

Selena looks briefly surprised. "Oh, it's like that, is it? Cal! I never thought it possible!"

"It's not like anything," Cal snarls. "We're just not handing her over to the Arrows."

She smirks, taking another bite of her apple. "'Course not, honey. I wasn't going to suggest it. I'm merely wondering why your brother doesn't just leave town." She raises a questioning eyebrow at Cupid. "If you left and assured the Arrows you would not pursue this . . . endeavor . . . perhaps they would leave you both alone."

"How did you know Lila was my Match? I thought the Arrows didn't know yet."

"Why else would you have brought a human girl here?" she says. "Probably not the smartest move, sweetie. The word is out that you have a Match, and the Arrows aren't the only ones against it happening."

Cupid frowns. "What about you? Are you on our side?"

Selena tosses the apple away. "Your company's policies and its consequences are of little concern to me. I will flourish under either outcome, as I have done in the past. For your own sakes, though, why don't you just leave town?"

I briefly wonder what she means by "either outcome," but Cupid interrupts my thoughts.

"I think it's a little late for that now."

"Yes, you're probably right," Selena says. "So, you want our protection? You know our price."

Cupid raises his eyebrows. "You've helped us without cost before. Do you remember the time in France? Before we dated? The Arrows were after the girl Cal was trying to prevent from matching."

Selena claps, delighted. "I'd almost forgotten about that. Cal *broke the rules!*" She glances at the matchmaking agent, and then at me. "It is probably hard to believe, but he can be a sweetheart sometimes."

Cal steadfastly occupies himself with a cheese tartlet, a flush of color on his usually pale face.

"There was a price, though," Selena says. "He didn't tell you?"

Cupid throws a questioning look at his brother, but Cal only shakes his head.

"Okay, we'll pay," Cupid says. "But maybe you could throw in a little something extra, for old time's sake. We need protection for Lila. I don't trust the Matchmaking Service to keep her safe, and Cal and I can't take on the whole force of the Arrows."

Selena nods. "Do you have a long-term plan—beyond getting the Finis, that is? Because without eliminating the entire group, they'll keep coming for you both."

Cupid grins. "I have the best plan ever."

"Whoa, let's back up a minute," I say, noticing Cal has tensed beside me. "They're not going to stop coming after me? Why don't we just tell them we're not going to get together and be done with it?"

"She's right, Cupid," says Cal slowly. "We can put Lila into protective custody at the Matchmaking Service, and you and I will go to meet the Arrows at the fountain and sort all this out. No one needs to get hurt." His eyes flash silver. "*Cupids cannot be matched.*"

"Has it ever occurred to you that I might be doing something for the greater good, Brother?" Cupid snaps, a storm suddenly behind his ocean-colored eyes.

"No," Cal snaps back, "it hasn't. Because you don't do anything unless it benefits you. What good can possibly come of this? We've had to expose our kind to a human, the Arrows are back in town, and now we're *all* in danger. You've had your fun, you've met your Match, now *please see reason.*"

They stare each other down, energy crackling between them. Selena coughs.

"Sorry to interrupt the domestic, boys," she says, "but do you want my help or not?"

Cupid raises an eyebrow at Cal. Cal stares at him a few moments, cold fire brimming in his gaze, then reluctantly nods.

"Good," says Selena. "I'll send out the message that Cupid's Match is under our protection—and that if anyone harms any human on our territory, we will come for them. It should be enough deterrent for the Arrows, at least."

"Excellent," says Cupid.

She looks at him. "You know if they can't get to Lila, they'll go straight for the Finis."

"Counting on it," he says, eyes sparkling with mischief. "Which leads to the second thing I want: its location."

She says nothing for a moment then shakes her head. "Sorry to disappoint—I don't know where it is. But I do know it's documented in a book: *The Records of the Finis*. It's probably a good place to start."

"Wasn't that the thing you were talking to that Curtis guy about?" I ask Cal. He'd mentioned it during his phone call when he'd driven us to the Love Shack.

Cal's shoulders tense.

"You've been looking for it, Brother?" asks Cupid.

"'Course I have."

Cupid's expression hardens. "Right. And what exactly were you going to do when you found it?"

"That hardly matters now, does it? I didn't find it." He looks up at Selena. "It's not in the Cupids Matchmaking Service archives."

"No, sweetie, it's not," Selena replies. "The original copy was destroyed. But one of my sirens had a little . . . *fun* . . . with one of your cupids about twenty years ago. An archivist." She licks her lips and smiles. "It's not common knowledge, but he was digitizing some of the older volumes before he became so consumed by the song of the sirens that he went mad."

Cal gives her a cool look. "I knew the guy. Carter Matthews. He left the Service after your lot got their hold on him."

She inclines her head. "Still comes here sometimes."

"*The Records of the Finis* was one of the volumes?" asks Cupid, tearing a piece of bread from a baguette and putting it into his mouth. He's clearly less bothered about the whole siren-driving-someone-mad thing than his brother is.

"I believe so," says Selena. "If you can access his login on the Cupids Matchmaking Service server you should be able to find it."

Cal pulls out his cell. "I'll message Curtis now."

The baguette flies past my vision and hits Cal in the side of the head.

Cal's eyes flash. "*What are you doing?*"

"Are you really *that* sure of Curtis's loyalties, Brother? The Arrows are in town, Lila is in danger, and everyone knows we are brothers. What if he decides to find the Finis first and make different arrangements?"

Cal sits, still and silent amid the low lull of chatter within the lagoon. Then he scowls and shoves his phone back into his pocket.

Cupid grins. "Looks like it's up to you and me. Just like old times, eh, Brother?" he says. "Although you'll have to get it for me. I'm banished. I'll never get into the building."

Cal fires him a dirty look. "Yes, please, allow me to be your personal assistant."

"Can't you just log in from here?" I offer.

Cal gives me a scathing look. "Of course not. The Cupids Matchmaking Service has details of every single human in the world. The system can only be accessed from inside the building."

I raise my hands. "Sorry. For a moment I forgot a dating service needed CIA-level security . . ."

Selena smiles as the three of us squabble. "Now, the small matter of my payment," she interrupts.

"Money?" I ask.

Selena laughs. "No, honey," she says. "We deal in information." She looks at me, her brown eyes burning into mine. "I want a secret. I want a secret about Lila. Something no one else knows."

I feel a bubble of dread in my stomach. *A secret?* I don't want to tell her anything.

"Of course," Cupid says. "The deal is done."

"You can't just . . ." I begin angrily, but then stop when he whispers something into Selena's ear. Selena's eyes twinkle hungrily. Cal looks from me to Cupid, his expression unreadable. Discomfort twists in my stomach.

When Cupid leans away from Selena, she looks at him for a moment before letting out a low whistle. "Well. I didn't see that coming."

I fire a glare at Cupid. "What did you tell her?!"

He looks at me, suddenly serious. "That's between me and Selena now," he says. "Sorry, Lila—we have to keep our end of the deal."

"That's ridiculous, if it's about me—"

Selena clicks her fingers, signaling that our session is over. Instantly, the male attendant who led us here emerges from the mist swirling about the pool.

"Please lead my guests out through the back exit," she says. Then she looks back at Cupid. "I take it you'll be meeting with the Arrows in the town square tomorrow?"

Cupid grins wickedly. "Of course—no one threatens me and gets away with it."

"I'll come too," she says. "It'll be a good way to emphasize the message—Cupid's Match is off-limits."

21

About an hour and a half later, we approach the exit to Forever Falls. My phone buzzes on the Aston Martin's backseat. *Charlie.*

I shove it into my pocket.

I'll deal with her and James later.

"Are you sure Selena can stop them from coming after me?" I ask.

Cal shakes his head. "She is just providing a deterrent to make them aim their forces at Cupid instead," he says. "But this won't be the end of it. *Cupids* cannot be matched. And we can't watch over you forever."

"You'll be fine," Cupid says to me. "The Arrows won't risk a war with the sirens. And if we can get to the Finis first, then there's nothing they can do to me." He grins. "Simple. But maybe I should take Lila to my house tonight. Keep her safe. Just in case—"

"*No,*" Cal and I say in unison.

The roads get narrower as we drive into Forever Falls. Cupid is making so many twists and turns that I'm not sure he knows where he's going.

"You're going the wrong way," I say after we take yet another wrong turn.

"Just making sure we're not being followed," Cupid says, peering out of the side mirrors.

Finally, we pull up to my driveway, and Cupid turns in his seat.

"Going to make sure there are no Arrows lurking. Stay where you are." He jumps out, leaving Cal and me alone.

Cal twists around, his face apologetic. "I'll sort this out, Lila," he says. "He's stubborn, with a complete disregard for others . . . but he can't continue to put you in danger like this. Sooner or later he'll either see sense or get bored. When he does, he'll leave town and everything will go back to normal. I just need to make that happen before anyone gets hurt."

"What's the deal with the Arrows anyway? I know it's against your rules and everything, but would it really be so bad if we're matched?"

Cal frowns. Outside, Cupid appears to check for a person underneath a plant pot.

"Do you *want* to be matched with Cupid?" Cal asks finally.

"Of course not," I say a little too fast.

A disappointed look crosses Cal's face. "Your pupils dilated," he says. "You find him—"

"Jeez, Cal," I say. "What is it with you and eyeballs? It's not that. It's just . . ."

It's just that despite the danger, and the Arrows, and James kissing Charlie, this is the first time I've really felt alive since Mom died. I bite my lip, annoyed with myself for thinking it.

"I don't know," I finish lamely. Then I look at him squarely. "Nothing will happen with Cupid and me, okay?"

Cal nods stiffly as Cupid's face appears at the car window.

"Coast is clear," he says, opening my car door.

"'Night, Cal," I say as I step out, but he just makes a non-committal sound.

Cupid walks me to my door. Inside, the light in the front room flickers as though the television is on. I hope that Dad has fallen asleep on the sofa; if he's still awake then I'm in trouble—it must be nearing one in the morning.

Suddenly, I'm aware of how close Cupid is standing. I can feel his body heat through the wrinkled blue shirt, and as the fall breeze circles us, I catch his summery scent mixed with dried saltwater. His eyes blaze fiercely, and I take a small step away from him, my back hitting the front door.

Cal is right, I need to be careful.

A rustling comes from inside the house.

"Looks like Dad's awake. All evening I was worried about the Arrows," I say, "but this is how I'll meet my untimely death."

Cupid's face brightens, the intensity of his gaze replaced by amusement.

"Well, I guess I'll be off!" he says. Then he leans forward conspiratorially. "Parents don't tend to like me." He flashes me a grin and walks backward down the driveway. "I'll see you in the morning."

"What—?" I begin, but he's already getting back inside the Aston Martin.

As the engine starts up, I turn back to the house and take a deep breath. I slip through the door and make to tiptoe to my room.

"What time do you call this?"

I turn around. My dad is standing at the foot of the stairs in his robe, his dark, gray-streaked hair ruffled at the back, as though he's fallen asleep on the couch. Though his expression is serious, I catch a glint of humor in his eyes.

"Sorry, Dad."

He shakes his head. "Half past one in the morning . . . I'm guessing it was a good party then?"

"It was . . . interesting."

He gives me a look. "Interesting, huh? Are you drunk?"

I shake my head.

"Good. Do anything you'll regret in the morning?"

I followed a love god onto the balcony and now I have a group of cupids trying to kill me. But I shake my head.

A smile tugs at his lips though he tries to contain it. "Well, get to bed then. We'll talk more in the morning."

I hurry up the stairs.

"Teenagers," I hear him mutter to himself as I disappear from view.

♥

During the night I am awoken by a vibrating sound.

I jolt upright, my heart thudding, and creep toward my window. *Have the Arrows found me?* As I peer out onto the tree-lined street, something stirs in the shadows. I catch the glint of a quiver and the black of an arrow, and inhale sharply. But then the shadows shift, exposing Cal standing stiffly in the cold.

He has dressed entirely in black, camouflaged to match the darkness, though he can't do anything about his blond hair, which catches the light of the streetlamps. His silvery gaze catches mine, and for a moment we are frozen, staring at one another. Then he takes a step back into the shadow of the nearest tree and disappears from view. I feel a smile tugging on the corner of my lips.

Cal is standing guard. Despite Selena's promise, he's still making sure the Arrows don't get to me.

I consider bringing him down a hot drink, but he doesn't seem exactly pleased that I've spotted him. I watch for a couple of minutes before turning away and getting back into bed.

As I settle back into the warm haze of sleep, my phone buzzes again. Eyes half closed, I fumble across the bedside table, almost knocking over an old glass of water, and pick it up.

"Hello?" I say.

"Lila," says Charlie quickly.

My eyes jolt open as I inwardly curse myself for not switching my phone off before bed. I'm not sure I'm ready to talk to her yet. Nerves mixed with anger tangle in my stomach. *I hate this. We never fight.*

"Listen, Lila," she says before I can hang up. "Something happened—"

"I know. You and James. I saw you kissing."

Saying it aloud somehow makes it real and my body stiffens. She lets out a soft groan.

"Oh God, I'm so sorry, Lila—"

Something ignites in my stomach and I sit upright. "Have you ever kissed him before?"

"What? God, no! It's just—"

"You liked him though, didn't you?" I demand. "Is that why you were always telling me my relationship was boring? That I needed excitement? Is that why you were so interested when you thought I'd *made out with Cal or something*?!"

The words tumble out of my mouth, hot and angry. Words I didn't even know were there. And I don't even know if I'm allowed to feel this way. They kissed because of the Capax. It makes it worse, somehow.

"Lila, it was never like that. I swear!" Her voice trembles.

It only works if feelings are there to begin with.

"Wasn't it?!" My mind is flying over the past year. It reinterprets every joke they shared, every time she called in at the diner without me, every time she mentioned him.

"Lila, you have every right to be angry with me. But it's not what you think. It was—"

"Oh? I have a right to be angry? Thanks."

"Lila. Please . . . it's hard to explain it. You'll think I'm mad."

"Well how about you try to explain it because—"

"It was the arrow!"

I fall silent. All I can hear is her heavy breathing on the other end of the line.

"What did you just say?" My voice is barely louder than a whisper. My body is cold.

"It was . . . it was the arrow. I was hit by an arrow. So was James."

Blood starts to pound in my ears. *She saw the Capax that hit her?* Neither of us speaks for a moment; my mind is still trying to process this information.

"I know it sounds crazy," she says, "but there were these—these people, and they were shooting arrows, I swear it. I got hit. Other people got hit too . . . and then the arrows just disappeared. But after that, all these feelings that I've been trying to hide, they all just came rushing to the surface, and . . ." Her voice wobbles. "Oh God, Lila, I'm so sorry."

As she starts to cry, something tightens in my chest and makes the back of my eyes hurt. I don't know what to think. I don't know what to feel. I don't know what to do. She's my best friend; we tell each other everything. And if she's seen the arrow, maybe this is the perfect opportunity to talk about what's been going on with someone who isn't a paranormal matchmaking agent or a love god.

This isn't her fault, the rational voice in the back of my head tells me.

Still, she didn't have to kiss *him*, another voice demands.

I stare blankly at the reflection of my conflicted face in the ornate dresser mirror. Charlie continues to sob. I exhale.

"I know," I say.

"You . . . know?"

"I saw them too."

"It's going to sound crazy, but I've been thinking," she says, her voice quavering. "One of the new guys at school's name is Cupid."

"Yeah."

"And then people got hit by disappearing arrows that made them all start making out." I can practically hear the cogs working in her brain. "Like, some kind of love arrows. Cupid? Is it real?" she says.

"*Yes,*" I breathe out, feeling a weight lift. "You're not going mad, Charlie," I say. "Look, there's a lot I have to tell you, but you have to keep it quiet. I'm serious. No gossip blogs or newspaper articles or telling *anyone.*"

"Okay," she says with a sniffle.

As the dawn breaks, I fill Charlie in on what's happened over the past few days—the Cupids Matchmaking Service, Cupid, Cal, the Arrows, the bar called Elysium, and lastly, Cupid's plan to meet the Arrows in the town square with Selena. She exhales slowly as I finish.

"So, you're Cupid's Match?"

There's something almost triumphant in her voice, and I feel a small spark of annoyance that it's probably because she thinks the way is clear now for her and James. But then she continues speaking and I'm sure I imagined it.

"Dude," she says in a low voice, "that is some serious . . . I mean, whoa."

"I know."

"And they're meeting the Arrows later today? Are you going too?"

"There's no way they'd let me come. But I wish I could. There's something about this whole thing that just seems . . . weird. I mean, weirder than all the rest of it, even. Like there's something they're hiding from me."

"It does all sound a bit far fetched," agrees Charlie. "Maybe we should follow them, see if we can get some answers." I can almost hear her grin on the other side of the phone. "We don't need their permission, do we?"

22

The events of yesterday flood back as soon as the light of dawn creeps through my blinds. Even though I should be keeping away from Cupid, I feel an unbidden twinge of excitement when I remember him saying he would see me today. I push it back —he came to find me knowing that it would put me in danger. The fact that he looks like he walked out of a fashion magazine doesn't change that.

Realizing I'm not going to get back to sleep, I get out of bed and walk over to my window, scanning the street for any signs of Cal. He's gone.

I don't expect Dad to be up when I creep down to the kitchen, but he's fully dressed and standing over the kettle. He starts when I step on the stair that creaks.

"You're up early!" we say in unison.

Dad grins, though I notice a strain around his eyes. He passes me a cup of instant coffee as I sit down at our small wooden table.

"I'm meeting Eric for breakfast," he says, "before I play with his bowling team this morning."

I'd passed on Eric's message from the Love Shack and told Dad it would be good for him—but I hadn't actually expected him to go along with it. "That's great, Dad!"

He smiles, but then looks down at the flowered mug in his hands and leans against the counter. "Yeah. Listen, Lila. I know . . . I know I've been no fun lately." He meets my eyes; his are a pale, washed-out gray. "I forgot the pancakes. I'm sorry."

I attempt to shrug off the uncomfortable moment. Dad and I don't share feelings. "It's no big deal."

"It is," he says, face serious. "I feel like since your mom left us, time's just . . . stood still. But I want to get it moving again. I want to try."

I swallow the lump in my throat. I know how he feels.

He squeezes my shoulder, then gulps down his coffee and puts the mug in the sink. "I was also thinking of asking Eric if he could get me a trial shift on the door at the Love Shack. Apparently, they're a person short. But I know you kids hang out there. I don't want to cramp your style."

I grin at him. "As long as you don't do any dad-dancing I think we'll be cool!"

He chuckles. "Can't promise anything."

As he's pottering around, my phone buzzes on the table. There's a text from an unknown number. My heart skips a beat. *Cupid?*

I read the message.

Come outside.

"I know that smile," Dad says. "Tell James I say hi. Have a nice day, sweetheart." Dad kisses my forehead then heads out of the kitchen. I hear him close the front door.

And then a horrifying thought hits me: *Is Cupid outside? What if Dad runs into him?* I *really* don't want those two to meet.

I hurry after him, lurching onto the driveway barefoot. Dad is already halfway down the street. When I see the yard is empty, I feel a wave of relief, although a bit of disappointment too. I'm just about to head back inside when Cupid's Aston Martin appears. He pulls up to the end of my driveway and rolls down the window.

"I thought that you might have taken off, fled the town."

"That probably *would* be the sensible thing to do," I say, "but then I thought if anyone should leave, it should be you."

Amusement glints in his eyes. "I'll win you over yet, Lila Black," he says. "Now go get your shoes on and get in the car."

"And why would I do that?"

He leans toward me. "Because it would make me feel bad if something were to happen to you."

"Not enough for you to leave town, though."

He smirks. "I told you—it's not that simple. Now come on. Cal and I will be combat training until our little meeting this evening, and you're going to join us," he says. "You're going to learn how to fight like a cupid."

♥

Twenty minutes later Cupid drops me off at the front of his house before he goes to park his car in the garage. To my amusement, Cal is standing at the kitchen stove flipping pancakes when I enter. He's still dressed in his clothes from last night—dark jeans and a skintight turtleneck that emphasizes the slender muscles in his back. He must have come here straight after his patrol outside my house.

I grin as he turns around and I take in the flour-covered apron. Cal and pancakes are not a combination that I ever would have put together.

"Morning, Lila," he says.

"Morning, Cal," I say, taking a stool at the breakfast bar.

"Breakfast," he says, looking at the frying pan.

"I love pancakes. My mom used to make them for me."

He gives me an embarrassed half nod as he plates one up for me. I drown it in some golden syrup he's left on the counter.

"Your plan to get Cupid to leave worked well then?" I say sweetly.

He narrows his eyes. "I have no intention of getting rid of him until we've dealt with the Arrows. And besides, I knew you would both be incapable of following simple instructions and staying apart. That's why I've had to disrupt my day to supervise the pair of you."

"He said we're doing combat training so I can fight like a cupid," I say. Elbow on the granite bar, I pick up my fork and point it in his direction. "Getting people to fall in love is aggressive work, is it?"

"We have always trained in archery. It is traditional." His chest puffs up a little, a hint of pride in his tone. "And as the largest global organization of paranormal beings, we are also called upon to police the rest of the mythological world. Being a cupid is about more than matchmaking."

"Okay. If you say so." I shrug, chewing on a forkful of pancake.

He narrows his eyes. "I do."

He grumpily whisks up some more batter, the metal of the whisk clanging loudly against the bowl. I wonder for a moment if I should tell him about my conversation with Charlie but decide against it. He seems to be in a bad enough mood as it is—I doubt he'll be happy that another human now knows about the cupids.

"I thought it would be messier here . . . after the party, I mean," I say, attempting a different conversation.

"I have a party cleanup service on speed dial," Cupid says as he wanders in from the hallway leading to the garage and tosses his car keys onto the side table. He slips his sneakers off and pads around barefoot. He's taken off the leather jacket he wore on the drive here and his white T-shirt clings to his hard torso. I hurriedly bring my gaze back to my plate to stop myself from gawking.

"Of course you do," I say.

The corner of Cal's lip quirks upward before he resumes his cold demeanor.

"Mmmm, pancakes," Cupid says, sliding onto the stool beside me and ignoring the waves of irritation coming from his brother.

"Thanks for looking out for me last night," I say to Cal, trying to distract him from murderous fraternal thoughts.

"I don't know what you're talking about." He turns to Cupid. "What weapons have you got?" he asks, changing the subject.

"Not many," Cupid says, shrugging. "Just my bow from back in the day, some training weapons, and a few black arrows."

Cal throws him a stern look. "You shouldn't have *any* weapons at all—you're banished. But still, that's not enough."

Cupid raises an eyebrow. "Well, Brother, I think that's where you come in."

Cal's silvery eyes flash irritably but he nods. "Fine, I'll go get my bow and stock up on arrows. I can probably get hold of an old Sim as well. Just . . . don't get into any trouble while I'm gone."

He looks pointedly at me, then, still wearing his apron, turns on his heel, heads out of the back door, and strides down the foot-path. Cupid and I watch him in silence for a moment, then my supposed Match turns to me and grins.

"So, Lila, what kind of trouble shall we get into?"

I roll my eyes and shrug. "Drinking coffee wouldn't be last on my to-do list."

Cupid laughs and slides off the stool, then makes his way over to a metallic contraption on the counter. He pushes a white mug into the coffee maker and presses a button. A whirring noise sounds and moments later the smell of freshly ground coffee fills the room.

"You didn't sleep much?" he asks as he swaps in another mug and presses the button again. When I shake my head, he nods knowingly. "Too busy thinking about me, I'd guess," he says. "I don't blame you, I *am* pretty dreamy."

"Yes, there's nothing dreamier than a guy who turns you into a target."

He places the mugs on the bar and looks at me thoughtfully.

"I guess it's a lot to take in," he says. "Cupids, sirens, matches . . ."

"Arrows turning into ash, people trying to kill me."

"Not to mention your boyfriend hooking up with your best friend."

I groan and place my head in my hands. "You're really not one for tact, are you?"

He slides onto the stool beside me again. "No," he says seri-ously. "It's never been my strong suit." He pauses then adds, "If it makes you feel any better, you're handling the situation remark-ably well."

I look up—noticing the way his tousled hair is brushed back and up from his face, but a strand still flops onto his forehead. I meet his eyes. "It doesn't make me feel much better," I reply, "but I appreciate the sentiment."

He leans toward me, resting his arm on the surface of the breakfast bar. "Your boyfriend was no good for you. You deserve better than that. I don't know what Cal told you about matches, but being matched with someone—it's stronger than that. People fall in and out of love all the time, but when you meet your match, it's different. It's two souls pulling toward each other, their fates tied. The matchmaking agents help those souls find each other, but they will always try to seek each other out on their own. Your boyfriend wasn't your match, Lila—you could never have been happy with him."

I'm suddenly aware of how close he is. I can feel his warm breath on my face, see the outline of each of his eyelashes. My heart is thudding against my rib cage.

Is he right? Is my soul being pulled toward his? Is that why I feel this way?

I think about Cal and the Arrows; the insistence that we should not be matched.

If it's because our entwined souls would create some sort of combustible force, it wouldn't surprise me. Right now, I can feel fire pumping from my heart, racing through my veins.

"Why is everyone so set against us being matched? I'm expected to just go along with all this, but no one is telling me anything."

He drags his gaze away from mine and takes a sip of his coffee. "It's nothing. It's a breach against the Matchmaking Service company policy, that's all. These cupids take their rules very seriously." He grins. "Me? Not so much."

The spell breaks. There's something he's not telling me, but before I can press further, Cupid rises to his feet.

"Follow me," he says. "I have something to show you."

I look at him curiously then jump down to the ground, clasping the coffee mug as I follow Cupid down a hallway to a door on the left. Inside is a black spiral staircase leading toward a basement.

It's pitch black at the bottom. It smells old and musty down here, forgotten. For a moment, I feel a pang of unease, despite my instincts telling me that Cupid isn't as bad as everyone is making him out to be.

"Do you often take girls down to your dark, creepy basement?"

I hear him fiddling around with something on the wall and then suddenly the room is filled with light.

Cupid throws me a sideways look. "Just the ones I want to train in combat."

I release a breath I hadn't been aware I was holding. We are standing at the edge of a large space that must stretch beneath the entire house. Its décor wouldn't look out of place at the Cupids Matchmaking Service, with large stone slabs for a floor and grand, templelike columns supporting the ceiling. Deep-pink gym mats cover the center of the room and there are a number of black and fuchsia targets surrounding them. Beyond a row of weights, I notice a large bow mounted on the wall—much like the one Cal showed me back at school—and a display case of arrows.

A collection of computer monitors dominates one corner of the room, while what I assume to be a statue haunts the other. An old sheet has been placed over it, concealing it from view.

Something about it gives me the creeps. Cupid sees me looking but doesn't say anything, just walks toward the center of the room. I follow him and see that the entire wall to my left is a mirror.

"Welcome to my combat training room," he says as I approach the pink gym mats, still clasping my cup of coffee. "When my brother returns, he should have a Sim. It's what they use at the Matchmaking Service to train new recruits. I can program similar conditions to what we'll be facing later today and we can have a run-though. You can stand in for Selena." He steps onto the mat, his eyes flashing excitedly.

"Now, you want to learn how to fight like a cupid? Take off your shoes. Let's see what you're made of."

"You want me to fight you?" My gaze involuntarily darts to the muscles in his arms.

His face cracks into a grin. "Yes."

23

"Fine," I say. "I'd like nothing better than to kick your butt."

I slip off my shoes and place my coffee cup on the stone floor. Taking a tentative step onto the pink mat, I look squarely at Cupid.

"Kick my butt, huh?" he says as he begins to circle me. "You know, the day I met you, I broke into the principal's office."

"Probably not the strangest thing you've done since you got here," I say. "What's your point?"

He raises an eyebrow. "I've seen your file."

"That's private," I say as I move in step with him, the mat spongy against my bare feet.

"You were a model student up to a couple of years ago," he says, not taking his eyes off my face, "but something changed."

He pads slowly around me, his movements more elegant than I would have imagined for someone so solidly built. His face is thoughtful, curious.

"Your grades dropped, you withdrew, and there were even a

few accounts of antisocial behavior—apparently we've *both* tangled with your school quarterback, Jason. What changed?"

When I don't answer, he continues.

"It was because you lost your mother, wasn't it? I'm sorry," he says.

I don't want to talk anymore. Not about this. I want to fight. I clench my jaw and lurch toward him, attempting to strike. He jumps out of my way and I overstep. When I spin back around, he's looking at me thoughtfully.

"You were hurt by love," he says, "and so you withdrew from love. I'd wager that's why you ended up with James."

I raise my arm again but he grabs my fist, spins me around, and pulls me back against his chest. I can feel his steady heartbeat thudding against my back and his warm breath against my cheek. I am furious, rage pumping through my veins, but there's something mixed with it—a fire.

"How strange it is then," he whispers into my ear, "that *I*, Cupid, should be the one to find you."

For a moment I'm frozen in his arms. Then I regain my senses and pull away; spinning around to face him. His eyes are watching me and the rise and fall of his chest quickens.

"You're mad at love?" he says. "Well, fight me then."

I stare at the person who knowingly put me in danger, mocked my relationship with James, and delved into my personal files, and yet at the same time, makes my soul feel *alive*. I fly at him, throwing my arms around his waist with my full force. He stumbles back a few steps but doesn't fall—he's too strong, too steady on his feet. Instead, he grabs my shoulders and lifts me up. I cry out as he slips a bare foot behind one of my legs and slowly tips me off balance. I grab his upper arm as he gently lowers me to the ground.

For a moment he is leaning just inches from my face. My heartbeat pounds in my ears as his eyes linger on my lips.

Then he pulls me quickly back up to my feet and steps backward on the mat.

"You'll have to do better than that," he says. "The Arrows won't be so easy on you. Fight me."

I swing for him but again he dodges, grabbing my arm and twirling me around as though we are dancing. He laughs when I spin back, and I feel a small smile tugging at the corner of my lips despite myself. He gives me an encouraging nod.

"Use my weight against me," he says. "Do what I just did, knock me off balance."

I feel an energy in the air, an electric crackle between our bodies. I run at him again but this time he doesn't dodge away. I grab his arms like he did mine and they tense beneath my fingers. Quickly, I hook my foot around his leg and pull while pushing at his torso.

Cupid doesn't resist, and falls back against the mat, bringing me tumbling down on top of him. For a moment we stay there, my body on top of his. I can feel the rise and fall of his chest and smell the light scent of fabric softener mixed with the intoxicating scent of danger.

I'm surprised to see a new openness in his eyes.

Then, before either of us can speak, a sharp cough comes from the entrance of the underground room. Cal is standing by the stairs, emanating disdain. A large brown satchel is slung over his shoulder.

We scramble to our feet.

"Glad to see you two are taking this whole thing seriously." He gives Cupid a look and walks toward us, throwing the bag onto the floor beside the mats. Then he thrusts what looks like a small USB stick into Cupid's hand.

"I thought you were going to L.A.?" says Cupid, his tone a little accusatory.

"No. I stored an old Sim and some arrows in my school locker last week in case there was trouble," Cal replies. "And I knew that you couldn't possibly be trusted on your own for the next few hours if I went to the Matchmaking Service."

"We were just training," I say quietly. For some reason I feel a bit guilty.

"Sure you were. I'm sure my brother was showing you some very useful *tips*."

He stalks off to the monitors in the corner of the vast room as Cupid and I share a look. Cupid shrugs, the vulnerability wiped from his face, as we turn to follow Cal.

"Don't ask," he whispers. "The inner workings of my brother's mind are just as much a mystery to me."

When we reach the array of screens, Cupid slips the USB into the computer and then slides into the leather office chair in front of the monitors.

"What are you doing?" I ask as pink letters begin to emerge on the black screens. "Is that some kind of code?"

Cupid doesn't look at me; he only nods and starts typing on the keyboard. "I'm tweaking this to set up a similar situation to what we'll encounter later," he says. He looks at Cal. "This is an outdated version."

"Will it run on the screens?" I ask before Cal can retort.

Cupid spins his chair around to face me and grins. "Nope."

He pulls the stick back out, fiddles with it for a moment, and then shakes it. Three small, metallic objects tumble into the palm of his hand.

"Put this in your ear. It sends a signal to your brain that causes a kind of controlled hallucination." He passes one of the objects to me and one to Cal. "We'll all see the same thing. Cal and I will be with you the whole time."

Cal looks at me and forces himself to smile. "It's a bit weird the first time, but you can stop the training by just taking the chip out."

I look down at the thing in the palm of my hand. It's cold to the touch, and I notice some small engravings around the sides.

"Ready?" asks Cupid.

I take a deep breath and nod. Then I raise my hand and slip the small, alien object into my ear.

24

At first, nothing happens. We're still in the exercise room. Then I blink and everything changes. Cupid reaches for me as I stagger backward, grabbing my arm to stop me from falling.

"Easy there."

I swallow, blinking up into his face before taking a cautious look around. The floor is now cobbled stone, the chair Cupid was sitting on is now a bench, and a worn-out diner stands at the other side of the space. We're in the Forever Falls town square, desolate and painted in twilight. Or we almost are—something's not quite right. I walk over to bench, suddenly realizing why the square looks slightly different than it should.

"This isn't in the right place," I say, running my hand along it.

Cupid nods. "The program creates a kind of blanket. Wherever there are objects in the actual room it covers them with an image of something that won't look out of place in the hallucination. There's a chair in the room, so the program shows you the bench in the square."

"It feels like a bench, though," I say, "and it's longer than the chair. Can I sit on it?"

Cupid nods. "Your brain is telling your senses that all of this is real, and your body will act accordingly. Probably worth bearing in mind for when the CuBots get here."

"CuBots?"

"Someone from the Matchmaking Service very creatively combined the words *cupid* and *robot*. They're basically the programmed enemies in the Sim. They aren't real but they can still hurt you."

I look at Cupid, alarmed.

He smiles gently. "Don't worry, it's only a sensation. Once you take out the microchip any pain experienced will go away."

Oh, well, that's completely fine then . . .

I continue to gaze around the square—it all looks so real. The worn fountain stands in the middle like always, a tired trickle of water dribbling into the stone pool below it. If it wasn't completely deserted, I could have almost fooled myself into believing I was there.

"This is so weird," I say, peering up at the orange sky. "What happens if I leave?" I locate the place where I remember the stairs to be, which now looks like the alleyway that leads to the Love Shack.

"The program will re-create this image in the next room you enter," says Cal. He looks at his brother. "Now, where did you put the weapons? And when will the CuBots arrive?"

"They're in the diner." Cupid nods across the square. Romeo's looks just like it does in real life, complete with paint peeling from the pastel-pink window frame and its name above the door in faded black lettering. "The CuBots should arrive in about five minutes."

He heads over to Romeo's and Cal and I follow, our footsteps echoing against the cobbled stones. I peer into the window of the florist's as we make our way by. Bert and Bradley, the store owners, are usually a permanent fixture behind the flower-packed counter at the far end of the space, but now the place is dark and deserted inside.

"Do you ever feel like loading one of these up and just going nuts inside it?" I ask Cal. "Like really trashing the place? Just for the fun of it?"

Cal looks affronted, chest puffing up beneath his black turtleneck sweater. "No!"

Cupid opens the door to the diner. The inside looks exactly the same as the one in the real square—checkered floor, red booths, scratched tables. I've spent so many evenings in here, drinking shakes with Charlie while we waited for James to finish his shift, trying to get a phone signal on my cell. I feel a slight turn in my stomach as I think of my life before Cupid and Cal stormed into it.

"How does it look so realistic?" I ask Cal to distract myself.

"You saw back at the Matchmaking Service that we have extensive amounts of surveillance. The program uses that to re-create the square."

We follow Cupid until we get to the counter. Cupid swings himself over then ducks behind it, disappearing momentarily from view. Seconds later he throws a bag onto the countertop.

Cal unzips the satchel and empties it; three bows, three quivers, and a number of arrows fall noisily out. There are a couple of Capaxes, an Ardor, and about ten black Cupids' Arrows.

"Do they work on you guys?" I ask.

Cal nods. "Yes, but differently than they do on humans. The

black arrows kill all cupids except for my brother and me. When hit by a Capax, a cupid will find it very difficult to suppress the truth. And the Ardor causes immense pain."

Cupid looks at me. "Probably worth mentioning that the Sim thinks you're a cupid. If you get hit by a black arrow you'll be fine. Die in the Sim and you'll just come to in my combat room. Get hit by the Ardor and, well . . . just don't."

"Okay. Don't get hit by the Ardor, got it."

The brothers arm themselves with a bow each and a number of arrows. Cal looks suspiciously at the third bow.

"Selena won't be using weapons," he says to Cupid. "Should we really be letting Lila play about with one?"

"*Play about*? If I'm going to be attacked by some crazy pro-grammed enemies that can cause me immense pain, I'll be taking a weapon, thanks very much."

I swipe the bow off the counter. It's cool to the touch, and heavier than I imagined; when I almost drop it, I try to smoothly pass the movement off to Cal's critical eyes as me weighing the weapon. Then I scoop up a quiver and fill it with arrows. I sling both over my shoulder.

"They look good on you," Cupid says, his eyes twinkling.

"I've literally no idea how to use this," I reply under my breath, hoping Cal won't hear me and take it away.

Cupid waves his hand dismissively. "You'll be fine."

Cal, however, looks troubled. "We would never expose a new recruit to danger like this on their first attempt. Even experienced cupids have been traumatized from getting hurt in a Sim. What if she gets hit by an Ardor? What if she forgets to take out the chip?"

Cupid gives him a look. "She's my Match," he says simply. "She'll be fine."

"Yes, and that's *sound* logic," mutters Cal.

I'm nervous, but surely it's no different than a virtual reality game . . . one that could hurt you, I guess. I'm just about to reassure Cal when I hear voices coming from outside.

"Remember, whatever happens, it's not real, Lila," Cal whispers, pulling me down and out of view.

"Come out, come out, wherever you are!" a male voice calls from the square.

My palms go clammy.

Cupid grins. "They're here," he says, jumping back over the counter to crouch beside Cal and me. He shares a look with his brother then starts moving toward the window, keeping low.

"Come out to plaaaay." The voice is cold and inhuman.

My breathing quickens. After Cupid makes it to a spot beneath the shop front, he turns and gestures for us to follow.

"Stay low," whispers Cal.

I nod and we head through the booths, making sure to keep below the window line. When we reach Cupid, we flatten ourselves against the wall beside him. Moments later, a shadow passes over us. One of the CuBots must be just outside the diner. I feel a delicious surge of adrenaline. I think I should be scared, but I'm not; I'm excited. I look at the two brothers.

"This is like paintballing."

Cal doesn't look impressed. "This is a serious Matchmaking Training Simulation," he says as the shadow of the CuBot passes over us again.

"Fine, it's just like paintballing, except much more serious and creepy."

"And we use arrows," says Cupid. He peers up out of the window. "There are six of them." He pauses and looks at me in an uncharacteristically serious manner. "You're not trained, so we don't expect anything of you. Just learn from us, and try not to get hit." He looks at Cal. "Long time since we've done this, eh, Brother?"

Cal narrows his silver eyes and grunts in response.

"Ready, Lila?" Cupid asks.

I take a deep breath and nod, lightly running my fingers along the bow slung over my shoulder.

Cupid grins. "Let's go!"

25

I spot the CuBots immediately when we burst into the square. There are six standing by the fountain—three guys and three girls. They could almost pass as real, but there's something not quite right about them. As they simultaneously turn to look at us I realize why. Their eyes are completely black.

"Whoa, creepy," I whisper.

One of them, a blond, shoots the first arrow. Cal reaches for his quiver, while Cupid pulls me out of the arrow's path before grabbing his own weapon. Seconds later, two black arrows fly toward the enemies in the center.

One of them hits its target and the victim falls into the pool of water.

The other misses.

The five remaining CuBots sprint toward us. After giving me a quick look, Cupid runs to meet them. He grabs a redheaded male by the throat and throws him down to the ground, stabbing his chest with the bow.

Beside me, Cal fires another arrow, bringing down another target. He draws another arrow, but the next CuBot is too fast; he tackles Cal to the ground as one of the final two agents, a girl with a long white braid and hollow black eyes, starts toward me.

My heartbeat begins to quicken. I raise my bow.

"It's not real," I mutter to myself. "It's not real."

Except it is real; if I get hurt the pain will be real.

I aim the arrow, the fletching tickling my cheek. Then I release.

It flies wildly over the agent's head and sinks into the wall of the bus shelter. Now only inches away from me, the CuBot raises an arrow, but I thrust my bow up into her face and send her reeling backward. I throw the bow aside—I don't know how to use it and it's slowing me down—and grab another arrow. I'm about to thrust it into her when the CuBot crumples to the ground. Behind her is a grinning Cupid, his bow raised.

"You're welcome!"

I nod in thanks but can't help feeling a pang of disappointment. I could have dealt with her.

There's grunting behind me and I spin around. Cal and one of the creepy-looking guys are still grappling on the floor. The CuBot is on top, hitting Cal's head repeatedly against the cobbled stone. A streak of blood snakes through his pale blond hair. Adrenaline surges through my veins and suddenly the excitement is mixed with panic. *I need to do something.*

I still have the arrow from before in hand. With all the strength I can muster, I thrust it into the back of the enemy. He cries out as the arrow turns to ash between my fingers. It's a Capax, not one of the deadly black arrows, but it serves as enough of a distraction for Cal to throw him off.

I glance to my left as Cupid plunges a black arrow into the

heart of the blond male he now has pinned to the ground by the flower shop. He looks as though he is enjoying himself. As he gets up off the floor he brushes his hands together, the ash sprinkling the cobbled stone.

"Lila!" Cal yells, lurching to his feet.

I turn just in time to see the dark-haired agent loading an Ardor just a few feet away. She points it at me and my breath catches in my throat. Then she shoots.

It almost happens in slow motion: the gold-and-red arrow coming toward me, the panic, the anticipation of immense pain, and then Cal. He hurls himself in my path, the torture arrow sinking deep into his shoulder. An unearthly scream escapes from his mouth as he falls to the floor.

As Cupid rushes forward to plunge a black arrow into the shooter's chest, I rush over to Cal, who is writhing in agony, his pale features flushed, his eyes watering.

This was the fate in store for me.

I grab his arms. "Cal! Cal—take the chip out!"

He ignores me, his body convulsing. "Cal!"

His unseeing eyes finally find me and I can see him struggling to focus on my face. "You're okay," he says.

Then his eyes close and he slips into unconsciousness.

"Cal!" I grab his shoulders and shake him. "Cal, wake up!"

Cupid approaches. He brushes his hands against his jeans, wiping the last of the ash on the denim. As he crouches on the cobblestone, he rolls his eyes.

"My brother, ever the dramatic one."

I look up at Cupid, my heart racing with worry. "Is he going to be okay?" I ask. "What do we do?"

"He'll be fine, he's a trained agent—this shouldn't traumatize him too much." He sighs. "Unlike what I'm about to do, which I think will give me nightmares for years to come."

Cupid grabs Cal's head and Cal's eyes spring open, wide and fearful. His body begins to convulse again and he grunts in pain.

"Hold him down."

I pin Cal's arms to the ground as Cupid pushes his brother's head to the side so his cheek is flattened against the stones. He looks into Cal's ear, a disgusted expression on his face. Then, in a sudden movement, he plucks out the small microchip. Cal stops struggling, and exhales in relief. He rolls onto his back, looking marginally embarrassed.

Cupid flicks the chip at Cal's chest. "There's brother bonding," he says, "and then there's just being downright gross. Lila—you can take your chip out now."

As he stands up and puts his hand to his ear, I pull out the alien object from my own. Instantly, I'm back in Cupid's combat training room, crouched near the dark-pink mats. Cal has got to his feet and stands rigidly nearby, brushing himself down.

I stand up. "Are you okay, Cal?"

"I'm fine," he snaps.

"Thank you—for saving me."

His cheeks flush and he looks at the ground. "Yeah, well . . . I didn't think you could handle it."

Cupid comes over to pat his brother on the back—much to Cal's evident annoyance—then looks at me and grins.

"Not bad for your first attempt. Now, let's go again."

♡

I spend the afternoon with Cupid and Cal in the training room.

We go through the Sim three more times, and Cupid shows me how to use a bow and arrow. I shoot one of the CuBots on my third attempt and experience a surge of exhilaration like nothing I've felt before.

By the time we're done, I'm exhausted, and can do little more than sit on one of the kitchen stools nursing another cup of coffee. Even though nothing in the Sim was real, my body aches. The rich evening light shines through the glass front of the house and makes the array of arrows scattered across the breakfast bar sparkle. I watch as the brothers examine them.

They both changed after training. Cupid now wears a white V-neck T-shirt under his leather jacket and Cal has on a maroon sweater with a gray collared button-down peeking out beneath. Both have a bow slung over one shoulder. Cupid selects a Capax from the counter.

"I think we should take some of these," he says. "Aim to capture one of the Arrows and get them to talk. See what they know about Lila and anything they've found out about the Finis."

Cal gives a sharp nod—after the incident with the Ardor he's been even more abrupt than usual. He seems about to say something when his phone buzzes; he looks down and purses his lips.

"Crystal," he mutters, pressing the Ignore button and stuffing the phone back into his pocket. I feel a stab of anger as I wonder if she is calling Cal about her *assignment*, aka matching my boyfriend. Cal interrupts my thoughts.

"We'll drop Lila off at home on the way."

I hesitate for a moment. "I was thinking of going around to Charlie's."

"Awkward," says Cupid, pulling a face.

"That could work," says Cal. "It's probably best that you're not alone."

For a moment I feel a stab of guilt at our plan to follow the brothers to the square. I've had fun today—shooting arrows, fighting pretend cupids, and getting to know them both a little better.

Still, though, there's something they're not telling me. And that's putting my life, and the lives of the other residents of Forever Falls, in danger. I want to know what's going on.

26

After Cupid parks the Aston Martin at the bottom of Charlie's drive, he turns around in his seat when my fingers are on the door handle.

"Stay safe," he says. "We'll deal with these Arrows then come back to let you know how it went."

"You sure you'll be okay?" I cast my gaze between him and Cal.

Cupid grins. "We've dealt with worse than this in our time," he says. "Plus, they can't kill us without the Finis, which is always a bonus."

Cal just continues to stares straight ahead. As I open the door, I pause to give him what I hope is a reassuring squeeze on the shoulder. He tenses momentarily; I sigh and let go, climbing out of the car.

"Good luck," I say.

Cupid waves before driving off down the street. As I head toward the house, Charlie flings open the front door and rushes to me.

"Are we going to follow them?" she asks.

She's dressed differently than usual—in skinny jeans and a black top instead of one of her stylish dresses. She seems to be resolute about not meeting my eyes—I guess she still feels bad about James.

"We'll need to set off now to catch up with them," I say. "You ready?"

She looks down the street. "Yeah, just give me a minute. I need to go and get something."

As Charlie goes upstairs, I head into the living room. I move one of Marcus's construction magazines off the floral couch and onto the glass coffee table, then throw myself down into the cushions.

As I'm waiting, my eyes pass over the cheesy family photos on the wall. Much to Charlie's embarrassment, her mom makes them pose for them every year in her photography studio. My favorite is the one hanging to the right-hand side of the decorative mantelpiece; in it a sulking three-year-old Charlie has her back to the camera while her dad and a young Marcus laugh in the background.

As I'm looking at it, I frown. There are marks in the wall beside it, and on the floor below it there is a thin dusting of ash—despite the fact they have a gas fireplace. I walk over and trace the holes in the plaster with my finger.

Arrow holes?

My skin prickles. Something doesn't feel right.

It's then that it comes back to me. "Only cupids or humans who have been shown the arrows can see them," I say softly.

"That's right."

I spin around. Charlie stands in front of me, a bow in her hand. In it is strung a single black arrow.

My eyes widen. *The Arrows must have got to her.*

"I'm sorry, Lila," she says calmly. "I have to do this. You can't be matched. They told me what would happen if you were." She's pulling her arm back to shoot when there is a flicker of movement behind her.

"Drop the weapon, Charlie," says a familiar voice. "You're a cupid now—get pierced by this and you die."

Crystal stands behind my best friend, the black Cupids' Arrow in her hand pressed against Charlie's throat. She's wearing the white suit I first saw her in at the Cupids Matchmaking Service, but now there is a quiver full of arrows slung over her shoulder. Her expression is set. I can see it in her face; she'll really do it, she'll kill Charlie.

Panic swells in my chest. I don't want to get shot but I don't want Charlie to die either.

Crystal pushes the arrow closer to Charlie's skin. "*Drop it.*"

With a sigh, Charlie lets the bow clatter to the ground. I release a breath as Crystal grabs Charlie by her hair and pushes her onto the couch. She keeps her arrow pointed at my friend's neck.

"You okay?" Crystal asks me.

"Yes," I say, forcing my voice to sound normal. "I never thought I'd be pleased to see you again. What are you doing here anyway?"

Crystal spares a quick glance in my direction as Charlie whimpers on the sofa.

"Charlie was part of my assignment—"

"To match with *my boyfriend*."

She sighs and flicks her hair over her shoulder. "Yes, that was the assignment. I've been monitoring the two of them. I was pretty sure the match had been made successfully last night after what happened with the Capax, but I thought I'd double check after my shift, just to be certain. That's when I discovered the surveillance went momentarily down in the early hours. That was suspicious, so I came here to check it out."

I cast my gaze back to Charlie. She's watching Crystal warily, a mixture of vulnerability and anger on her face. I attempt to touch her arm to reassure her. She flinches.

"What did they do to you, Charlie?" I ask softly.

A defiant look appears on her usually soft face. "You're dangerous. You have to be stopped."

I feel a stab of hurt. I turn to Crystal. "Have they brainwashed her? Is she really a cupid now?"

Crystal keeps her gaze on Charlie. "Yeah, she's a cupid. Seems as though they shot her in here." She nods to the marks I noticed in the wall by the mantel. "And no, she's not brainwashed—not as such. She's a new cupid, so she's more susceptible to our laws. And she's not exactly wrong." Crystal looks at me. "You *are* dangerous."

I feel frustration building up inside of me. "What do you mean?! *No one is telling me what is going on!*"

"I'll get to that, but first—where's Cal?"

"He and Cupid went to go fight the Arrows at the square. Why?"

A dark look crosses her face. Charlie struggles for a moment but Crystal pushes her back down with ease. "Why do they think the Arrows will be at the square?" she asks quietly.

"I guess because the Arrows think I will be there with them."

Crystal raises her eyebrows. Suddenly I understand what she is getting at.

"But I'm not there, I'm here. And if Charlie is one of them . . ."

Instantly, Crystal swipes another arrow from her quiver and jams it into Charlie's throat. Charlie and I cry out instantaneously.

"What are you doing?"

Crystal turns to me as the arrow crumbles to ash between her fingers. "Calm down. It's just the Capax. We need answers, and we need them fast. What happened?" Crystal asks Charlie sternly.

Charlie purses her lips. After a moment of internal struggle, she blurts, "The Arrows came after the party. They must have followed me. They shot me with a black arrow. They told me that Cupid had a Match, someone from the high school, and that they'd turned me to help them find her. They said they'd read my blog and if anyone could find out who it was, it would be me. Then they left."

Tears have started to form in her eyes.

"Then what?" Crystal insists.

"It started to come back to me—being hit by an arrow at the party."

Crystal nods. "That's normal after being turned. Then what?"

"And then I remembered the Love Shack and the Ardor. And Lila acting weird and going after Cal. I didn't know for certain, but I thought she might know something. So I contacted her, and she told me everything."

I feel a flare of anger. She's supposed to be my friend, and yet now she's betrayed me twice.

Crystal leans in close, menacingly. "And did you tell the Arrows who she was?"

Charlie reluctantly nods.

"And, final question—*where are the Arrows now*?"

For a moment Charlie says nothing. She looks like she is trying to fight the urge to speak. A tear spills down her cheek, but when she turns to me, her watery eyes are triumphant.

"They're on their way," she says. "They'll be here any minute."

27

Crystal plunges her hand into the pocket of her white trousers and pulls out her phone. She throws it to me.

"Call Cal," she instructs, her voice urgent as she pulls Charlie to her feet then swipes Charlie's bow off the ground. The blond's eyes are darting anxiously around the room as though expecting one of the Arrows to jump out any second.

I do what she says, my heart thumping in my chest.

Cal picks up. "What is it, Crystal?" he says sharply. "I'm kind of in the middle of something."

"Cal! It's me, we're in—"

Before I can say anything else, Crystal pushes me backward into the mantelpiece and the phone skitters out of my hand. A shattering sound fills my ears as Charlie's front window explodes into tiny shards of glass. I look up just in time to see a black arrow plunge into the wall by my head then turn into ash.

They're here.

A tanned, muscular male in a black suit jumps through the broken window into the living room, long dark hair tied back from his face. As he runs toward me, quiver jouncing over his shoulder, my eyes dart across the room to Crystal. She's thrown Charlie back onto the couch and has her bow raised, ready to shoot. Then she fires.

There is a whooshing sound and for a moment I think her arrow is going to hit its target. But then the Arrow agent advancing toward me dodges, grabs me by the throat, and slams me into the wall. Pain bursts across my back. I grapple against his grip, struggling to breathe as he raises a black arrow.

Over his shoulder, I see that a female Arrow with dark wavy hair has just tackled Crystal to the ground. She can't help me.

I manage to knee my attacker in the groin. When he grunts and momentarily loosens his grip, I take the opportunity to thrust my weight forward. Then, using Cupid's move from earlier, I hook my leg around his and push.

He falls heavily to the floor, almost taking me with him.

I stumble over him and start to make my way to Crystal, who has thrown off the female agent, but another pair of hands grab my shoulders from behind. As Crystal launches a Capax, I pull my head out of the way so that it plunges into my second attacker's shoulder. Whoever it was flies backward.

Crystal pulls Charlie to her feet and looks at me urgently.

"We need to go. My car's down the street. GO. NOW!"

We take off out the door, the three black-clad agents close behind. As we hurtle toward the street, arrows stream through the darkening sky around us. Crystal points her car keys at a pink Bentley parked on the road, and I hear the sound of the doors unlocking. She throws Charlie inside and then looks around for me, pulling her own bow back up and sending a few arrows flying back toward our pursuers.

Just when I think I'm going to make it, the muscular agent suddenly grabs me again and I go flying to the ground. I feel a searing pain in my knees as they scrape against the concrete. I try to climb back to my feet but the Arrow is upon me.

He turns me over so that I'm lying on my back then puts his foot on top of my stomach, holding me in place. I cry out, struggling against his weight as he raises his bow and points it directly at my heart.

"For crimes against cupids, I sentence you, Lila Black, to the Cupids' Arrow, then death," he says in a thick Italian accent.

I fight with everything I have, clawing at his leg, but I can't break free. Panic consumes me. There is a sudden whooshing sound and for a moment I think I'm hit.

I scream.

But then the agent crumples to the ground beside me.

I lurch up into a sitting position and look around frantically. Then I see it—a black arrow jutting out of the agent's shoulder. It crumbles to ash. On the other side of the street, Cal stands with his bow raised, his blond hair illuminated by the light of a streetlamp that's just clicked on.

Relief fills me.

He gives me a subtle nod before powering down the pavement after the other male Arrow. Seconds later, Cupid appears by my side. He scoops me up onto my feet just as, a few feet away, Selena, her brown eyes blazing, snaps the neck of the female Arrow. She looks both beautiful and terrifying in a black tank top and skinny jeans.

Cal has now reached the end of the street and fires arrows into the darkness. The third agent is nowhere to be seen.

My heart pounds as I turn my gaze to Cupid. He looks at me steadily, a flash of concern behind his eyes.

"You okay?"

I nod, my breathing fast, then check to see that Crystal is all right. She is, but she's surveying Cupid and me warily. Cupid follows my gaze and nods at her in greeting. She merely scowls.

"What happened?" he asks, turning back to me.

"Charlie, she's a cupid now."

He exhales heavily as Selena approaches with Cal, whose expression is unreadable as I fully extract myself from Cupid's arms.

"About time!" Crystal says to Cal.

After throwing her a sharp look, he frowns. "We shouldn't have left you," he says. "I'm sorry."

"It's fine. I'm fine." I look at the three of them. My whole body is still shaking from the adrenaline. "What do we do now?"

Cupid runs his hand through his hair. "Let's get Charlie and Crystal back to my place. Selena—the other Arrow got away. Can you come back with us, see if Charlie knows anything about where he might have gone?"

The siren nods, then looks at me and smiles. "Glad you're okay, honey," she says before heading to Crystal's pink car.

"We need to hurry up and get a hold of the Finis," Cupid says. "And to do that we need to get that copy of the book from the Matchmaking Service." He looks at Cal. "And by we, I of course mean you."

Cal narrows his eyes. "I don't know when your problems suddenly became mine."

Cupid looks at me pointedly. "They're not just my problems. Don't you want to protect Lila?"

"*Want*?" Cal says. "I'm *assigned* to look after Lila. Despite having Selena on our side, the Arrows are *still* going after her.

I should have known their feelings about the match would out-weigh any fears of the sirens. This has gone too far. I'm taking her into protective custody."

"You're *assigned* to stop me and Lila from matching," Cupid says, "and until I get hold of the Finis, I'm not going anywhere."

"You *cannot* be matched. You know what will happen!"

"*Help* me, then!" Cupid says, passion sparking behind his eyes. "Help me get the Finis and I'll get out of town."

I look from one brother to the other. Cal's jawline is hard, his expression unwavering.

"If you get the Finis you'll leave?" I say to Cupid. "And the Arrows will get out of town? Everything will just go back to normal?"

Cupid looks at me, a hint of regret passing across his features as he nods. I feel a twinge of disappointment, but after everything that's happened, surely it's better for him to just go. Surely it's bet-ter for him to leave before these unbidden feelings deepen. We can't ever get together. That much is obvious.

"Nothing will ever go back to normal," says Cal, eyes fixed on his brother. "If the Arrows can't kill you, they'll go back to Lila. She's an easier target."

"So you'll watch over her," says Cupid.

Cal's chest rises and falls deeply beneath his fluffy maroon sweater. "She will *never* be safe—"

"She *will* if we make an arrangement with the Arrows."

"What kind of arrangement will they possibly accept?! You're not thinking straight."

Cupid's shoulders slump. "I'll swear an oath on the Styx. As soon as I have the arrow, I'll swear I won't come back to Forever Falls in Lila's lifetime. Draw up the paperwork. I'll sign it."

"An oath on the Styx is unbreakable," says Cal.

Cupid inclines his head, holding Cal's gaze. "I know I've caused a lot of trouble, Brother," he says. "I shouldn't have come here. But I had to find her, I had to know if it was true; I had to find my Match. You of all people should understand that. You fell for a human once—"

"Don't." Cal's tone is final.

There's a lull of awkward silence.

"I just want the Finis," Cupid says eventually, "and then I'll go."

A flicker of suspicion crosses Cal's face. "Why do you want it so much?"

Cupid pauses. "I don't want to die, Brother. If I get the Finis before they do, I'll have a fighting chance."

As he speaks, something flickers behind his eyes, something that makes me wonder if he has another motive. But then it's gone.

No one says anything for a few moments.

Finally Cal frowns. "It's the only way to get rid of you?"

Cupid grins, the tension broken. "Yup."

Cal exhales heavily. "Fine. I'll help you get this damn arrow. But then you get out of town." He looks at his brother distrustfully in the dim light. "And Lila is coming to the Matchmaking Service with me to find *The Records of the Finis*. I'm not leaving her alone with you."

28

As Cupid drives us back to his house, I look out of the rear window at the headlights of Crystal's pink Bentley. Dread mixed with guilt bubbles in the pit of my stomach as I think of the prisoner in the car. *What's going to happen to Charlie? Will she have to get a job at the Matchmaking Service like the other cupids? Will she always hate me?*

Thinking of her pointing an arrow at my chest makes my heart hurt. Charlie has been my best friend ever since I can remember. Even though she kissed James, I know we would have worked through it. But now it's like she's not even the same person.

"What's the Styx?" I ask, turning back around.

"Long story, but it's a mythological river," says Cupid. "You include a clause about it in any legal contract and the contract can't be broken. Pretty shady stuff. I didn't check the small print of an agreement I had going with this bull-headed guy back in the seventeenth century—ended up trimming his hedges for the next five months."

"So you really *are* going to leave?" I ask.

"Yeah." He catches my eye in the rearview mirror and sighs. "Yeah. Once I have the arrow."

Around ten minutes later we pile into Cupid's kitchen. Selena and Crystal take Charlie into the living room while Cal makes a round of coffees. It's completely dark outside now, yet Cupid lingers at the front of the house, cautiously scanning the grounds through the glass.

I perch on a stool at the breakfast bar, nervously clutching the mug Cal hands me. It's not until I take a sip of the dark, caffeinated liquid that I realize how tired I am. I look over at Cal as he leans against the counter somewhat awkwardly.

"What's going to happen to Charlie?" I ask. "They're not going to hurt her, are they?"

Cupid turns and the brothers exchange a glance.

"It won't come to that," says Cal stiffly, though his eyes don't look convinced.

Cupid slides onto the stool beside me, the sultry lighting of his kitchen casting shadows on his lightly tanned skin. He smells like leather and aftershave.

"Of course it won't; we just need to know what she knows and make sure she doesn't cause any trouble. That's why we've brought Selena." He looks at me. "She's very powerful. She can get the truth out of people quickly, and she can calm them down."

"Can I see Charlie?" I ask.

Cupid nods. "Just give Selena five minutes."

I put my coffee down and head into the hallway. I give my dad a quick call to let him know I'm okay. He answers from the Love Shack—apparently Eric has given him a trial shift tonight. I force a smile into my voice.

"That's great, Dad!"

"Thanks, sweetheart," he says. "I guess I better brush up on my dad-dancing skills. I'll see you tomorrow, okay?"

I tell him it's fine then stuff my phone into my pocket. After a deep breath, I enter the living room.

The floor is hardwood, and a maroon rug lays in front of the fireplace. Its roaring blaze is the only light in the room, seeing as the heavy velvet curtains are drawn. On either side of the mantelpiece, the walls hold built-in bookcases filled with an eclectic mix of volumes.

My focus is drawn to the center of the room. Beside the dark mahogany coffee table, Charlie is tied to a wooden chair. Selena kneels beside her. Crystal watches while perching on the edge of a leather armchair that matches the two long couches around the hearth.

"What is *she* doing here?" Charlie spits when she sees me. She twists her head viciously to glare at Crystal. "Aren't you going to do something about this? You're a cupid. You should know better."

"I've been a cupid a lot longer than you, and we don't attack innocent humans," Crystal says as Charlie fidgets against her restraints.

"Cupids cannot be matched," Charlie says, her lips thinning into a hard line.

Crystal crosses the room to stand in front of me. "They won't be." Then she gives a false smile. "I'm going to freshen up."

As her footsteps click up the spiral staircase, Charlie shrieks after her. "DON'T LEAVE ME HERE! DON'T LEAVE ME HERE WITH *HER*!"

How can Charlie hate me so much?

Selena leans over her and I hear a soft tune start up. Then, as instantly as she started screaming, Charlie begins to snore. I feel my own eyelids drooping and I fall back into the couch behind me.

"What's going on?" I yawn. "Why is she asleep?"

Selena smiles kindly. "Don't worry," she says. "Your friend is going to be all right. I sent her to sleep because she was getting agitated. It's not safe for her to be awake around you at the moment."

"Is she always going to hate me now?" I ask sadly.

Selena gives me a sympathetic look. "Attempting to pierce you with a Cupid's Arrow, believe it or not, was an act of mercy. But now . . . I do believe she will try to kill you."

"Is there a way to stop her from feeling like this?"

"The power from the arrow that transformed her is still surging through her veins. It's like a venom, taking control. As her body starts to get used to it, she'll become more open to reason. But she still won't want you to be matched with Cupid."

I shake my head. "But *why*?"

Selena walks over to the couch and sits down beside me. "She has been informed of the company policy."

"Right. That it's against the Cupids Matchmaking Service rules for cupids to get matched. But seriously, what's the big deal? So what if me and Cupid *do* get together? He doesn't even work there anymore."

Selena frowns. "They haven't told you?"

"Told me what?"

She sighs heavily.

"Do you know who the founder of the Cupids Matchmaking Service is?"

"I never really thought about it," I say. "I guess I thought it was Cupid—before he got banished."

"No, honey, it's not Cupid."

"Okay, so who is it?" I ask. "And why does it matter who owns the company?"

Selena looks as though she is trying to figure out how to explain something. The flames cast dancing light over her flawless skin.

"The company founder left many years ago, but the terms of the policy state that if the rules are broken, the founder will reseize control of the Matchmaking Service."

"Well, that doesn't sound too bad."

Selena smiles faintly. "You don't know the founder, honey." She leans forward until her face is just inches from mine. "Listen."

She hums a gentle tune and I feel myself leaning in even closer to her. I stare into her eyes—they are beautiful, dark and wild.

"There's something I need you to do," she says.

I nod, a wooziness coming over me. Anything she wants, I will do.

"Downstairs, in Cupid's combat room, there are some arrows. Do you know which ones I mean?"

I nod, thinking of the arrows mounted on the wall.

"I need you to go down there, get a black arrow, turn it on yourself, and—"

Suddenly a hand seizes Selena's neck and she is flung from the sofa onto the floor. She rolls over and leaps to her feet, her eyes glinting dangerously. I blink and it's like a film has been lifted from my vision.

I jump up from the couch. "Hey! You tried to hypnotize me!"

But she's no longer looking at me. Cupid stands by the door, his jaw tense, the muscles under his T-shirt bulging as he clenches his fists.

"You betrayed me," he says through gritted teeth. "Explain yourself." He takes a step forward but Selena stands her ground. She raises her palms in front of her, in a placating gesture.

"No need to get overexcited. I don't want a fight. It's just, I thought about what you told me in Elysium, and I think it's better if Lila—"

Cupid's eyes narrow. "Get. Out."

She nods. "Like I said, I'm not looking for a fight. But you're playing with fire." As she walks past Cupid, she catches my eye. "I'm sorry, honey. It really was an act of mercy. You'll find out soon enough."

"Wait!" I call when she reaches the doorway.

She turns and looks over her shoulder, arching a perfectly formed eyebrow.

"What about Charlie? You spoke to her—what did she say?"

Selena sighs, her eyes flitting to Cupid, who's still wearing a face like thunder. "She doesn't know much," she says. "They told her about the company policy, obviously. They are looking for the Finis, which they think is close by. And there are more Arrows on the way."

She turns to look at Cal, who's arrived in the doorway, looking confused.

"Keep an eye on your brother," she says.

And then she's gone.

29

"I really don't see why you feel the need to come along," says Cal.

We're back in the Aston Martin on the way to the Cupids Matchmaking Service to access the digital copy of *The Records of the Finis*. Cal clearly doesn't want Cupid here, but after a bickering match between them following Selena's exit, it seems he's decided it might not be such a bad idea to keep an eye on his brother after all.

While we're gone, Crystal is keeping watch over Charlie, who woke up just before we left. Crystal said she'd thought the initial influence of the arrow had worn off enough that she could reason with Charlie, though I'm sure I overheard her snippily tell Cal she'd have to lie about Cupid and me to do it.

"Getaway driver," Cupid says brightly. His dark mood seems to have vanished. "Plus, I don't trust the Matchmaking Service. Speaking of which, did you tell Crystal what we were going to the Matchmaking Service for, Brother?"

He gives a stiff shake of the head. "I thought she might alert someone, since she doesn't like you. I told her I was going to draw up the paperwork about you leaving town," Cal says. "Which I am—once we've found out where this stupid arrow is."

I sink back into my thoughts as Cal mutters under his breath about what a pain in the ass his brother is.

I don't know what to think. Cupid doesn't trust the Matchmaking Service. Selena doesn't trust Cupid. Cal doesn't trust Crystal. And I don't trust *anyone* in this whole mythological mess . . .

"So, what's the plan again?" I ask from the backseat.

"You'll come in with me," says Cal. "There won't be too many cupids about at this time of night, so hopefully we won't run into too many questions. We'll say that you have an appointment with me in my office. I can access Carter's login from my computer. We'll print off the document, then get out of there." He throws a warning look at Cupid. "And Cupid will stay in the car."

Cupid grins. "Me going in there is a one-way ticket to the Matchmaking Service dungeons. And I really don't want to end up there . . . again."

Cal doesn't return the smile. "Do you know what I'm risking for you? If they catch us with *The Records of the Finis,* they'll know it's to help you. I'll be banished, or worse."

"It's not me that you're risking yourself for," Cupid says quietly.

I wonder what he means by that as we pull up to the side of the road, just down the street from the dating service.

Cal stares stiffly ahead. "I don't have a good feeling about this."

Cupid laughs. "You don't have a good feeling about anything."

Cal ignores that and turns in his seat to face me. "Come on, let's get this over with." He fires a look at Cupid. "And you, you stay in the car. I'm serious."

That just prompts Cupid to make a big show of exiting. "You sure you want to do this?" he asks, sidling back to open my door while Cal huffs and slams his own.

"Sure," I say. "This mystical arrow is the only way I can get you to quit bugging me? I'm in. Let's figure out where it is before they do."

Cal stalks around to our side, his face twisted with fury. "I told you to stay in the car."

Cupid holds his hands up in surrender as I climb out of the Aston Martin. "I'm just going to walk you to the door. If you get caught, you'll need my help to get out."

He gives his most charming smile, which Cal counters with a humorless stare.

"Fine," he says. "Just stay out of sight."

Cal stalks off toward the Matchmaking Service. I watch him go, his hair pale in the moonlight. I think back to what he said about risking his place at the Matchmaking Service.

"You really are infuriating, you know?" I say, looking up at Cupid. "Couldn't you have just done what he asked?"

A smirk tugs at his lips. "I know, I know, I'm sorry. I've condemned you to a half hour with Moody Cal, the even-worse version of Sullen Cal." As I shake my head and start toward the building, he falls into step beside me. "I just need to make sure you're both okay. None of this is how I expected it to be," he says. "When I came to Forever Falls, I thought . . . I don't know what I thought."

The sadness I glimpsed on the balcony has returned to his eyes. And now it seems there is regret mixed in there too.

"What's wrong?" I ask.

He shakes his head. "Have you ever been sure that what you

were doing was *right*, but then as everything starts to fall into place you begin to wonder whether it was worth it?"

"I entered a hot dog–eating contest when I was fourteen," I say. "Threw up for the entire evening afterward."

He gives a surprised laugh. "Well, you know exactly how I feel then."

I look at him seriously. I'm guessing his question was referring to coming here—to finding me. "Who is the founder of the Matchmaking Service? Selena said that person would take over if we were, you know . . ."

"Matched?"

I nod, feeling heat grace my cheeks despite myself. His eyes burn into mine for a few beats, but then he waves his hand dismissively and drags his gaze away.

"Won't happen," he says. "The founder is gone. People need to stop worrying about it."

Suddenly Cal spins around ahead of us and takes several strides back.

"Brother?" Cupid says, amused.

"Cupids can't be matched," Cal says sharply. "I trust you know that. I'm taking part in this escapade because I want Lila safe, and because as much as I hate to admit it, I don't want you killed. But know this: once you have the Finis, I want you out of Forever Falls. I want you gone."

A strange look passes over Cupid's strong features as they stand face to face, tension crackling between them. Not for the first time, I wonder if it's going to develop into a physical fight.

Then Cupid takes a step backward and shrugs. "Let's just get the Finis. We'll deal with all that later."

"Yes, we will," Cal replies.

We carry on in silence until we reach the glass shop front of the Cupids Matchmaking Service. *I can't believe how much has changed since the last time I was here.*

Cupid lingers by the neighboring wedding boutique, eyeing the excessively frilly dress with a look of bored intrigue.

Cal looks at me. "We get the copy of *The Records of the Finis*—then we get out. Ready?"

"Ready."

30

The bell tinkles as we step inside. It looks the same as last time, except now Curtis is sitting beneath the long, golden arrow at the front desk. He's casually flicking through a newspaper and doesn't look up.

"We're not taking on—"

"Any new clients at this time. Yes, I'd heard," I say.

On seeing Cal, Curtis hurriedly shoves his paper beneath some files by his monitor. Then his dark eyes narrow on me.

"Cupid's Match," he says.

"Yes," says Cal, "and proving to be more difficult than I'd expected."

He says it a little too genuinely, in my opinion.

"I'm showing her some of Cupid's files in a hope to get her to take this more seriously."

"Be careful how much you divulge," Curtis says. "She's a human."

"I'm quite aware of that," Cal says, voice clipped.

Curtis shrugs and pushes a clipboard across the stone desk. "Well, she'll have to sign in."

The sign-in sheet is a blank piece of paper with only two Italian names at the top. Today's date is written beside them. *Are the Arrows already here?*

"We don't get many visitors," Curtis offers in brusque explanation.

"I can't imagine why. You're all so friendly." I scribble down my name. "You had two visitors tonight, though."

I feel Cal tense beside me. "Visitors?"

Curtis takes back the clipboard. "Couple of cupids from the Italian branch. In town on business. They wanted to use a computer so they could access the server. I let them use yours seeing as you haven't been in the office all day." There's something a little accusatory in his tone.

Cal's features give nothing away as he strides through the door beside the reception desk. I hurry after.

"The Arrows?"

"They must have found Carter," he says, jaw hard. "They could have easily learned he used to work in the archives, and Selena said he still visited Elysium. We should have taken him in. We need to hurry."

A few of the cupids rushing around the desks and stone columns look at us as we enter, but no one says anything to us as we head to Cal's office. I sit down in his red armchair, casting my gaze around his little section of the Matchmaking Service as he switches on his computer. Other than the chipped mug beside the kettle, there's nothing personal in here—it's all just files and office equipment.

"You should get a plant or something," I say as he slowly types something with two slender fingers. "Spruce this place up a bit."

"I had a plant once. It died," he says, deadpan, eyes fixed on the flat computer screen.

"Oh." *Well, that's the end of that conversation then.* I fiddle with a loose red thread on the arm of the chair. "Find anything?"

"I'm in his files. He's scanned a lot of books in. But I can't . . . ah, got it."

He clicks something. Then his face blanches.

"What is it?" I say.

He curses under his breath. "It's not there. The Arrows must have wiped it after they left."

"Curtis said they used your computer to log in?" I say. "Have you checked for deleted files? They could still be on there."

He looks at me blankly. I lift myself from the armchair and go stand behind him. "Just go back to the desktop . . . no . . . no, don't click there. See that little bin icon? . . . No . . . not that one . . ."

He moves the mouse wildly about the screen and I bite back the growing spurt of frustration. It reminds me of the time I tried to show my grandma how to send an email.

"What are you doing?! Just get out of the way!" I slap his hand off the mouse and lean over him, feeling his irritable breaths on the back of my neck. "How do you have all this surveillance technology and not know how to use a computer properly?"

I navigate to the recycle bin. A jolt of relief passes through me: a file named "Records of the Finis" is at the top of the list of recently deleted PDF files. I click on it and the scanned pages of the book fill the screen. Luckily, it seems that the Arrows' technology skills are just as modern as my grandmother's.

"I can use a computer fine," mutters Cal. He nudges my arm in a battle for dominance of the mouse. Moments later, a whirring sound fills the room as the printer on the filing cabinet behind the armchair springs to life. "But it's not like I grew up with my face glued to a screen like you kids today . . ."

"You just grew up shooting arrows and playing with abacuses, I guess."

"Abaci."

"What?"

"The plural of abacus is abaci."

My lip twitches and he flashes me a grumpy look. Seconds later, he crosses the room and swipes the printed document from the tray.

"Want me to delete the file permanently?" I ask.

He inclines his head as he skims through the pages. When I look back at Cal, his usually steady hands are trembling.

"Cal? What's wrong?"

"We need to get back," he says, his face paling. "The Arrows might be there already. Once they've found out where she's put it, they'll kill her."

I frown. "What do you mean? Who was the last cupid to have the Finis?"

Cal looks at me, panic in his silver eyes.

"Crystal," he says. "It was Crystal."

PART 3
THE FINIS

31

My search for the Finis led me to London.

It was said that there was a beast in these parts—part man, part something else entirely—that had stolen the final arrow and hidden it within his abode.

A thick fog was in the air when I arrived during the dead of night. I'd had to dress the part, and my long, blue skirts made a scratching sound as they dragged across the pavement. I was afraid it would be hard to fight dressed in this way, and I clutched at the special sword that hung under my cloak for comfort.

As I navigated the roads, I wondered whether the humans who had built these streets realized they had unknowingly provided him with a labyrinth. I had to marvel at his power—he had made them do it; he had made them create a vast maze out of terraced houses, shadowed alleyways, and dead ends.

It was a place where it was easy to get lost, and impossible to escape.

The beast had always liked a labyrinth.

I progressed onward. I knew that his home would be at the very center. That's where he would keep the weapon that would kill anyone who shared the blood of Cupid. I hid by a wall as two police constables in tall helmets passed by.

"The Ripper is still at large," I heard one say, their voices muffled in the fog. "Four murders and counting."

I hurried on, clutching the sword even tighter. The humans thought a man had committed the grisly killings, but it was no man.

It was the beast.

The one we knew as the Minotaur.

It was over an hour before I realized I was getting close. The alleys and snicketways grew closer together and before long I reached a tall, wooden fence. At the foot was a pool of liquid. I bent down and studied it.

Blood.

This had to be it.

I pulled myself over the rotting fence and landed on a carpet of dead leaves that led to a mansion. It was tall and foreboding, the roof crumbling in parts. I doubted any human had ever set eyes on it; it was too far hidden.

I took a deep breath and made my way toward the large, wooden door. I had just grasped the cold metal knocker when it opened of its own accord, permitting me entrance into a hall lit dimly by oil lamps. The air smelled damp and musty. I moved forward through the doorway ahead.

Then I stopped still in my tracks in front of a room with a roaring fire.

A long table stretched across the room. On top of it, a feast of food had been laid. At the end was a figure leaning back in his chair, his booted feet resting on the table. His face was hidden by shadow.

The Minotaur.

"Crystal!" he said, his voice as smooth as silk. "How nice of you to drop in."

Then he leaned forward and revealed a face I was not expecting. The face of a man.

His skin was dark and smooth, and his eyes were a hypnotizing brown. I suddenly felt exposed despite my layers of clothing.

He was wearing a shirt with the sleeves torn off, revealing black tattoos that covered his bare, muscular arms. His hair was shaved close to his head, and across his left cheek and eye I could see a long, ugly scar that did nothing to detract from his overall beauty.

In a sudden movement he swung his legs off the table and grabbed a jug. He looked at me and smirked.

"Wine?"

Without waiting for my response he poured red liquid into a nearby goblet. I approached the table and sat down beside him.

"How did you know I was coming?"

He cocked his head to the side, and I turned to see a wall of monitors depicting areas within his London labyrinth.

He, like the cupids, had access to technology ahead of the time.

"You've come to kill me," he said, grinning and exposing bright white teeth, "but first, let us dine."

He made an exaggerated sweep of his hand to gesture at the food before us.

I looked at him curiously. He had an eccentric air, and I was close enough now to notice the black liner accentuating his eyes.

"You're not what I was expecting," I said.

"You were expecting part man, part beast?" He wagged a long finger at me. "Tut tut, Crystal. You should know that is the stuff of fairy tales." A dark look crossed his face then. "But this is no fairy tale. And there is a beast within me," he said quietly. "One that I cannot control."

His eyes glazed over for a moment, and then, with a sudden swipe, he pushed my goblet of wine across the table toward me.

"But let us worry about that later," he said. "Drink."

Cautiously, I took the goblet and sniffed the liquid within. And then, for some reason I cannot quite explain, I drank.

That was my first meeting with the Minotaur.

I dined with him on each of the three nights that followed.

Though I knew him to be dangerous, there was something that made me yearn to be around him. We talked about life, and death, and politics, and gods, and I learned more about him in that short space of time than I believe I have ever learned about anyone.

It was on the fourth night that we knew this charade had to end—one way or another.

"So, are you to kill me?" he asked over a feast of meats. "I deserve it, you know." Then he leaned forward and lifted one finger in an exaggerated fashion, as though he had just had an idea. "Though perhaps we could come to some sort of . . . agreement."

I waited, saying nothing.

"I have something you desire," he said, "and you have something I desire. I know what you keep hidden about your person," he said, cocking his head toward my body. "You got it from the

Oracles, I presume: the Sword of Aegeus. The one sword that can kill me."

My eyes widened in surprise. "You would swap the Finis for the sword?"

"Yes."

I nodded sharply. "Then the deal is done."

That night, we made the exchange and I took the Finis from London.

I hid it in a place where no one would expect to see it.

A place where I could watch over it.

A place where the Arrows would never find it.

♡

"We need to get back," Cal says again. "They'll kill her."

He takes off without another word and I sprint after him. When we reach the reception area, we halt in our tracks.

Curtis is no longer sitting at the high stone desk. He is standing in the center of the floor, blocking our only exit from the Matchmaking Service, and pointing a black arrow straight at us. A quiver full of more arrows hangs over his shoulder.

"Find what you were looking for?"

32

Curtis's eyes skim over the pages tucked beneath Cal's arm, but his arrow remains pointed at us.

"That's it, isn't it? *The Records of the Finis*?" When Cal says nothing, he continues, "I've been watching you from the surveillance room over the past few days. The others may have trusted you with preventing the match, but I knew you'd betray us for your brother. I've seen you—helping him, entering Elysium together, hanging out at his house. Why else were you looking for the Finis other than to make sure he was unstoppable?"

Cal takes a step in front of me. "Curtis. You don't want to do this."

"Why are you doing this, Cal? Your loyalties should lie with us, not *him*."

Cal stands rigidly, his arm muscles tense beneath his maroon sweater. "The Arrows are here," he says softly. "They're looking for it, and they may well find it. Whatever his sins, Cupid doesn't deserve to die."

Curtis's hand tightens around his bow so hard that his knuckles whiten. "*Cupids cannot be matched*," he says. "Reinforcements are on their way. I'm arresting you, Cal. You've betrayed us."

He turns his gaze to me, his eyes wild.

"As for the Match, we no longer shoot humans . . . but I'm sure the Service will forgive me in this exceptional circumstance. Two black arrows and she'll be dead," Curtis says. "Then the match can never be made." He raises the bow higher. "Forgive me."

Cal pushes me farther behind him as my heart pounds.

"I can't let you do this," Cal says. "What do you think Cupid will do to you if he finds out you killed his Match?"

Curtis shakes his head sadly. "I have to   "

"Excellent question, Brother," Cupid asks from the doorway. He turns to Curtis. "What do you think I'm going to do to you?"

Curtis's eyes widen in alarm and he twists and releases the first black arrow. It plunges into Cupid's chest.

"Stay back!" he says. "Stay back."

Cupid pulls out the black arrow with a grunt. "You know you can't kill me with that," he says as it crumbles to ash in his fingers.

Curtis swiftly pulls out a new arrow, loads his bow, and releases. This one hits Cupid in the stomach. Cupid grunts again but continues to advance.

"You can't escape," the receptionist says, though there is more than a glimmer of fear in his voice now. "There are more of us than you."

I hear movement behind us and spin around. My stomach drops. Three more cupids line the entrance to the office, each with a bow and arrow in their grasp. My heart rate quickens.

"Cupid," says Cal sharply, catching his attention.

There is a moment's pause before I hear Cupid sigh heavily. "Are we really going to do this?"

"You could come with us voluntarily," says Curtis, his voice unsure. "We'll put you on trial. It will be fair."

"As convincing as that sounds, I'm afraid I have other plans . . ."

In a flicker of movement, Cupid rushes at the agent blocking our exit and spins him in front of him as though he is a shield. At the same time, Cal grabs the back of my neck and pushes me to the ground to avoid the flurry of arrows streaming over our heads toward Cupid.

Two Ardor arrows sink into Curtis's chest. As he shrieks with pain, I look back frantically at Cal, who pulls me to my feet as Cupid throws the receptionist into the three cupids behind us. Then Cupid darts back out onto the street. Cal and I sprint after him, staying low to the ground as another arrow whooshes above our heads.

I run as fast as I can toward the Aston Martin, my legs screaming with the effort. When we reach it, Cupid is already in the driver's seat, turning on the engine. I throw myself breathlessly into the back as Cal scrambles into the passenger seat. As the car accelerates, I peer through the rear window. One solitary female cupid watches us from the middle of the road, a sour expression on her face.

Cal peers over his shoulder. "You okay, Lila?"

I shoot a glimpse behind us again. The road is now completely empty.

"Yes," I say. "Why aren't they following us?"

Cupid looks at me in the rearview mirror. "I don't know if you noticed," he says, "but they're pretty scared of me. They're prob-ably regrouping, working on a better plan of attack. They know force won't work when they can't kill me. Though I guess I was right—Lila isn't safe from the Matchmaking Service after all."

He throws an I-told-you-so look at his brother, then immediately frowns. "What did you find out in there anyway? Please tell me you found the copy."

"Crystal," says Cal quietly. "Crystal was the last cupid to have the Finis."

Cupid's eyes widen and then he steps on the accelerator hard enough that I'm thrown back against the leather seat.

"What will happen to her?" I ask. "If we don't get back in time?"

Cal's angular face is paler than usual and his jaw is clenched.

"They'll start with the Capax," says Cupid, "to try and get her to tell the truth about where she put the Finis."

"She's a trained cupid, though," says Cal. " She'll fight it. And then . . ."

He stops, looking sick.

"The Ardor," says Cupid quietly. "They'll torture the answers out of her."

My stomach turns as I remember Cal's reaction in the simulation and the receptionist's shrieks just moments before. "And then when they have what they need, they'll kill her so that she can't tell us."

Cupid puts his foot down even harder on the pedal, but it still feels like the hour we spend hurtling down the freeway takes forever. The streetlamps are streaks of white light as we finally race through the town square and approach his home. A terrible thought loops through my mind throughout the drive: *What about Charlie? Is she safe? Will they take her too?*

After Cupid skids to a halt in front of his house, we rush out. There is still a light on in the kitchen, and all looks undisturbed as we race in.

"Crystal!" Cal shouts. "Crystal, are you here?"

Then we open the door to the living room. My stomach plummets; there's obviously been a struggle. The armchair is overturned and books from the shelves are scattered across the hardwood floor. Across the far wall, the roaring fire illuminates what looks like a smear of blood. I turn to Cal, whose expression is unreadable even though his silver eyes blaze.

Then I catch a movement in the corner of the room. I brace myself, spinning to face whatever threat is lurking there. Charlie steps out from behind the bookcase, and her dark eyes meet mine.

"They took her," she says. "They took Crystal."

33

Cupid walks up to the overturned armchair, pushes it back on its legs, and sits down. He looks up at Charlie, his eyes narrowed.

"Why didn't they take you?"

The flickering light from the fireplace casts threatening shadows across his hard jawline. Cal takes a step forward, placing himself between Charlie and me, his fists clenched by his side.

"I would like to know the answer to that too," he says.

Charlie shakes her head. "I . . . I don't know. They untied me, then said they'd be in touch."

"She's lying," says Cal. "She knows where Crystal is."

Suddenly he lunges toward her, but Cupid grabs his brother's arm. Although alarmed, Charlie doesn't flinch. I can see some of my old friend in her stubborn expression, but there's a strange new power there too; a distance. I want desperately to believe we can bring her back again.

"Let's all calm down," I say. "If Charlie was part of this, surely she wouldn't have stayed. Wouldn't she have got out of here if she was helping the Arrows?"

As Charlie looks at me, her face hardens. For a moment, we stare at each other and then she flies at me, wrapping her hands around my neck and ramming me into the wall. Cupid jumps to his feet, but not before I headbutt her and tackle her to the ground.

As I do, it releases some hidden emotion in me, something lurking since I saw her kiss my boyfriend at the party. I pin her arms against the maroon rug as she fights me, her dark eyes flashing.

We stare at each other, breathing hard, ragged breaths. And then the anger seeps away, replaced by sadness at her mask of hatred.

"Charlie, stop it! Just stop it!"

Suddenly, the tension leaves her body. I think maybe she's listening to me, that I've reached her somehow, but then I follow her gaze. Cal has a black arrow pointed her throat.

Cupid crouches down, and I relax my hold on her.

"Listen, Charlie," he says, speaking slowly, as though explaining something to a child, "you must be feeling confused right now, angry too. But the Arrows are not the good guys. They're the ones who did this to you. And they're the ones who have taken Crystal. Now, we're going to get her back, but we need your help to do it."

She narrows her eyes as she focuses on him; her breathing is fast and shallow. "You can't be matched."

Cupid shakes his head. "They made it up, Charlie. They've been trying to kill me for years. And now they're trying to get Lila, too, because they know that hurting her will hurt me." He looks at me, his face serious. "I've been looking for my Match for a long time."

I feel trapped in his gaze for a moment, but the words he is saying . . . I know they're not true. The Arrows want to kill me because us breaking some corporate rule will force a change in leadership. But I still don't understand why that's such a bad thing. Or why Cupid seems to want it to happen.

"That's what Crystal said too," says Charlie. She looks at me, the hate behind her eyes slowly dying. "I just . . . I feel like . . ."

"Brother, some help here," says Cupid, clicking his fingers impatiently at Cal, who, though still holding the arrow, has a glazed look. He blinks, then drags his gaze toward Charlie.

"You feel like your blood is boiling in your veins," Cal says, "like you need to attack—to protect the cupids, to stop what the Arrows have told you will come to pass. That's natural for a new cupid. But we're not your enemy. Neither is Lila. In the next twenty-four hours or so you'll feel yourself again."

Cupid wiggles his eyebrows. "Only cupid-ier."

She looks warily at the black arrow then at the three of us.

"Why did you stay here and wait for us?" I ask suddenly. "If you really hate me this much?"

"Crystal's my friend," she says. "Before I went to camp we hung out a bit while she was working at the diner."

While you were hanging around my boyfriend, I find myself thinking.

"And I don't hate you," she adds, holding my gaze. "What I did—hating you didn't come into it."

Cupid nods and gives what he clearly thinks is an encouraging smile. "Well, that's a start. Why don't you take a seat and tell us what happened?"

Neither of us moves for a moment; we are frozen in the fire-light, me straddling Charlie on the ground. Then she gives a small nod. I take a breath then slowly stand up.

Cupid looks at me and I see the question in his eyes: *Are you okay?*

I nod, though my head is throbbing from where I just smacked it into Charlie's face. I step over a broken stone ornament of two figures riding a wolf, and a tipped-over trinket box marked by an engraved *P* before taking a seat on one of Cupid's leather couches.

Cupid pulls Charlie to her feet.

"We don't need to tie you up again, do we?" Cupid asks.

Charlie gives him a withering look but shakes her head.

"Know that to try anything else like the stunt you just pulled on Lila would be very . . . unwise."

He nods at the armchair, and Charlie tentatively sits down. The brothers take a seat on either side of me, Cupid sinking back into the cushions while Cal perches on the edge, spine straight and stiff. He twirls the black arrow vacantly with his long fingers, his eyes focused on the smear of blood on the wall.

"Cal," I say sharply, hoping to snap him out of it.

"I should have told her," he mutters, staring at his feet. "I should have told Crystal we were looking for the Finis."

"You couldn't have known, Brother," Cupid says, his tone unusually gentle. Then he looks at Charlie. "Now, I could use a Capax arrow on you, but I imagine you've had enough of being treated like a human pincushion. If at any point I think you're lying, though . . ."

"Okay, I get it," Charlie says. "Now, do you want me to tell you what I know or not? Because I think they're going to hurt Crystal, and we need to get her back."

Cupid nods. "Go ahead."

"We were talking when Crystal had me tied up—thanks a bunch for that, by the way . . ."

"No problem," Cupid says.

"And there was a noise outside. Crystal went to check it out. When she ran back in, she looked scared and shut the door. Then she looked at me and said something . . . weird."

Cal leans forward, suddenly alert. "What did she say?"

"She said, 'I wasn't always a receptionist.'"

"Does that mean anything to you?" I ask Cal.

He shakes his head, frowning. "I don't think so," he says quietly. He looks back to Charlie. "Did she say anything else?"

Charlie shakes her head. "Three people burst through the door—two girls and a guy. One of them grabbed Crystal and she fought him. She threw him into the wall."

Charlie gestures at the streak of blood with her head and I see a half smile appear on Cal's face; he seems satisfied that she at least caused some damage to her kidnappers.

"I thought they would attack me, too," Charlie continues, "but they ignored me. There was a struggle and they dragged her out of the room. Then one of them cut through the rope binding my hands together. She told me to get out of here, and that she'd be in touch when she needed me. She said they had an assignment for me."

"What assignment?" Cal asks sharply.

Charlie pauses, an internal struggle evident on her heart-shaped face. "I think they expect me to bring Lila to them at some point, on their orders."

I cast a look at Cupid, who's suddenly wearing a triumphant smile.

"Charlie?" he says. "Would you like a coffee?"

Charlie looks surprised, but she nods. "Sure."

"Lila, Cal—come help."

He gets up and walks out of the room. Cal and I share a look then follow him into the kitchen.

"Subtle . . ." I say.

Cupid shrugs. "Subtlety has never been my strong suit."

As he leans over the breakfast bar, his arms on the counter, I find myself staring at his shoulder muscles. He catches me looking.

"So," I say, before he can make any kind of remark, "you think that the Arrows are going to contact Charlie?"

"Yes. And we can use her to lead us to Crystal. We'll just need to keep an eye on her. Make sure she doesn't revert back to her murderous tendencies."

"No way," Charlie says from the doorway. "I'm going home. I've had a *really bad day.*"

Cupid shakes his head. "Sorry, Charlie. It's not safe, and I can't risk you doing anything stupid." He turns to me. "You, too, Lila," he says. "The Matchmaking Service has shown its true colors, the Arrows are out there, and Selena tried to harm you. You're not going home either."

"Fine by me," I say—though my stomach clenches at the thought of spending the night with Cupid. "Definitely not keen to have my house turned into some mythological battleground."

"Oh God," says Charlie. "My parents! My living room! The Arrows jumped through the window."

"Yeah, they like to make an entrance," says Cupid. "But Crystal made a few calls when we first got here. It'll be sorted by now."

Before Charlie can say anything else, Cal slams his hand

against the breakfast bar. "I'm not happy with waiting for the Arrows to get in touch."

Cupid shrugs and makes his way over to the coffee machine. "What choice do we have?" he says. "Neither of us can get into the Matchmaking Service now. We're both wanted men."

Cal scowls. "You're hardly wanted."

34

Charlie, on seeing that she doesn't have much of a choice, calls her mom then reluctantly heads to bed in one of the house's spare rooms. Cal skulks down to the combat room, presumably to blow off some steam, while Cupid begins clearing his living room of evidence from the attack.

Meanwhile I sit alone in the kitchen, nursing my coffee.

My mind replays the events of the day, which culminate in Cupid's insistence that I spend the night, here, with him. Given all that's happened, it should be the least of my worries, but there's something about Cupid that plays with my emotions; perhaps it's that expression of longing and sadness that crosses his face when he thinks no one is looking. I'm unsure of what to make of him. I do not think I can trust him, yet every part of me yearns to.

Cupid suddenly appears at the doorway, jolting me from my thoughts. After gesturing that I should follow, he leads me into the living room, which has regained its former elegance; if not for the smudge on the wall, it would be hard to believe that this was the scene of a vicious attack.

Cal has returned from the basement and is sitting tensely on one of the sofas, his pale skin lightly flushed and his hair damp. As I pass him to go and sit on the armchair, I catch the scent of fruity shampoo.

"I take it we're spending the night in here?" he says, looking at Cupid. "*All of us?*"

Cupid grins and looks at me. "Well, I have a nice big comfy bed upstairs if . . ."

He trails off as both Cal and I give him a withering look.

Cupid laughs. "Just kidding. I was planning on staying down here anyway, in case Charlie decides to go on a walkabout. If you insist on acting as our chaperone, so be it. I'd say take one of my spare rooms, Lila, but while Charlie still has the Cupids' Arrow pumping through her veins it's probably best you stay with me."

My heart thuds against my chest at the thought of sleeping in such close proximity to him.

"Take the other sofa," he offers. "It's more comfortable. I can take the chair."

I shake my head. "I'm fine." I hardly think I'll be able to sleep anyway.

Cupid shrugs and stretches out on the couch, his shirt riding up and exposing his hips and lower torso. He catches me looking and grins, placing his arms behind his head.

"Now," he says, "time for pillow talk."

Cal sighs noisily and lies down on the second sofa before turning his back to us. "Time for sleep," he says shortly to the cushions. "We have a big day tomorrow."

Cupid holds my gaze, the light from the flickering fire dancing around his ocean-like eyes. I know exactly what he is trying to communicate.

I think sleep is the last thing on Cupid's mind tonight.

It's not long before Cal's gentle snores fill the room. I curl up in the armchair, determinedly facing away from Cupid and studying the objects—aside from books—decorating the shelves. There's an eclectic mix of knickknacks: a small, cheap plastic globe next to a bronze bookend shaped like a temple column; a tiny ornamental Roman helmet tucked beside *The Hitchhiker's Guide to the Galaxy;* a toy car that looks like it came from a McDonald's Happy Meal; and a bunch of James Bond DVDs mixed in with a collection of classic literature.

It's weird how attuned my body seems to be to Cupid; I can hear his breathing, feel his heat, sense his energy. Even without looking I know that his eyes have not moved from my profile.

After a while he sighs and gets up. I watch him out of the corner of my eye as he moves to the curtains, bends down, and picks out three folded blankets from a black cube-shaped footstool in the bay of the window. He walks over to Cal and casually throws one over him. I stare at him, surprised. I thought they hated each other.

Cupid notices me looking.

"Want one?" he says, holding out a blanket. It's cream colored and fluffy.

I take it, then watch curiously as he resumes his position on the leather couch, places his hands behind his head, and rests his bare feet on the arm of the sofa. He doesn't take his eyes off me.

"I don't think you're quite as bad as you make yourself out to be," I say quietly after a few tense moments have passed.

Cupid smirks. "*I* don't make out that I'm bad at all. It's my dear brother who likes to do that."

"You care about him, though."

Cupid shrugs. "He's my brother. He's a pain. But he's my brother."

"He thinks you shouldn't have come here."

Cupid sits up again and leans forward to look at me steadily. "Is that what *you* think?"

My mind is cast back to the past couple of days. Everything—Charlie becoming a cupid, Crystal being kidnapped—all of that is because of him.

"Yes," I say quietly. But as I say it, I know that it's not true. "You've caused a lot of trouble since you got here. Why *did* you come?"

His eyes don't leave mine. "To find you."

My face suddenly feels hot and I'm unsure if it's because of the heat from the fire or the energy that now fills the room. I shift in the armchair.

"Cal said you were banished from the Cupids Matchmaking Service because you obsessed over women. That you had extreme views."

Cupid lets out a short laugh. "Cal said that? He *was* always the dramatic one."

I frown. "They didn't banish you?"

Cupid grins. "Oh, they banished me all right," he says, then pauses a moment as though in thought. "I guess my views are extreme to them."

"What views? Dating?"

He gives another laugh as he shakes his head, then falls back against the sofa.

After a while I speak again. "I don't think you're my Match. I don't believe in that kind of thing."

Cupid shrugs. "I don't either, really—not like my brother does."

"Well, why did you come here, then?" I ask, surprised.

He looks amused. "Curiosity." When I don't reply, he looks at me, his eyes darkening. "I've seen matches. I've made matches. So I guess it's not that I don't believe in them," he says. "It's just, well, a bit depressing, isn't it? You only have one shot, with one person, and once that person's gone—they're just gone, and you're all alone?"

My mind drifts to my dad, lost without my mother. Cal matched them, so they must have been soul mates. And now my dad's soul mate is gone.

Cupid continues, "Sometimes I think that people should just be left to their own devices. All this matching . . . it makes it seem like everything is planned. I don't think love should be planned. Do you?"

"You're a cupid, and you don't think people should be matched?"

He smiles. "Hence the extreme views."

"If that's what you really think, then I still don't understand why you came here."

A shadow flickers across his face. "Whether or not I like it—and whether or not you believe it—a complex system that details the lives of *every single person* on this entire planet has determined that you and I should be together. So maybe I'm not into matches the same way as my brother is. Maybe I don't think love can be that simple. But still . . . in cupid terms, you *are* my Match. I had to find you, Lila. I had to see."

We both fall into silence. The only sounds in the room are Cal's muffled snores and the crackling of the fire. I fiddle with the tassels on my blanket.

"Why did Cal tell me you were dangerous? Because he knew the Arrows would come?"

"Partly," he says, "but partly something else."

"And that is?"

"He thinks that something bad will happen if we're matched."

"What does he think will happen? Is it about the founder?"

"It's something in the Matchmaking Service company policy—"

From the other sofa comes a sharp throat-clearing noise. I jump and spin around. Cal has turned over on his side and is glaring at us both.

"Can you please keep the noise *down*?"

He turns grumpily back around to face the back of the couch and Cupid makes a face at me. I find myself grinning back—I can't help myself.

"'Night, Brother," says Cupid, smiling. Then he lies back down on the sofa and pulls a blanket over himself. When he turns toward me, his face looks softer. "There's something about you, Lila," he says quietly. "I don't know what it is. But when I first met you—I felt something. And I think you feel it too."

I think back to the moment when I handed him the pen, the buzz that seemed to charge through my veins. I want to pull my eyes away but my gaze is locked on his.

"You don't like the idea of matches," I remind him softly.

Cupid smiles and rolls onto his back. He shrugs.

"I think maybe I'm starting to."

35

I don't know how I manage to sleep, but somehow I do. When I next open my eyes, the embers of the fire are glowing orange and early-morning light creeps in through the heavy red curtains. I jolt upward, pulling the blanket to my chest as I sense a pair of eyes watching me. Cupid is sitting upright on the sofa, a huge grin on his face.

"Jeez, Cupid," I say. "You nearly gave me a heart attack. Watching me while I sleep? That's not creepy or anything . . ." My eyes dart about the room. The other couch is now empty. "Where's Cal?"

"He went downstairs to train," he says. "And in all fairness, while you were dribbling and mumbling and snoring over there, it was really hard not to gawk!"

I give him a look. "I was not!"

He grins. "Fine, you weren't. You looked adorable, okay? Now—shall we go and wake our angry little cupid up? See if that arrow venom has left her system yet?"

We head up the black spiral staircase to the spare room, and I can't help but recall the last time I was up here. If I hadn't followed Cupid out onto the balcony, would things have turned out differently? Or would I still be here now, going to wake up my best friend, who has been turned into a cupid, after spending the night with a literal love god?

Before we reach the terrace, Cupid stops and knocks on one of the doors. I feel a knot of tension in my stomach as I remember the way Charlie looked at me last night.

"Come in," Charlie grunts from inside.

We enter a simple but elegant bedroom. The carpet and curtains are a soft white, and there is an ornate black dressing table with a mirror by the wall. Charlie is sitting cross-legged in the middle of the double bed, still dressed in the jeans and black top she was wearing yesterday. Her cell phone is in her lap.

She looks up as we approach, and when our eyes meet, I see something of the old Charlie in them: the sleepovers, the school detentions, and the gossiping during our lunch breaks all seem to flicker behind her expression.

She winces. "Did I really try to kill you yesterday?"

I feel a wave of relief and nod.

She puts her head into her hands.

"You're feeling better then?" I ask.

"Well . . . I feel different. It's all a bit of a blur. I don't really remember all of it. My head is killing me—probably because you headbutted me." She groans. "It's like having a really epic hangover."

"But without the fun from the night before," Cupid says, grinning.

She gives him a dubious look but then sighs dramatically. "Yeah."

He laughs. "It sucks, but that can be the case after the trans-formation." He inclines his head at the phone on her lap and his eyes narrow, the humor disappearing from his face. "Someone's contacted you?"

She beckons us over to show us a message from an unknown number.

"Well that's . . . interesting," says Cupid.

My stomach lurches as I read it. It's from the Arrows.

Keep an eye on the Match. We will take her soon. Be ready.

Half an hour later we're congregated around the breakfast bar; Charlie and I on stools, Cal standing, and Cupid leaning against the counter by his high-tech microwave, eating a bowl of Froot Loops.

We're all staring at Charlie's cell phone in the center of the granite island.

"Ask them if Crystal is okay," Cal orders. He's dressed unchar-acteristically casually in black sweatpants and a white T-shirt that's slightly too big for him. I wonder if he's borrowed the outfit from his brother.

Charlie looks at him warily, then taps out a message. She seems mostly herself again, though her body is angled away from me. Moments later, her phone buzzes in response.

She has not talked. This could take a while. Be ready.

Cupid looks relieved, Cal pained. I understand both of their reactions; the Arrows don't know where the Finis is yet—which is good—but that means that Crystal is still being tortured.

I take a nervous sip of the coffee Cal thrust into my hand as soon as I walked into the kitchen.

"They said you'd help them get to Lila," says Cupid. "Ask them about their plans for Lila."

Charlie types in another message and a couple of minutes later the phone buzzes again.

We know you are on the party planning committee. We need you to get us peacefully into the Forever Falls dance on Friday, and make sure she is in attendance.

"Tell them you'll bring her to them now," Cupid says. "But only if they tell you how many of them there are, how many weapons they have, and to give you their address first."

Cal and I both look at him.

"But in a more subtle way," Cupid says. "Obviously."

She keys in a message and we wait. It takes a good five minutes before we get the reply.

Too risky. Cupid will be watching her. Just get her to the dance. We'll be in touch.

"Interesting. They clearly want the distraction of the dance," says Cupid. "Gives us a bit of time to plan, at least." He places his cereal bowl in the sink and stares pensively into his yard for a moment. The morning light that streams through the glass paints his hair gold. "With lots of people in the same place, it'll be easy for them get Lila out undetected."

"Yeah? We'll see about that," I say, taking a sip of coffee. "I don't get it, though. Why don't they just ask Charlie to kill me now?"

Charlie suddenly appears very interested in the bottom of her mug.

"They think the Finis is within their reach," says Cal, heavily. "I imagine they'll want to hold you hostage so that Cupid will come to them willingly; you would be the easier one to kill, but he's the one they really want. This whole ordeal has given them a perfect excuse to go after him. Which means unless we can get a hold of the Finis, they're not going to be easy to negotiate with."

I frown at Cal.

"Hold me hostage? That's stupid—"

"It's not," says Cupid. "If they catch you, I'll come for you. I'll always come for you."

His eyes beseech mine but I look away. I can't let him draw me in.

"What about the whole unbreakable-oath-on-the-Styx thing?" I say. "We tell them Cupid will leave town once he has the arrow and he won't come back." My heart feels a little heavy saying it.

Cal pinches the bridge of his nose. "I think they've proven they're a little past accepting that now," he says.

"My brother's right," says Cupid. "They've hated me a long time. Our . . . *politics* are somewhat opposing. And they're not easy to reason with. Not when they have the upper hand. Which they do." He shrugs heavily. "They have Crystal, they think they have Charlie under their cupid-y thrall, and they have a plan. We need to get the Finis before they do."

Cal turns sharply to Cupid. "And you're *still* leaving town when we find it."

"'Course, Brother," says Cupid with a strained smile.

"How are we going to find the Finis when the only person who knows where it is has been captured by the Arrows?" I ask.

"It's all going to kick off at the dance. And they need me to get in, right?" says Charlie. "I have an idea."

After she tells us, Cupid leaves the room. He comes back carrying a pink-tipped arrow, which he places on the breakfast bar.

"We need to make sure you're not lying to us, Charlie," says Cupid.

She doesn't say anything for a couple of minutes, then she

nods slowly. "Fine." She picks up the arrow then lightly pricks her fingertip. She breathes in sharply as it turns to ash in her hands.

"Are you going to betray Lila?" asks Cupid.

"No. Are you going to leave town if we get the Finis?" she says.

Cupid looks at her warily then nods.

She turns to me. "They shot me with two arrows, tried to make me a killer, and took my friend. I won't betray you, Lila. Let's get these guys. Let's get Crystal back."

36

After breakfast, Cal uses one of Cupid's cars to drop Charlie and me off at the Forever Falls town square. He's heading back to Elysium, where he hopes to find that song-addicted cupid, Carter, in the hopes he might know something more about the Finis. Since he wants to look like he's on official business, he's changed back into his matchmaking-agent suit. The white brings out the dark smudges under his eyes.

He barely waits for us to shut the car doors before skidding out of the square and down the road toward Los Angeles.

"Bye, Cal," I mutter into the cloud of dust.

Charlie gives me a half smile as we head to the thrift store down one of the side streets. Seeing as Charlie's plan involves us attending the dance, we've decided to pick out something new to wear. It is when we are rooting through the dresses hanging on the clothes rack that I finally ask her the question I've wanted to ask since she was turned into a cupid.

"When you tried to kill me," I say, "it was because you said I was dangerous. You said the match couldn't be made—why?"

"It's all a bit blurry, but they told me it was a breach of the company policy and that the founder would come back." She shrugs. "It seemed really important to me at the time."

"Who's the founder?"

She shakes her head. "I don't know. All I know is that yesterday I was convinced that the founder coming back was a very bad thing." She looks at me squarely. "This Cupid guy, you like him, don't you?"

"No," I say a little too fast.

She arches a knowing eyebrow. "Sure you don't." A smile tugs at her lips before she turns serious. "Be careful, Lila. I have a bad feeling and I can't shake it. I dunno—it might just be from the arrow venom in my veins, but I'm sensing danger. Something is coming."

Charlie is right about Cupid, but something about him is so exciting, so intriguing. He's a mystery, a puzzle for me to solve, unlike James, where I've always known exactly how to put the pieces together—even if it never seemed quite right.

As if reading my mind, Charlie plucks a dress from the rack then looks a little sheepish. "Have you spoken to James?"

I shake my head. "I need to break it off with him but I'm dreading it. To be honest, I think a part of me has wanted to break it off for a while."

She nods seriously. "I know."

"What? And that makes it okay to kiss him, does—"

"No. 'Course not," she says hurriedly. "I just mean . . . well, you never seemed that on board with the relationship. Or that happy. That's all."

There's something a little pained in her voice, and for the first time it occurs to me that if Charlie and James are matched in the same way as Cupid and me, it can't have been easy for her to have watched our relationship from the sidelines. I barely even know Cupid, and yet the thought of him with someone else bugs me more than I would like to admit.

I sigh. "Maybe you're right. Have *you* spoken to James?"

"You mean in between being turned into a cupid and trying to shoot you with an arrow?" She offers me a half smile. "No. And don't worry, I'm not going to try to get together with him or anything."

"You're into him, though, right? Crystal said he was your match, in the same way that Cupid is supposedly mine."

"It's weird, but I feel different since I was shot. What happened—it wasn't right. You're my best friend. And I swear I wouldn't have done it without being hit by the arrow. If I could go back in time, I never would have . . . are we okay?" she says, cutting to the chase.

I look into her brown eyes and see the doubt and fear behind them. She kissed my boyfriend, and I in turn got her turned into a cupid. She tried to kill me, but I was the one who dragged her into this whole mess in the first place.

I smile. "I hope so."

She grins back, relief evident. Then she passes me a black strapless dress over the rack. "Here, try this on," she says, an amused challenge behind her eyes. "I bet Cupid will like it."

♥

"Good trial shift, Dad?" I ask as I enter the kitchen.

He turns around, briefly assessing the shopping bag in my

hand. "It was. Thanks, sweetheart," he says. He gestures toward the living room with a mischievous glint in his eye. "There's someone here to see you."

My heart bounces.

Cupid? I think as I head to the front of the house.

Surely not.

James is sitting nervously on the sofa. He turns to look at me, and his light-brown eyes are forlorn.

"What are you doing here?" I ask. "Aren't you supposed to be at work?"

He shakes his head. "The diner's closed down for the next couple of weeks," he says. "Some kind of maintenance issue." He takes a deep breath. "Listen . . . we need to talk."

I breathe in, pushing down the weird nerves that are rising up from my stomach. "Yes, we do."

I walk past him to perch on the edge of Mom's old armchair.

Silence twists through the air. My eyes skim over Dad's old bowling trophies on the mantelpiece to stop myself from staring at James. I don't know what to say. Evidently, neither does he. He's staring at the wooden floor between his sneakers.

"Did . . . did Charlie tell you?" he says finally.

"Yes," I say. "That, and I saw you."

He puts his face in his hands. When he removes them and looks up at me his brown hair is messy. There's something pleading in his eyes.

"God, Lila. I'm so sorry. I don't know what came over me . . ."

I do. It was the Capax. But still—

"You have feelings for her," I say blankly.

"I don't! I think maybe there was alcohol in the punch or something . . . I never—"

"Just admit it, James," I snap.

He flinches before sighing heavily. "Okay. Maybe. Maybe there was some feeling there. But I chose you, Lila. I *love* you."

"I love you, too, James," I say. "We grew up together. When you fainted in class in kindergarten, I was so worried about you I cried. In fifth grade, I slapped you in the face for drawing all over my favorite pencil case. And when Mom was ill, you were . . . you were my rock. You made me smile and you helped me get through it more than you will ever know." I bite my lip. "But I don't think we're *in* love. If I'm honest . . . I don't think we ever were."

He leans farther forward. "Lila, listen—"

"Please, James. Let me finish." I swallow hard. "I think we were friends. And we just kind of fell together because it was easy. Easier than going after what we really wanted. And when I lost Mom and felt like everything was reeling out of control, that's what I needed. I needed a friend. I needed something that wasn't complicated, or messy, or hard."

"So now you want something messy?" he asks, his tone hardening. "Is there someone else?! It's that Cupid guy, isn't it? I saw him gawking at you at school—"

"Life *is* messy. And look at *us*. *This* has become messy. You kissed Charlie!" I rub my face, hard. "I don't want messy for the sake of messy. But I don't want to live my life trying to avoid anything complicated just because I don't want to get hurt."

"So what are you saying? Are we . . . are we really breaking up?"

I swallow the lump in my throat. "Yes."

We stare at each other. I can feel the heat in my face and his cheeks are flushed too.

Then slowly, James nods.

"Okay," he says. "Okay."

He gets to his feet and I mirror him. We stare at each other for what feels like an eternity.

"I'm sorry for what happened at the party," he says, finally. "I should never have kissed Charlie."

"I'm sorry too. About . . . all of this."

We're standing a few feet apart in the living room we've spent so much time in together—and yet suddenly we're strangers.

"Do you think we can ever go back?" he asks. "To the way things were before we got together?"

He's kissed my best friend, Charlie has been turned into a cupid, and a paranormal organization wants me dead because I've been matched with a banished love god.

"I'm sorry, James," I say softly. "But I don't think we can."

♥

The next few days pass without much incident. Dad seems to enjoy his new job, Charlie doesn't try to kill me again, and James mostly avoids me after the breakup.

I don't get a chance to speak much with Cupid, as Cal hovers around him like an irritable shadow and leads him away every time he spots me down one of the locker-lined corridors. I wonder why they even bother to come to school at all, but on one of the rare occasions I manage to speak to Cupid, he points out that if they were expelled, then they wouldn't be able to attend Friday's dance, which could pose some problems for our plan to get Crystal back.

On Wednesday, Cal demands that we all meet him in the

library at lunch, whereupon he dumps a stack of books and papers in the center of the table. He didn't manage to find Carter at Elysium, but he did blackmail another cupid there into stealing a bunch of resources from the Cupids Matchmaking Service's library; amid the haul are company staff records, old photographs, and weapons books. We sift through them for the hour but can't make any sense of them, and the next day he doesn't bother asking for our help at all—only skulks off at lunch to pore over the yellowing papers alone.

When Friday finally arrives, the air is heavy with anticipation. During the afternoon, we meet in the school gym to help Charlie and the rest of the party planning committee set up the dance, with the idea that we'll also surreptitiously hide some weapons for tonight.

Cal grumpily helps me paint a banner, irritably flicking pink paint and looking at the paintbrush with open disdain. "Why is your mascot a lobster, anyway?" he grumbles. "Forever Falls isn't even by the sea."

"Oh, is that what that's meant to be?" I say peering over his arm at the pink splatter he's made.

He looks highly affronted. "Well, it's not finished yet."

"What's wrong with Shelly anyway?" I say, smirking as I continue with the black lettering.

"It's called *Shelly*? Shelly?! The Lobster?!" He shakes his head. "You humans really have no imagination . . ."

As he mumbles to himself, Charlie picks up a stack of speakers and effortlessly carries them past a muscular football player who is struggling to carry one. Charlie might not want to kill me anymore but I've noticed a few changes since she was hit by the arrow—the superstrength being one of them. I watch as she puts it down and marches across the gym to Cupid, no doubt to tell him off for playing on his phone rather than helping with the decorations.

"Speaking of nonhumans . . . will Charlie be okay?" I ask Cal.

He puts a paint-smudged hand through his hair. "It can take a while for the person affected to understand the weight of the transformation. Usually, an agent would have taken her into the Matchmaking Service by now to debrief and properly train her. But obviously neither Cupid nor I can do that now."

I frown, watching her worriedly. "Can't you get someone else to do it? What about the guy who got you the papers?"

"Right now she's our only chance of getting Crystal back. And our only chance of getting rid of my brother too." His expression hardens. "You really need to be more careful around him. He's no good for you, Lila."

Something shifts in his features as he looks at me. Neither of us speaks for a moment, and I sense the same loneliness behind his stiff exterior as I do behind Cupid's recklessness.

Then abruptly he stands. "I'm going to plant some weapons. Make sure no one notices what I'm doing."

I watch him stalk across the gray floor, then turn my attention to the rest of the room. There are a couple of girls from my class hanging up a banner, Charlie is instructing the guy doing the lighting, and a sophomore named Jane is plugging in the speakers. No one is paying attention to Cal.

Cupid notices me sitting alone and wanders over. As he reaches me, he thrusts a packet into my hand. "Balloons," he says unenthusiastically. "Charlie says we have to blow up balloons."

He sits on the floor beside me and we get to work. Before long we're laughing, racing each other with our balloon-inflating skills and generally having a lot more fun than I would've expected. Once or twice I catch Cal watching us disapprovingly from across the room, but I am never able to catch his eye.

When the end-of-day bell rings, I wave good-bye to Cal and Charlie, who are deep in discussion about tonight's events. They don't seem to want my input, and I want to go home and get ready, anyway. I'm halfway down the corridor when I hear foot-steps behind me.

"Lila?"

I turn around to find Cupid inches away from me. My breath catches in my throat.

"Yes?" I ask, looking up at his face.

He pauses and actually looks a little sheepish. "This may be a weird question after all that's going on, but . . ."—he grins wickedly —"will you go to the dance with me?"

37

For a moment I'm too shocked at the question to answer. Having a date to the dance seems trivial when a bunch of cupids are trying to kill us.

"We might as well have a little fun while we're being hunted," says Cupid. "I mean, what more could possibly go wrong?"

I groan and playfully slap his bicep. "Don't say that. Do you *want* to tempt fate?"

He laughs then gently places his hands on my arms, holding me still. His eyes bore into mine and as they do, the smile falls from his face. "Come on, go to the dance with me."

Every part of me yearns to say yes, but everyone seems so certain that my spending time with Cupid is a bad idea. What about the Arrows? And the plan? And Cal telling me that Cupid is dangerous?

"If everything goes to plan, we'll have the Finis soon, and then I'll be leaving town," he says. "We're meant to be together, Lila. Let us at least have one dance before it all ends."

His thumb gently strokes my arm, sending a tingle across the surface of my skin. I look up at him and drink in his features.

I wonder what his hair would feel like running through my fingers, what his lips would taste like . . .

Stop it, Lila.

"I thought you didn't believe in matches," I say.

He tilts my chin up with his finger so I'm forced to look into his ocean-colored eyes. "I said I was starting to."

I take a deep breath then pull myself away. I need to think. I need to compose myself. But then he wiggles his eyebrows and the corner of my lip tugs upward.

"Fine. I'll go with you," I say. "But I have a condition."

He smiles. "Anything."

"I don't get why the Cupids Matchmaking Service changing management is so bad. Who is the founder?"

I can tell I've taken him by surprise because he rocks backward—it's almost imperceptible, but it's there.

"If you go to the dance with me, I'll tell you afterward," he says. "I'll tell you everything."

"Tell me now."

He shakes his head. "I can't do that. I need more time."

I frown. "What do you mean?"

"Come to the dance with me tonight," he wheedles, "and tomorrow I'll tell you anything you want to know. *Anything.* I promise. Deal?"

He holds out his hand for me to shake and I stare at it. I have a strong feeling that whatever he has to tell me will change everything. I should demand he tell me now. I should tell him I'm not playing these silly cupid games anymore.

But I don't think I'm quite ready for it all to change. Not yet.

Let us at least have one dance before it all ends.

"Fine, deal," I say as his fingers clasp mine. "But tomorrow I want answers."

♡

Later that evening, I stand nervously in front of my bedroom mirror. I'm wearing the black strapless dress Charlie picked out and my hair is pinned up, exposing my bare collarbone and shoulders. I don't normally dress like this, and I feel oddly vulnerable without my usual jeans and Converse.

I should be more worried about what the Arrows have planned, but my mind keeps wandering toward Cupid. It's ten to seven; he should be here to pick me up any minute.

The doorbell rings.

"I'll get it!" I yell.

After one last look, I head downstairs.

The Cupid that is waiting for me when I open the door is different than any version I've seen before. He's dressed in a formal dark-blue suit, a light-blue tie, and a crisp white shirt. The dim light from the porch adds lighter shades to his dark-blond hair, and he's keeping one arm behind his back.

"Lila," he says softly, his eyes drinking me in hungrily. "You look . . . I mean—wow. You look great."

I shift uncomfortably. "Uh, thanks."

"Nervous?" He grins wickedly. "About the Arrows, I mean."

I give him a look. "Well, seeing as they're planning on kidnapping me tonight, a little, yes."

Something uncertain flicks across his expression. "I, um, got you this," he says. He brings his arm from behind his back and passes me a corsage of white flowers. After I take it carefully, he rubs the back of his neck. "You don't have to wear it . . . if you don't like it."

I slip it on my wrist. "I like it," I say. "Thank you."

His face brightens, a smile spreading across it. "Phew. I've never been to a high school dance before. Binge watched an entire season of *Prom Queens* this afternoon to make sure I was doing it right."

I laugh. "I'm sure Cal would approve of that use of time . . ."

"Who's this?" my dad asks, coming up from behind me and placing his hand gently on my shoulder.

I groan inwardly; I really hadn't wanted these two to meet.

Cupid extends his hand. "It's nice to meet you, sir," he says. "I'm Cupid."

Dad says nothing for a moment. Why couldn't he have a normal name?! I cringe, awaiting judgment. Instead, my dad chuckles lightly and returns the handshake.

"A joker, huh?" he says. "Well, I suppose we could use a cupid around here." He looks down at me, light humor behind his blue eyes, and kisses me on the forehead. "Have fun, sweetheart."

I smile, relief washing over me. "Thanks, Dad."

Cupid holds his elbow out for me to take. "Well," he says, "shall we go?"

I tentatively hook my arm through his. Despite the chill in the air, he feels warm, and when we reach his car parked at the end of the driveway, he opens the passenger door for me. I wave good-bye to my dad as Cupid walks around to the other side.

Moments later we're on the road. Neither of us speaks at first, and I can't help feeling a little awkward.

"All the weapons were hidden okay, right?" I ask after a few minutes of silence. "And everyone knows what they're doing? Charlie is okay with doing all this still?"

Cupid turns to look at me. "Don't worry," he says. "It should be simple enough. Charlie only added three of the four names she was given to the invite list. She's told them to arrive at different times so as not to arouse suspicion. One Arrow won't be permitted entry. As soon as we hear there's a problem at the door, I'll slip out, grab him, and take him back to my house. Bit of time with the Ardor arrow and he'll tell me where Crystal is being held. Then Charlie—who will be entertaining the remaining Arrows with her powerful skill of chatting complete nonsense—will help us organize a hostage exchange."

There's a knot in my stomach. It seems like Charlie's the one who is risking everything, and that doesn't seem right.

"They think she's on their side," Cupid says, reading the worry on my face. "She won't be in any danger."

"Is there nothing I can do?"

He shakes his head. "As much as it pains me, and as dull as it may render the latter part of your evening, it's better for you to remain with my brother. The Arrows want at least one of us; it's better if we don't make it too easy for them. Don't worry—we'll enjoy the dance until they get there," he adds, as though my main concern is spending half the evening with Cal. "Cal will keep you safe while I'm gone, and I'll make sure I'm back for the last dance. Promise."

He gives me a winning grin.

"Well," I say dryly, "I suppose that's okay. I mean, as long as you're back for the last dance."

He looks at me intensely. "I'd battle a Roman legion to get to dance with you."

I feel my cheeks heating up and look away. Out of the corner of my eye I see Cupid smirk as he turns his gaze back to the road.

"I'd like to see a few Arrows try and stop me," he says.

38

Ten minutes later, we enter the gym.

The space has been transformed from its usual dull gray to a shock of vibrant pinks. There are blinking white fairy lights draped around the DJ booth in the corner, and a huge banner reading *Welcome Back to Forever Falls!* covers the far wall—to Cal's credit, his lobster ended up looking surprisingly good. The pink, black, and white balloons that Cupid and I blew up this afternoon have been hung around the room in bunches, and a flashing, fuchsia strobe light illuminates the hundreds of students already here.

We immediately spot Cal sitting alone on one of the benches. He also looks different—more grown-up in dark-gray suit and a black shirt that makes his light hair look even brighter than usual. He's done something different with it, too, brushed it away from his face.

"Charlie's over there," he says, gesturing across the room.

I turn and see my friend, wearing a floaty magenta dress, dancing.

Cupid raises an eyebrow. "You know, when I said to keep an eye on her, I didn't mean sit on a bench and stare at her like a creep. Go dance! Have some fun for a change."

Cal scowls and takes a sip of the pink punch he must have got from the drinks table. "I think you're having enough fun for the both of us." He pauses, then looks at me. "You look nice, Lila," he says formally.

"Um, thanks," I say, taken aback by the compliment. "You don't look too bad yourself."

"Yeah. Well."

He shifts his gaze back to the dancing, and I look up at Cupid who shrugs.

"Come on," he says. "Let's go dance."

I'm about to accompany him when I feel someone's eyes on me. James is in a black suit, watching us with a sour expression from across the room. I look away and take Cupid's hand as he leads me into the crowd. We have enough drama going on tonight without James getting mixed up in it all.

Cupid smirks. "I think someone's jealous," he whispers in my ear.

"Well, he shouldn't have kissed my best friend, then."

Cupid's eyes twinkle. "Worked out all right for me."

As we get closer to Charlie, she pulls her phone out of her sleek black purse and looks at it. I reach for her arm, smiling, but when she turns to me, her eyes are wide.

"The Arrows are already inside," Charlie says. "They hit Mr. Butler on the door with a Capax and slipped in while he was flirting with Ms. Green. I knew they were into each other!" She catches sight of our faces. "And totally not the point. . . . They've asked me to bring you to them now, Lila. They're creating a distraction so I can slip you away from Cupid."

"A distraction?" says Cupid. "That doesn't sound good."

"Are they in the gym?" I wildly scan the crowd. "What do we—?"

Before I can finish my sentence, a sudden burst of screaming erupts from the edge of the dance floor. The whooshing sound of hundreds of arrows flying through the air fills my ears. Students begin scrambling over one another, aware that something is going on even if they can't see the Capaxes. When those in front of the pack discover the door to the school's sports fields is barricaded, the panic increases. Cal bolts toward us through the crowd. He shares a look with his brother.

"Brother," Cupid barks, "look after Lila. Charlie, tell them you're coming and follow me. We need to get them out of the gym." When his eyes find my face, he looks as though he wants to say something.

"I'll be okay," I say firmly. "Be careful."

He nods and pushes his way through the dance floor toward the source of the commotion. I reach for Charlie's hand and squeeze it. She nods. Then she's turning and following Cupid toward the gym exit.

Cal grabs my arm. "We need to get out of here."

We start to move, Cal just ahead of me. I'm getting jostled about in the crowd, and it's hard to see where I'm going. Then I hear a loud whoosh and feel a sudden searing pain in my shoulder.

I stop, filled with a weird sense of euphoria as I look down, my eyes momentarily blurred. An arrow juts out from my body.

Huh?

I grasp it and pull it out, watching as it crumbles to ash between my fingers.

"Lila!" Cal catches me in his arms as I begin to fall to the floor.

When I open my eyes, Cal's face is close to mine. All around us people are wandering back to the dance floor as a Daft Punk track blares from the speakers. The pink lights still flash on and off in time to the music. I blink a couple of times trying to figure out what is going on.

"Lila?" says Cal gently. "Lila, are you all right?"

"I . . ."

Suddenly I notice Cal's arms, which are cradled behind my back, supporting me. Despite his slender frame, I can feel the strength radiating from his tensed muscles. When I look at him curiously, he hurriedly pulls me up toward him so that my feet are flat on the ground.

"Are you okay?" he asks again, stepping back.

"Yeah," I say, rubbing my head. "Yeah. I'm fine. What happened? Did I faint? Where's Cupid? Where's Charlie?"

"They went after the Arrows," Cal says slowly. "I know you can't remember, but you were just hit by a Capax, Lila."

I stare at him, confused. "No, I wasn't. I can see the arrows, you know."

Cal nods slowly. "Yes, you can see them," he says, "but you're still human. Remember what I told you before. When a human is hit by an arrow, they forget about it."

I frown. *The Capax? I feel fine.*

Around us the harsh pink lighting mellows as "Can't Help Falling in Love" by Elvis Presley begins to play. It permeates my mind, soft as a dream, and a smile spreads across my face.

"My mom used to love this song," I say. "It was my parents' first dance at their wedding."

Cal taps his leg anxiously, his gaze darting about the gym as people pair off to dance together. There's something about him that's different than usual. He seems brighter somehow.

He shifts a little as I step toward him.

"Dance with me," I say.

His eyes widen. "Uh, Lila, we should probably get out of here. Hide somewhere and wait for Cupid and Charlie to get back."

I shake my head. "We're here now. The Arrows seem to be gone, and Cupid knows where to find us."

I take another step toward him. He doesn't move back, but I can tell by the expression on his face that he is troubled.

"Lila, this really isn't a good idea. You're not thinking straight. It's the Capax."

I look up into his eyes. "It's just a dance."

I hold up the palm of my hand. After a moment of looking at it blankly, he moves his hand toward mine. Our fingers briefly entangle but then he pulls away, flinching as though my skin burns.

I give him a look, then put my other hand around the back of his neck. I can hear his breathing deepen as he slowly places a hands at my waist. I move my body closer to his and look up into his eyes. We begin to sway in time to the music.

"When we were back at the Matchmaking Service you showed me a mug," I say. "It had *World's Best Boyfriend* on it. You were in love once?"

He hesitates, then nods.

"What happened?"

He pulls back a little, seemingly lost for words. "Lila, I really don't think . . ."

"Tell me."

Cal sighs then relaxes, bringing his mouth closer to my ear. "It was a long time ago. I had feelings for a human. It wasn't allowed. The founder was still in charge, and set out to punish us. The only way to save her was to turn her into a cupid," he says bitterly. "So I did."

I feel his tensed shoulder muscles under my fingertips.

"Afterward, she didn't love me anymore—not like she did before. I broke it off and returned to the Matchmaking Service. She joined a Matchmaking Service in London." He looks away as though embarrassed, his eyes shining. "She used to send me gifts on the anniversary of the day I turned her. The mug was one of them."

I gently pull his face back toward mine.

"Do you still love her?"

He shakes his head. "Not anymore. Not like I did."

We look into each other's eyes for a few moments. With anyone else I'd feel uncomfortable being so close, but somehow with Cal it feels okay.

"Lila, this isn't right. We shouldn't be . . . you've been hit by the Capax."

I move closer and lightly touch the side of his face. He leans into me, his forehead just barely touching mine. Then suddenly he springs away. He looks over my shoulder, clearly mortified.

I turn around.

Cupid.

He's no longer wearing a jacket, and his shirt sleeves are rolled up over his muscular arms. His hair is slightly ruffled, and there is a pink bruise emerging over his left eye, as though he's been fighting. And as soon as I cast my eyes on him, I want to be close to him too; to run my fingers down the muscles in his back, taste his kisses, feel his lips brush against mine.

"Cupid."

I am consumed by fire; my skin is alight with it. My heart thumps so hard against my rib cage it feels like it's trying to leap through my chest and into his. He looks at me and then at his brother.

"She was hit by the Capax," Cal says.

I take a step toward Cupid, my eyes fixed on his face. I have never wanted anything more than for him to kiss me.

Something is playing out behind his solemn expression. Then he swallows hard and forces a smile onto his face.

"Come on, lovebug," he says, placing a firm hand on the small of my back. "Let's get you back. You need to sleep this off." He shoots his brother an unfriendly look over his shoulder. "I took out a few of the Arrows, but there could be more. We need to get back. There's been a change of plan, and I don't think either of you are going to like it."

"Where's Charlie?" I ask suddenly, though thoughts of my friend are clouded and far away. My skin feels like its burning where Cupid touches me.

"Yeah, that's where the change of plan comes in. I'll explain in the car."

He steers me through the crowd and out of the gym, Cal following closely behind, his eyes cast to the ground.

39

I wake up in the middle of the night to find that I'm in a large four-poster bed. The sheets are silky against my skin. It's dark, but the window across the room lets in the light of a full moon outside. It illuminates a pile of tattered books on the side table.

I'm in Cupid's bed.

I force my mind to go over the events of the last few hours: the Arrows, the strong pull I felt toward Cupid, and then finally being sent to bed to sleep off the effects of the Capax. I put my head in my hands, cringing hard.

Oh God, did I dance with Cal?

Then my breath catches as I remember what happened to Charlie. When things didn't go to plan, Cupid said they'd had to improvise. They'd faked a fight between the two of them until the Arrows had realized their chance to grab me had passed and invited her to go with them. And she went.

I can't believe Cupid didn't stop her. He said she'd be safe, that we could track the GPS on her phone and that would lead us to

Charlie *and* Crystal. But I don't like this at all. I don't want her to be in such a dangerous situation.

I slide out of bed. I need to know whether they've found her yet—I need to know my friend is safe. I quickly check my phone to see if she's messaged me, then pad across the hardwood floor to the door. I'm still wearing my dress, and my hair is tangled around my shoulders. I must look a mess right now.

From the doorway I hear raised voices coming from downstairs. I creep along the hallway and make my way down the twisty staircase.

"I've reread Crystal's account in *The Records of the Finis*," I hear Cal snap. "And the Finis can kill *anyone* who shares the blood of Cupid. That's what it says."

There's the flutter of papers as Cal presumably drops the document onto the breakfast bar.

"What's your point, Brother?" asks Cupid.

"It's not just me who shares your blood, is it? There's another. If you're doing what I think you're doing . . ."

"And what's that?"

There's a pause.

"You *want* the match to be made," says Cal, lowering his voice to an angry whisper. "You *want* the founder back. And you want the Finis. You don't want it to protect yourself, you want it to kill—"

"So what if what you're saying is true?" says Cupid. "Wouldn't it be better? To not live in fear anymore? You and Amena could be together again."

"I don't feel that way about her anymore," snaps Cal.

There's a pause.

"Well, after that display at the dance, it *does* seem you've moved on," Cupid says, and I note a hint of jealousy in his tone.

Cal doesn't reply for a moment. Then, "You shouldn't be put-ting so many lives at stake," he says quietly.

Thinking I hear footsteps approaching, I hurry back down the hallway. "And you *especially* shouldn't be putting Lila's life at stake," Cal's fading voice says as I slip back into the bedroom.

My heart is thumping fast. I don't think I can trust Cupid anymore.

What is going on?

I want to get out of here, but I can't leave yet, not when Charlie is in danger. When I hear footsteps start down the hall, I run to the bed and leap back in.

There's a light rap on the bedroom door and my body tenses. I don't want either of the brothers to know I heard them. Especially not Cupid. Not yet, not until I know what I need to do.

There's another rap.

"Lila?" Cupid's voice comes into the room. "You awake?"

I don't reply. He knocks again.

"Lila?"

Taking a deep breath, I sit up. I scoot back toward the head-board and pull the silky sheets to my chin. "Yes?"

Cupid opens the door. He's changed out of his suit and is now wearing baggy gray sweatpants and a white T-shirt. He approaches the bed and sits down on the edge, placing a stack of folded clothing beside him.

His breathing seems heavy. I wonder if the argument he has just had with Cal has got to him.

"Have you managed to track Charlie yet?" I ask in a voice as even as I can make it.

"There's something interfering with the signal," he says, "but she'll message us when she can. She'll be safe, don't worry—they think she's one of them."

My heart drops. I want to find her. I want her back.

Cupid says nothing for a moment. "I just wanted to check you were okay," he says.

"I'm fine."

Cupid looks at me curiously. "Are you sure?" When I force a smile, he points to the stack at the end of the bed. "I've brought you some clothes," he says. "Just an old T-shirt and some of my shorts. I thought you'd be more comfortable."

I nod again. He seems to study me for a moment.

"I know you're worried about your friend, but she'll be okay. We'll get her and Crystal out of there before you know it. Trust me."

I force another smile—my cheeks are starting to scream.

"You danced with my brother," he says after an awkward silence. His voice is a little strained, and before I can answer, he stands up. "It was just the Capax," he says, then walks briskly to the door.

"Cupid?"

He looks over his shoulder.

"Who's the founder of the Matchmaking Service?"

A look of suspicion creeps onto his face. I wonder if he's realized I've overheard his conversation.

"We made a deal, Cupid."

He nods sharply. "In the morning," he says. "We'll go to the Love Shack first thing and I'll tell you everything." He smiles but it doesn't reach his eyes. "Get some sleep."

♥

Cal is sitting at the breakfast bar when I come down several hours later, clutching a cup of coffee and staring vacantly at nothing. He looks like he hasn't slept all night. *The Records of the Finis* sits in front of him. He jumps when I walk in.

"Hi, Cal." The air between us feels charged. I know we're both thinking about our dance last night.

"Lila," he says shortly, giving a sharp nod in greeting.

"Any news?"

He shakes his head. "We think Charlie has no phone signal wherever she is. We just have to wait it out, hope she manages to send us a message today." He goes back to staring at the papers on the table.

"What are you doing?"

Cal runs an agitated hand through his hair. "Just trying to find some clue as to where Crystal might have hidden the Finis. When she was taken she said, 'I wasn't always a receptionist.' What does that mean?"

"What was she before she was a receptionist?" I ask.

He shrugs. "An agent," he says. "Like me. Before that, a human. But that doesn't help at all."

I think for a moment. "When did she become a receptionist?"

"I don't remember. There'll be a record of it somewhere, though." He looks up at me, his silvery eyes a little brighter. "Hey. That might actually help!"

I give him a half smile. "The tone of surprise is a bit insulting," I say, heading toward the door. "I'm going to walk home. I want to get changed and check in with my dad before we go to the Love Shack."

"Dressed like that?" he says. "Won't he be a bit suspicious as to where you've been?"

I look down at my combo of huge white T-shirt, baggy shorts, and heels.

He sighs then gets to his feet. "Come on, I'll take you."

I follow him to his Lamborghini. On the road things get awkward again. My mind flashes back to our fingers entwined, our foreheads touching. I feel heat rushing to my face and try to distract myself, looking out of the window.

"You're meeting Cupid today, aren't you?" he asks suddenly.

I nod.

"He's going to give you some answers?"

I nod again. Cal sighs heavily as he pulls up outside my house. He looks like he's holding the world atop his slender shoulders.

"I won't try to stop him," he says. "It's against procedure for our organization to divulge secrets to humans, but nothing is worse than the consequence of you matching with him. It's about time you learned the truth."

I wonder if his heated conversation with Cupid last night has changed his perspective on things. I step out of the car and turn back to look at him seriously.

"Yes, I think it is."

40

Half an hour later I'm walking down the alley toward the Love Shack. The florist's flowers perfume the air, and the overly sweet scent mixes with my nerves and makes my stomach turn. I have a feeling that whatever Cupid is about to tell me, I'm not going to like it.

I let Eric stamp my hand, then I walk inside.

The place looks even tackier in the daytime. The sunlight struggling through the covered windows illuminates the sticky patches dotting the floor. The pink colors, vibrant at night, seem washed out and tired. And the faint aroma of stale alcohol and lime wedges doesn't seem right this early in the morning.

It's pretty much empty, and I see Cupid as soon as I enter. He's sitting at a pink table on the other side of the room.

I take a deep breath then make my way toward him. He's wearing jeans and a wrinkled black cotton T-shirt that looks like he pulled it off the floor this morning. His hair is messy and there's a slouch in his posture. I pull out the stool opposite him and sit down. He smiles at me, but it is strained.

Neither of us speaks for a moment as one of the waiters appears with a pot of coffee. Cupid pours the dark liquid into two mugs then looks at me intensely.

"So, Lila," he says, "what do you want to know?"

I think of all the things I want to ask him, wondering where to start. I take a sip of my coffee then look up at him.

"Why is it so bad that the founder comes back?" I ask. "Why is Cal so afraid that will happen?"

"He thinks it will mean the end of the world."

I raise my eyebrows. "Will it?"

Cupid holds my gaze. "Perhaps."

"Is that what you want? Do you want the world to end?"

"You heard us talking last night," Cupid says. When I say nothing to confirm or deny that, he continues, "I did want the founder to come back, but not to end the world. I wanted to *save* the world. But now . . ." He looks at me sadly. "I didn't expect to feel this way . . . about you, about us, about anything. I don't want to put you in danger, Lila. I'm just worried it's too late."

I feel my heart rate accelerate and my skin prickles. The answer to my next question should tell me everything I need to know.

"So . . . who *is* the founder of the Matchmaking Service?"

He runs his hand through his hair. "She goes by a lot of names," he says. "Aphrodite, Venus—she's the original goddess of love." He looks at me darkly. "Or, as Cal and I refer to her, Mother."

Neither of us speaks for a moment. I stare at Cupid across the table. He looks at me darkly.

"Venus? As in the goddess?"

He nods, his eyes watchful. "She's insanely powerful, extremely dangerous, and nearly unstoppable."

"And she's . . . *your mother*?" I should have paid more attention when we did mythology at school.

Cupid sighs. "Look," he says, "I know this is a lot . . ."

"And she's coming back? If we're matched? *Why*?"

"Breathe, Lila," says Cupid. "I can explain." Without asking he pours some more coffee into my mug. "Let's take this one step at a time. What would you like to know first?"

"Oh, I don't know, the end of the world thing might be a good starting point."

Cupid pauses then takes a sip of his own coffee. He runs his hand through his hair again.

"It doesn't have to come to that. But if we're matched—then she *will* come back."

"And why is that so terrible?"

"It's hard to explain," he says, "but the old gods don't belong in this world. In the old times, they roamed free and ruled over all. They had no regard for the lives of humans—they commanded countless sacrifices, massacres, wars . . . Venus was one of the most powerful and sadistic of them all. The goddess of love."

His eyes burn into mine.

"And there is nothing more powerful or sadistic than love."

I take this in, then push on with my next question. "Why will she come back if we're matched?"

He rubs his chin. "There was a shift around two thousand years ago. The old gods left, went dormant. The reason why was never clear—maybe it was because people stopped worshipping them, or maybe they just became bored of this life. But they still watch over us. They have their eyes everywhere—in their statues, their remaining temples, and through those who still serve them. They lie in wait for an opportunity to return."

He pauses, waiting for me to process what he has just said. Then he continues.

"About a millennium before they went away, Venus founded the Cupids Matchmaking Service. It was the most efficient way for her to remain powerful. She gained power every time a match was made, and every cupid, upon getting hit by an arrow, entered into a contract with her. They were sworn to serve her in secrecy by making those matches, and in payment they received eternal strength, youth, and beauty. They're still bound by that contract."

I frown. "But where do I come into all of this?" I ask. "Why will she come back if we're matched?"

"Cupids are forbidden to fall in love themselves. It was the rule she enforced most severely, punishing and torturing anyone in her service who broke it."

I look at him, confused. "Why?"

He shrugs. "She said it was a distraction—that it would prevent the cupids from wholeheartedly serving her. I always wondered if there was more to it, though—some kind of power behind a cupid being matched that could be harnessed against her if it was discovered."

"But she's gone now."

Cupid's face is unusually serious. "Yes," he says slowly, "but before she left, she wrote the company policy. In it she listed rules, which if broken, would mean she would come back to bring order to the Matchmaking Service. And one of those rules was—"

"No cupid must ever be matched," I say, remembering the words carved underneath the stone statue in the Matchmaking Service. The statue was Venus. That was why Cal seemed so uneasy around it.

"Would that really mean the end of the world, though?" I ask.

"If she's just bringing order to the Matchmaking Service, is that really so bad?"

Cupid shakes his head. "You don't know what it was like in the old days. Do you really think a god would be satisfied with reigning over one organization? We're talking mass human sacrifices, wars over love, forced worship at temples erected in her name, more cupids created, more Ardor arrows punishing humans. She'll take back the Matchmaking Service . . . and then she'll take back the world."

I stare at him, my brain whirring. I'm trying to make sense of everything, but it's still not all fitting together. "Before, you said you *wanted* her to come back? If she's so bad . . . *then why*?"

A dark look crosses his face. "I want to put an end to her," he says, "once and for all. For thousands of years we've lived in fear, bound by her rules, knowing she could come back and destroy lives at any moment. She's been more lenient with me breaking rules because of who I am, but she wouldn't be able to ignore this one. Cupid himself finding his Match!" He shakes his head ruefully. "What would the others think if she didn't enforce her own most revered policy? If I break this rule, she *will* return."

"You want to draw her back and then kill her with the Finis."

He nods and a wave of nausea, cold and clammy, settles over me.

"You want to kill your mom?!"

He reaches for my hand over the table but I pull it away. "Lila, listen, yes. But—"

"That's horrible," I say quietly. "She's your mother."

His lips tighten. "You don't know what you're talking about, Lila. She's a monster."

My heart thuds in my chest. I don't know what to make of any of this. I can't relate to it, none of it—not a goddess returning, not wanting to kill your own mother. I rub my face, trying to make sense of it.

"So, this will happen if we're matched," I say. "But what counts as a match? We already went to the dance together."

Momentary amusement flashes across his face. "It takes more than that, lovebug."

I look at him, feeling heat rise to my face. "Oh!"

Cupid laughs. "No, not that. The match is made when both parties develop feelings—feelings beyond a superficial attraction. It's made when they begin to fall in love."

I frown and shake my head. "I really don't want to bring back an ancient goddess so that you can kill her."

Cupid looks at me seriously. "Don't fall in love with me then."

I think back to last night—the urgent need I felt for him, the fire in my veins. And then I feel rage boiling in my stomach, knowing that he used me, that he put me in danger for his own needs. I fix my eyes on his.

"Don't worry, I won't."

The words come out coldly enough, but I don't know if I mean them. Despite everything, as he sits there, his ocean-like eyes fixed on my face, I still want him. I can't help it. *I still want him.*

"Okay, good," he says, "and I'll try to do the same."

"God, Cupid. How could you do this? Everything that's happened, it's all your fault." I abruptly rise to my feet, letting the stool fall back on the floor behind me. A couple of the waiters turn to look at me but I ignore them. "I'm done," I say. "I'm done with all of this."

If we continue to spend time with each other we *will* fall for each other—that is what Cal was trying to prevent all along. And if that happens, it could mean the end of the world.

He jumps to his feet, and I see the regret in his expression. "Lila, please . . ."

"No, the match cannot be made. I need to stay away from you." I shake my head. "I can't believe I started to actually feel something for you."

Cupid makes as though to reach for me, but stops when he takes a good look at my face. "I'm sorry," he says, trying to keep his voice even. "I didn't know you. I didn't expect to feel this way. I never intended to put you in any danger. I thought it was the only way to free my people, to return *home*."

I glare at him. "You used me to try and resurrect an ancient goddess!" Something suddenly occurs to me. "That's what you told Selena, back at Elysium. That's the big secret. That you were going to use me to bring back Venus. That's why Selena tried to turn me into a cupid."

He takes a deep breath then nods. I want to walk away from him yet something in his eyes holds me in place.

"When I get the Finis I'll leave, I swear it," he says. "If that's what you want. But please, stay with me until then. As long as we don't develop any more feelings for each other, Venus can't come back—but the Arrows are still out there. You're in danger, Lila."

I shake my head again, a tornado of anger and sadness rising through my body. "I need to go."

I spin around, barging right into Cal's hard chest. For a moment he looks like he's going to tell me off for not looking where I'm going, but then he sees my face and shuts his mouth. His silver eyes flicker to Cupid, looking lost behind me, and a grim satisfaction crosses his face. Then he turns his gaze back to me.

"Charlie got in touch," he says. "I know where she is. I know where they're keeping Crystal."

41

"Where are they?" I ask.

"Romeo's," says Cal. "Just around the corner. Come on, we need to go. *Now.*"

He turns on his heel and heads back out of the Love Shack. I race after him, feeling Cupid fall into step beside me. I try to push my feelings of anger away; I need to focus on Charlie.

"Will they be okay?" I ask Cupid, trying to keep my voice even.

"Charlie will be fine. Crystal . . . I don't know. After this amount of time, well, it's hard to say what state she'll be in."

We catch up with Cal in the alleyway and burst into Forever Falls square. The run-down diner stands there as usual in the corner. It looks unusually dark inside.

"Weapons?" asks Cupid.

"Three black arrows and a Capax in my backpack," Cal says.

Cupid nods and we head toward the building. When we reach the diner, there's a sign on the door reading *Closed for Maintenance.* I recall James saying earlier that it would be closed all week. It would be the perfect place for the Arrows to set up base without being detected. The phone signal has always been bad there, which is why it took Charlie so long to get in touch. I wish I'd thought of it sooner.

"You don't have to come inside with us," Cupid says. "What we see in there . . . it might not be pretty."

Cal looks at his brother sharply. "Well, we can't just leave her alone out here. What if one of them comes out to find her? She's safer with us."

Cupid looks at me awkwardly. "Sorry, scrap that. Looks like you're coming along after all."

"Of course I'm coming. My best friend is in there."

Cupid takes a quick look around to make sure no one is about, then puts his hand on the door handle. "Lila," he says, his eyes burning into mine, "about before . . . I really am sorry."

"This isn't the time for that," I say quickly, heart pounding. "Let's just get Charlie and Crystal back."

He nods then throws his shoulder into the door. There's a cracking sound and it flies open. The three of us walk into the empty diner. The last time I saw the inside of this place was when I was in the Sim. I think back to the training and the black-eyed demons within. My hands shake slightly and I stuff them into the pockets of my jacket. *I managed to fight the fake Arrows, but can I fight real ones?*

Cupid passes the booths and makes his way to the door behind the counter. Cal and I follow. We enter a narrow hallway that smells of damp. There are wooden stairs leading upward, and a murmur of voices comes from above.

Putting a finger to his lips, Cupid slowly leads us up the rickety staircase. My heart pounds as the steps creak below my feet.

We emerge into another dank hallway lit by a flickering bulb. There is one door at the end.

The voices are louder now.

Cupid moves forward. Despite his size, I notice the lightness in his steps. When Cupid stops by the door, Cal silently unzips his backpack and slips out a black arrow. Realizing my eyes are on him, he raises his pale eyebrows in question.

I nod. *I'm okay.*

He smiles thinly and we move toward Cupid. We wait outside the door, trying to listen to what is being said.

"She's made it pretty clear where it is," says an accented male voice. "I've let the other Arrows know; they'll go collect the Finis. Our job is done. Let's just dispose of her."

I notice Cal's grip tighten on the black arrow.

"No!" I hear Charlie say and my heart leaps in my chest. There's an awkward pause. "I just mean, well . . . what if you're wrong?"

There's a murmuring.

"She's right," comes another voice, this one sneering and female. "Our people can't get the Finis now—there'll be too much security. They'll head there at midnight when there's a shift change. If it really is where she says it is, then we'll kill her. If not, we can ask her some more questions."

As Cupid turns to say something to us, the floorboard beneath him creaks. Silence suddenly falls on the other side of the door.

"There's someone outside," the first voice announces. "Get Crystal out of here."

Cupid barges through the wooden door. Instantly, Cal jumps forward and throws the arrow like a spear over his brother's shoulder. I hear a grunt as it hits its target, then a thud.

One down.

Cupid grabs another arrow from his brother's bag as Cal moves into place. I rush into the room behind them. Charlie leaps to her feet, catches Cupid's eye, then swipes a gold-and-red Ardor from the floor. She jams it into the nearest Arrow's shoulder, causing her to scream in pain.

"Lila!" shouts Cupid. "Get Crystal!"

My eyes dart about, logging five Arrows: one fighting Charlie, three on their feet by a tattered-looking couch, and a fifth—hit by Cal's arrow—on the floor. I search the shadows for Crystal as the two brothers rush forward and tackle an Arrow each, Cupid jamming his weapon into the neck of a woman in a sleek, tailored suit.

The last Arrow, dark haired and wiry, turns around and leaps over the sofa, rushing toward the far wall of the room. I follow him with my eyes and see Crystal slumped over a wooden chair, unconscious. Without hesitation I run toward her, racing the Arrow. He gets to her just before me and turns, a sneer on his face. He doesn't seem to have any weapons, but he is a good head taller than me.

"I'll be back for you later, Lila Black," he says, his accented voice dripping with disdain.

Then he scoops Crystal off the chair and makes his way toward the door. I look about frantically, trying to find assistance, but Cupid, Cal, and Charlie are all fighting a small but fierce Arrow who has picked up an arrow and has Charlie pinned to the ground by the couch.

I stand frozen for a moment, not knowing what to do. Then I notice something shimmering by the wall. Stacked in front of the peeling wallpaper is a bow and a quiver full of red-and-gold arrows.

Ardors.

They must have been using them on Crystal, I think with a wave of nausea.

I grab the bow and an arrow, pulling back and aiming at the back of the cupid carrying Crystal. He's moving quickly and I can't afford to miss. I take a deep breath then let go. There's a whoosh as the arrow hurtles through the air, then a thunk as it plants itself in his back.

I feel a wave of satisfaction as the male lets out a strangled cry and falls to his knees, dropping Crystal unceremoniously onto the floor. Cupid, having just knocked out the remaining Arrow with a swipe of his fist, looks up at me, impressed.

The four of us rush toward Crystal and the screaming Arrow. Cupid places his fingers against Crystal's throat, checking for a pulse. He nods to himself, satisfied.

She's alive.

"It's too late. We know where it is!" shouts the Arrow in his thick accent, his words laced with agony.

Cupid reaches into Cal's bag and pulls out the pink-and-silver Capax. He jams it into the already tortured male.

"*Where is it?*"

The cupid only laughs. "You really think the truth arrow can make me talk?" he pants against the pain. "I'm a trained . . . Arrow. I serve *Her*. I'll never tell you where the Finis is. More of us are coming, and you'll never get away."

Cupid sighs and scoops up Crystal. "I believe him. He won't talk. Time to go."

Cal looks down at the writhing Arrow and gives him a contemptuous look. Then he punches him square in the jaw.

"That's for Crystal," he says as his target thuds backward against the floor.

Cupid raises his eyebrows. "Nice punch, Brother."

Cal nods rigidly, but I notice the half smile on his face. "Thanks."

Once we burst out into the square, we don't stop running until we reach Cupid's car. Piling inside, Cupid lays Crystal down over Charlie's and my laps in the backseat. He starts the ignition and we race toward his house.

"Are you okay?" I ask Charlie.

She nods but I notice her trembling hands and smudged makeup. She's still wearing her magenta evening dress but the fabric is creased. Her jet-black hair is no longer in its updo, but messily tumbling down her bare shoulders.

"I kept trying to make excuses to leave but they weren't having it. They clearly didn't trust me. I couldn't tell whether they knew I was on your side. I thought they would kill me."

I squeeze her hand then look down at Crystal. Her skin is clammy and there are red smudges around her swollen eyes. Her closed eyelids flicker and every few moments she moans. "Will she be okay?"

Cal looks over his shoulder, his brow furrowed. "I hope so."

Cupid catches Charlie's eye in the rearview mirror. "So, where is it? Where is the Finis?"

Charlie shakes her head. "I don't know," she says, looking momentarily queasy. "Crystal just kept saying the same thing over and over again. It was like she was trying to tell me something without telling the rest of them, only they must have figured it out."

"What did she say?" Cupid asks.

"The same thing she said to me back at your place: 'I wasn't always a receptionist.'"

42

Once we're back in Cupid's living room, we lay Crystal on the couch opposite the fire. Cupid goes to make us coffee and Charlie, after her traumatic evening, goes upstairs for a nap.

Cal crouches beside Crystal as I perch on the edge of the armchair. He brushes a damp strand of hair out of her face with surprising tenderness.

"Crystal? Wake up," he says. "You need to wake up."

Her breathing seems to steady, but she remains in her weird, Ardor-induced coma. As Cal continues to entreat her, Cupid enters the living room. He passes me a mug.

"Get out of the way, Brother," he says, putting his own coffee mug down on the table and shoving Cal aside. He shakes Crystal by the shoulders. "Oi! Crystal! Time to get up!"

She doesn't stir. He taps her on the face.

Cal slaps his hand away. "Hasn't she been through enough?!" he hisses.

"We need to find out where the Finis is before the Arrows get it," Cupid replies.

"Well, your technique is clearly not working."

Cupid huffs and gets up, looking unusually irritable as he sits on the edge of the other sofa. Cal begins pacing around the room.

"Will you sit down, Brother?" Cupid snaps after a few minutes of silence.

Cal glares at him, then suddenly walks out of the room without saying anything.

"What do we do?" I ask.

"The Arrows said they'd send someone to get the Finis at midnight," Cupid says. "Unfortunately, we can't ask Crystal where they'll be going, what with her being unconscious. When they have it, they'll come straight for us. Not to be dramatic or anything . . . but they'll kill us all."

He smiles weakly. For a moment, despite our earlier fight, I want to reach out and touch him, to tell him that everything will be okay. But then I remember what will happen if we develop true feelings for each other: Venus will come back. And the Arrows are coming for us. So nothing is even close to okay right now.

I wrench my gaze away from his and glance at the clock on my phone.

"If she wakes up soon, can we get the Finis before they do?"

Cupid runs a hand through his hair. "I suppose . . ."

"We can't count on it," Cal interjects from the doorway. He walks back inside and dumps a pile of books, papers, and photographs on the coffee table. Cupid groans.

"Oh great, your stacks of useless information."

Cal's jaw clenches. "Have you got a better idea?!"

Neither of us speak.

"Well?" he says. "What are you waiting for? We have less than twelve hours to find the Finis or we're all dead. Let's get to work."

We spend the entire day in Cupid's living room. By ten o'clock, the living room is a mess of papers and documents. I sit on the floor by the coffee table, skimming through the printed pages of *The Records of the Finis*.

Two hours until midnight.

Cal crouches on the floor beside me, flicking through sepia photographs while Cupid slumps in his armchair, his eyes bleary as he looks through an especially thick file marked *Employee Details*. Crystal is still unconscious on the couch behind us. Dirty coffee cups cover every available surface. After a while, Cal sighs and drops the picture he was examining.

"Anything?" he asks us.

"It would help if we knew what we were looking for," says Cupid, throwing the file down on the floor. "Let's try and wake up Crystal up again." He makes a move to rise, pushing his muscular arms against the sides of the chair.

Cal glares at him. "And what do you suggest we try now?"

They stare at each other for a moment before Cupid shrugs, slumping back down in his seat.

"Fine," he says. "You've got me. I have no idea."

We fall back into silence for a few moments before Cupid speaks again.

"Anyone want another coffee?"

I pass my mug to him and he strides out into the hallway.

Cal frowns. "There *must* be something," he says, going back to the photographs on the coffee table.

I peer over them. Some are faded and sepia toned, others are bright and new. They all seem to be depicting the same posed shot of a group of cupids.

"She said she wasn't always a receptionist. That *has* to mean something," he mutters. As he reaches behind me for the file Cupid dropped on the floor, I pick up a sepia image from the top of the pile to examine it more closely.

It shows the reception area of the Matchmaking Service. The image is faded, but I can make out a male in his early teens standing in Crystal's place behind the desk. I scan the rest of the picture, trying to find her, but she's not there. There's something else about the room that looks different, like something is missing, but I can't put my finger on what it is.

I glance down to the corner of the image, where *March 1887* is written in black marker. *Why does that year mean something to me?*

I frown and pull *The Records of the Finis* toward me, turning to the earmarked pages that give Crystal's account of her meeting with the Minotaur. *Whitechapel, London, 1888* is written at the top of the page. The year after the photograph was taken.

Cupid saunters back into the room carrying two steaming mugs. He places one down before me and throws himself back into the armchair.

"Cal," I say, "the file you're looking at—it has employee details in it?"

He looks up at me sharply, seeming irritated by the interruption. "Yes?"

"So presumably it will have the dates when cupids started working for the Matchmaking Service?"

"Yes. But what good is that?"

"Does it have the date when Crystal stopped being an agent and started being the receptionist?"

He studies me a moment, then looks back down at the file and flicks through it. He stops on a page and scans it for a few moments.

"January 1889," he says. "But I don't see why that is important."

1889. Just after her visit to Whitechapel to retrieve the Finis.

I ignore him and grab the sepia photograph, studying it again. Then I turn back to the pile on the coffee table, sifting through the photographs until I find the group shot from 1889. Sure enough, Crystal is there, smiling in the center.

I look up and grin, realizing now what else was missing from the first image.

"It's important," I say, "because I know where the Finis is."

♥

The street in front of the Matchmaking Service is quiet beneath the lit streetlights. The clock on the dashboard of Cupid's car reads eleven forty. We have twenty minutes before the Arrows get here.

"You really think it's in the Cupids Matchmaking Service?" Charlie says from her spot beside me in the backseat.

I nod.

"And you want me to break in?"

"No. Yes. Well . . . kind of."

Cal looks at us in the rearview mirror. "It's not a break-in. You are welcome there."

"Unlike any of us," Cupid adds.

"Thanks to your brilliant plan of resurrecting a goddess," I say.

Cupid makes a dismissive sound as Charlie says, "What?!"

"If you're quite finished," Cal says.

He turns to look at Charlie. "In normal circumstances, one of the cupids would have brought you in already, usually the one who turned you. Because that was someone from the Arrows rather than a cupid from our L.A. branch, I expect that Crystal would have been assigned as your mentor."

"And you want me to take the Finis?"

"No," says Cal. "To take it yourself would be a one-way ticket to banishment. We can't ask that of you. You just need to get the receptionist to leave the desk *before* midnight, which is when they usually swap shifts. Once the area is clear, we'll do the rest."

She nods. I'm grateful that after everything that's happened to her, she's still willing to help.

"Be careful. We only have one shot at this," Cal warns.

"So no pressure or anything," says Cupid.

As Charlie opens the door of the car and steps out onto the street, I marvel at the simplicity of Crystal's clue. She was giving us the answer this whole time. When she'd got back from London with the Finis, she must have maneuvered herself to work in a position where she could watch over it at all times.

It was the arrow hung over the desk. She'd hidden it in plain sight.

"Wish me luck," Charlie says.

I watch as she walks down the street toward the Cupids Matchmaking Service, then glance at the quiver full of arrows by my side. My heart beats fast as I think about the potential fight ahead.

"Good luck, Charlie," I say quietly.

We sit in tense silence for a few minutes before Cal exhales loudly. He grabs his bow from the satchel beside me and opens the car door.

"I'm going to try and get a bit closer, see if I can see what's going on." He looks at me and then at Cupid. "Behave yourselves," he adds sharply before stepping out of the car.

We fall into silence again as Cal moves stealthily down the sidewalk. Cupid turns to look at me, and, despite myself, I find my gaze wandering toward his lips. Despite everything, I still find myself wondering what they would taste like.

"You're still angry with me," he says.

"I have to be," I say. "What's the alternative?"

He gives me a sad smile. "You forgive me, give us a chance, and we live happily ever after?"

I force a laugh. "This isn't a fairy tale. Love isn't a fairy tale. If I give us a chance, Venus comes after us and I'm guessing we don't live at all."

"What is a fairy tale without a monster to defeat?"

I shake my head then drag my gaze away. "You used me. When you get the Finis you need to leave."

He sighs heavily. "You have my word. As soon as we have the final arrow I'll get out of town. The Arrows will come after me, Venus won't return, and you'll never see me again."

Even though it's what I asked of him, his words make me feel like I've been punched in the stomach.

He has to go. But I want him to stay.

I rest my head on the leather headrest and nod. "Okay."

He reaches over the seat to try and take my hand but I don't let him. *I have to be strong.* I feel my anger coming back, and I seize upon it gladly. It doesn't matter that he now seems to have acquired a conscience—he used me to try and resurrect an ancient goddess, he made me feel something for him, and now he is leaving me behind.

"You should never have come here," I blurt, fixing him with my stare.

He looks momentarily hurt. Then a flash of annoyance crosses his face. "Well, I'll be leaving you in good company at least," he retorts coldly. "I would have thought you would appreciate some alone time with my brother."

I stare at him in shock but before I can respond, my phone vibrates. It's Charlie. She's inside.

43

Cupid immediately snatches his bow and quiver then climbs out of the car and slams the door behind him.

When I get out of the car and sling my own quiver over my shoulder, I note the distinctive lack of black arrows. It's not the Arrows we're dealing with this time around, and Cal doesn't want the members of the Matchmaking Service to be harmed too badly; they were his colleagues and friends, after all.

"Let's go, then," says Cupid. "We don't have much time."

We walk down the street in heavy silence, me half running to keep up with his long strides. We spot Cal just ahead, feet away from the Matchmaking Service entrance. On seeing us approach, he nods in our direction then slips through the door.

Cupid and I jog after him to the glass shop front. It's empty inside. Immediately, my eyes home in on what we came here for: the long golden arrow that hangs above the reception desk.

The Finis.

Cal is already inside, passing the neon-colored armchairs and sprinting toward the high stone reception desk. Cupid opens the door and we both hurry inside as Cal pulls himself up and reaches for the arrow.

"How long have we got?" I ask.

"Not long," says Cupid, not looking at me.

Then Cal has it in his hand. He pulls, and it detaches easily. He looks at us, a triumphant expression on his face. And then the alarm starts.

"Dammit!" Cal mutters, his face panic stricken as he leaps down in front of us, slipping the Finis into the quiver over his shoulder. "*Run!*"

Cupid pushes me ahead of him. I'm just behind Cal going through the exit when there's an inhuman shriek of pain behind us. I spin around as Cupid falls to his knees in the center of the reception, four Ardor arrows embedded in his back. Curtis stands in the doorway from the office, a large bow raised. Agitated, he's shouting into his headset for more agents to come.

He swipes another arrow from his quiver as voices raise behind him.

Cupid looks up at us. "Go," he splutters, his face red, his eyes unfocused. "Get out of here."

The exit is just behind me. I share a look with Cal, who shakes his head quickly, trying to tell me not to do what I'm about to do. *But I can't leave him.*

I race back inside, dodging an Ardor that Curtis sends my way as more agents spill into the reception area. Cal bites out a curse and sends a stream of arrows over our heads. I throw Cupid's arm over my shoulder.

But Cupid's too heavy—I can't lift him and he doesn't respond to my desperate pulling. Cal's arrows are buying us time, but now the agents are advancing toward us. My eyes find Charlie, who is watching the scene unfold in horror from the back of the room. Our eyes meet but she does nothing, her expression uncertain.

"*Help me!*" I scream at her.

Nothing.

Another arrow slams into Cupid's shoulder.

His eyes water and he's stopped making any sound. I grab his face, forcing his gaze onto me. "Cupid! Come on. Get up!"

The nearest agent reaches for Cupid's shoulder. He is tall with striking blue eyes. He looks strong. And merciless.

This is it. We're done for.

Then he cries out in pain as an arrow is thrust into his neck. Charlie stands over him, her brown eyes shining fiercely. She throws Cupid's other arm around her shoulder as Cal hits the two other agents reaching for us in quick succession. Her cupid strength makes all the difference, and with Cal covering us with his rain of arrows, we manage to move Cupid out to the street.

"Get him to the car," says Cal. "I'll try to hold them off."

Cupid starts to regain consciousness as the three of us move toward the Aston Martin. An Ardor skims past my arm, snagging some of the material of my leather jacket. Cal is still behind us, sending arrows back toward our pursuers.

"Get him in the back!" Cal calls. "I'll drive."

We push Cupid into the backseat beside me and Charlie runs around to the passenger seat. Then Cal sprints to us, turning his back to the arrows hurtling his way. He makes it to the car and throws himself inside, immediately locking the doors as arrows ping against the outside of the vehicle. Soon, two agents are banging on the hood.

"You are under arrest! Get out of the car."

Cal ignores them and starts the engine, then puts his foot down on the accelerator.

"The match must not be made!" an agent cries, but he's forced to jump out of the way as we power off down the road.

Cupid's head lolls onto my shoulder. He is whimpering quietly, and there is a thin sheen of perspiration across his forehead. Charlie is muttering in the front seat, her head in her hands. "Oh God, oh God," I hear her quietly repeating to herself.

I reach out and grab her shoulder in what I hope is a reassuring manner, then I look out of the rear window. The road is dark for a couple of minutes, but then I see two cars—a Porsche and a Jaguar—roar into view behind us.

"Cal," I say, "they're coming."

He accelerates. The car skids around a sharp corner, throwing Cupid on top of me.

"Where are we going?" I ask, pushing a groaning Cupid back into an upright position.

"Don't know!" yells Cal.

I glance over my shoulder again. Another car has joined the chase and they're all gaining on us. The night is filled with sounds of screeching brakes and beeping horns. They're closing in. We're going to get caught.

Then suddenly they drop back. I blink in confusion.

"Cal . . . what's going on?"

His expression in the mirror is equally confused. Then his phone buzzes. Keeping his eyes on the road, he pulls it out of his pocket and throws it onto my lap.

"Read it."

I read it aloud:

Contacted the Matchmaking Service. I've bought you some time.

But there's a condition—they want something in return for their leniency. I said I'd make the arrangements. Come back to the house. I'll explain everything. Crystal.

"Atta girl, Crystal," Cupid mumbles, his head rolling back to rest on the back of the seat.

A wave of relief crosses Cal's face. He turns the car around and heads back toward Forever Falls. I look at the screen and frown, then key in a reply.

What do they want in return?

Seconds later the phone buzzes with Crystal's response.

Cupid.

44

I stare blankly at Cal's phone, a sinking feeling in the pit of my stomach. Then I glance at Cupid, whose head is still lolling against the seat. His eyes are closed and his breathing is fast and shallow. My eyes find Cal's in the rearview mirror.

"Their condition is Cupid," I say quietly as he drives. "The Matchmaking Service is letting us go back safely because Crystal told them they could have Cupid."

To my surprise Cal gives a noncommittal shrug.

"I thought as much," he says as we reach the sign reading *Forever Falls*.

"What? You mean you're okay with this?"

His angular features harden. "You don't understand *anything*, do you? They were hardly going to let us off with no consequence. You've learned by now what happens if Cupid is matched, I presume? He's been on their undesirable list for years. You should be thankful it's not *you* they're after."

I sit in stunned silence for a moment before Charlie turns around.

"Maybe he's right, Lila," she says tentatively. "I'm new to all this—but if those Arrow guys are after you and Cupid because they think you're going to get together . . . well, they'll have no reason to try and kill you if he's in custody."

I open my mouth to retort but Cupid rolls his head toward me and looks at me with bleary eyes. "S'okay, Lila."

I look at him. His face is flushed and his body is as hot as a furnace. "Cupid? What can I do to help you?"

"He'll be fine," says Cal. "The Ardor just needs to work its way out of his system. Crystal recovered."

I look up at him. "Are you seriously going to let them take him? When he's like this? He can't defend himself. What will they do to him?"

Cal takes a turn and I realize we are approaching the hill by Cupid's house.

"They'll put him on trial. It's no less than he deserves."

Moments later Cupid's house looms before us. Cal parks the car outside the front door.

"I can't believe you're even contemplating this," I say angrily. "What's wrong with you? He's your brother! And he said he was leaving town after he got the Finis, anyway."

Cal looks sharply over his shoulder. "My brother says a lot of things he doesn't mean."

I shake my head. "He gave me his word. He really will leave. I told him there was no future for us."

Uncertainty flickers behind Cal's silver eyes. We stare at each other for a few tense moments.

"Does that change anything?" I finally ask.

Cal sighs and opens the car door. "Maybe," he says. "Let's just get him inside and see what Crystal has to say."

He comes around to the back and grabs his quiver, which has the golden Finis bunched in among the other arrows. Then he throws Cupid's arm over his shoulder and hauls him up the driveway, reminding me again of his understated strength. Cupid is bigger, yet Cal holds him upright with a casual ease.

Charlie and I follow the brothers back into the house.

Crystal is sitting at the breakfast bar when we enter, stirring a mug of coffee. Her skin looks unusually pale and there are dark circles under her otherwise bright blue eyes. In front of her is a narrow, black case. Her gaze slides across all of us, lingering on Cupid, then resting on the quiver slung over Cal's shoulder.

"You found it," she says, her voice a little weak.

Cal nods, still supporting Cupid, whose head has drooped onto his chest.

"What happened?" he asks her.

"I told the Matchmaking Service about the Finis, and how the Arrows tortured me to gain possession of it. The Matchmaking Service agreed to pardon you and Charlie for your involvement, and they have issued an arrest warrant for the members of the Arrows involved with my kidnapping, so they should be off your case, for the time being at least."

"But they want Cupid?" I say quietly.

Crystal turns to look at me. "Yeah," she says. "And they want the Finis."

Cal's features darken. "They'll kill him."

Crystal shrugs. "Maybe," she says, "or maybe not. I don't think they want to. They'd fear a backlash if they were wrong. I think they'll do something worse."

"Put him in a Sim you mean," Cal says quietly, color leaving his face.

I look at Cal questioningly, and he tries to school his features into something less horrified.

"They can sentence someone to time inside a Sim—trap them inside their own mind."

Nausea fills me. "Look, maybe Cupid's been selfish in coming here, but he doesn't deserve this," I say. "The match hasn't been made. No harm has been done. Can't you just let him go?"

Crystal pinches the bridge of her nose, eyes cast down to the granite breakfast bar. "Not when we can't guarantee he won't come back."

"He won't," I say.

"And what am I supposed to say to the rest of the Matchmaking Service, Lila?" she asks. "That I let him go because his Match told me to? I'll end up on trial myself."

"But—"

"Tell them he escaped." Cal's voice is low.

Crystal snaps her head toward the two of them. Cupid groans, his face flushed, and I can't tell if he's trying to join the conversation about his fate, or whether he's just in pain. Cal shushes him.

"I'll make sure he leaves in the morning," says Cal. "I'll have him swear an oath on the Styx not to come back in Lila's lifetime." He takes a deep breath and looks uncomfortable. "Please, Crystal."

She eyes Cupid warily. "He'll never agree to that."

"He will," I say. "He was going to before."

"Is that true?" asks Crystal.

Cal gives a stiff nod. They hold eye contact. Then Crystal exhales.

"Fine. But he leaves first thing," she says.

Relief floods my system as Cal agrees, but it's weighed down with sadness. It's the right thing to do, I know that. We can't risk developing any more feelings for each other. But the oath is so definite; if he swears it then there's no way I'll see him again. Ever. And that hurts.

Cal watches me for a moment before turning back to Crystal. "What about the Finis?" he asks.

"I've kept it hidden for so long," says Crystal. "I never wanted the other cupids to get a hold of it because I feared what they would do with it. It's our one fail-safe way to destroy *her* if she comes back."

"Venus?" I say. "You're worried the cupids might destroy the Finis even if Cupid and I don't get together? "

"A way to show their loyalty—and now that Cupid has matched, who's to say another cupid won't one day find themselves in the same situation. Which is why we can't give it to them."

A half smile creeps onto her face. She opens the case sitting on the breakfast bar to expose a golden arrow that looks exactly like the arrow that hung above the reception desk.

"We're going to give them a replica."

45

A few hours later I sit on the edge of Cupid's four-poster bed. The moon shining through the window paints him with ghostly light. He is fast asleep, and finally peaceful. I find myself watching his chest move up and down under the silky sheets.

Not long ago Crystal headed over to the Matchmaking Service with the replica of the Finis. She'd had it made years ago just in case she ever had to switch the two. Her parting words were, "The match must never be made."

I plan to join Charlie in the spare room shortly, but I want to say good-bye first. As I'm watching, Cupid opens his eyes slowly, then smiles.

"You shouldn't be here," he says. "Not that I'm complaining."

"Are you feeling better now?"

"Mm-hmm," he says sleepily. "Much better now."

I smile, then stand and start to walk toward the door.

"Lila."

I look back.

"Stay with me. Just for the night. Just once."

My breath catches in my throat. I know I shouldn't, yet the vulnerability in his voice stops me still in my tracks.

"We won't do anything," he says softly. "Just lie here. Lie here with me."

"The match can never be made," I whisper.

I turn to look at him. He props himself up on the pillow, his eyes blazing into mine. "I know."

He's going in the morning, I remind myself, *then I'll never see him again.*

Tentatively, I approach the bed and sit down beside him. I can feel his warmth. Smell his scent. Every part of me longs to touch him, to stroke his cheek, to brush my lips against his. But I can't— not now, not ever.

I lie down beside him, my head sinking into the soft pillow.

My breathing hitches at the intensity of his gaze, at the way his eyes, filled with want, flick down to my lips. I don't think anyone has ever looked at me that way before.

Heat spreads unbidden through my body. I try to stop it. I swallow hard, pushing it down before it consumes me.

"You shouldn't look at me that way," I say.

"I know." A smile spreads across his face but his eyes remain fixed on mine. Then he sighs and turns onto his back, rubbing his face with both his hands. "I know."

I roll onto my back, too, staring up at the dark oak posts of his bed, and the shadows they cast on the ceiling above. His arm brushes against mine as he lays it between us.

"I should go," I say—even though I know I won't.

"Don't. I'll be good. I promise."

I breathe in deeply, tasting the faded scent of his cologne on my tongue. The window opposite us is slightly open and a cool, moonlit breeze ripples the thin white curtains. I watch them for a moment as they reveal glimpses of the infinite stars outside.

"When you leave town . . . where will you go?" I ask.

He gives me a half smile. It doesn't reach his eyes.

"I'll probably just hit the road again. See where it takes me. I've traveled a lot since I was banished. I could never find a place to settle." He grins. "Plus, I knew Cal and the Matchmaking Service always had eyes on me—so I liked to make things difficult."

"Yeah. I noticed that . . ." I say. "Where have you been?"

"Where haven't I been? I've visited every continent. More than once."

"Even Antarctica?"

"Even Antarctica."

"What's it like?"

"Chilly."

I laugh and turn to face him. "I never would have guessed."

He rolls onto his side too. "It's beautiful," he says.

The tension starts to build again between us and I avert my gaze down to his chest.

"I always wanted to travel," I say, bringing the conversation back on track. "I told myself I'd go somewhere last summer. And then I told myself I'd go somewhere *this* summer. Only I never actually did." I shrug. "Maybe after graduation. Just for a few months. But . . . I don't know . . ."

He frowns. "Why don't you know?"

"I don't know if I can leave my dad. Plus, every time I think about planning it, it makes me think of Mom."

He looks at me, suddenly serious. "Why?"

I meet his eyes, something heavy inside me. I don't like talking about Mom, yet something about the close comfort of his body and the concerned furrow of his brow makes me want to, for once.

"She had this wild, adventurous heart deep down, and she always used to talk about seeing the world. But she never did it. And then, between the hospital visits, and the chemo, and . . ." I swallow, something thickening in my throat. "She never got the chance. When she was ill, just before the end, we used to . . ."

I sigh and roll onto my back. I've never told anyone this before.

"What?" he says softly.

"It sounds stupid. We used to play pretend," I say. "I'd lie in bed next to her and we'd talk about all the places we were going to go, the things we were going to do, the sites we'd see, and the food we'd eat."

He moves his hand, his little finger brushing against mine. "That doesn't sound stupid at all."

"We never had much money," I say. "But my mom left a little for me. I was going to use it to go to some of the places we talked about, only every time I think about it . . . I always worry I'll get it wrong. I'll go to the wrong place. It won't be like we talked about. I won't live up to her expectation of it."

Somehow, saying it makes some of the weight in my chest lessen. He moves his hand completely over mine, enveloping my fingers in his, and squeezes.

"You have so much time, Lila," he says. "If you do something, and you get it wrong, then you try again. Nothing is permanent." He glances at me. "When I'm about to do something I always think—what's the worst that can happen?"

I turn back onto my side to face him. "Is that what you thought when you came to Forever Falls?"

"Yeah." He raises his eyebrows. "What's the worst that can happen? I resurrect an ancient goddess who'll want to destroy the world. No biggie."

The corner of my lip twitches. "Yeah. No biggie."

"I am sorry, you know. I know I can be reckless. I guess it's easy to be when you don't have anyone, anything, to care about . . . but still, I can't quite find it in me to regret it," he says. "I know my brother thinks I shouldn't have come here. I know a lot of people think that. But regardless, I'm glad I met you."

"Yeah. Me too."

"I think you have a wild and reckless heart, Lila," he says, finally. "Like your mom."

"I miss her," I say, something tightening in my throat.

"I know."

He squeezes my hand again, and his fingers are warm and safe around mine. We fall silent for a while.

"So . . ." he says. "When all this blows over, where we going to go?"

"We can't—"

"I know."

I meet his gaze, his face close to mine. He gives me a reassuring smile. I take a deep breath.

"Okay. Well . . . I always wanted to go to Europe. Italy maybe."

"Good choice. I'll meet you in Rome. By the Colosseum. There's a great pizza place nearby . . ."

We make our pretend plans well into the night; we'll see the pyramids in Egypt, and ride tuk-tuks in Bangkok. We'll wander around the Louvre in Paris, and see the northern lights in the Arctic Circle. We'll eat, and party, and Cupid will show me the places he grew up in.

Finally, as my eyelids become heavy, silence descends. For a moment we look at each other and he is so close I can count each eyelash. Slowly, and unsurely, he reaches for my hand, enveloping it in his. My skin tingles where his touches mine.

"I wish things were different, Lila." His voice is heavy in the darkness.

I swallow hard. "Me too."

♡

When I wake up, the room is still dark. I hear the patter of rain against the window. I turn to look beside me. The sheets are rumpled and Cupid is no longer there. I climb out of bed and pad barefoot out of the room. A shadow flickers across the hallway leading to the terrace. I creep to the glass door.

Cupid is pacing back and forth in the darkness. His gray T-shirt is wet with rain and clinging to his muscular frame. He has his head in his hands.

I step onto the terrace, feeling the chill against my bare arms. "Cupid?" I touch his shoulder. He flinches and jumps backward.

"Stay away from me!"

I feel a flash of hurt. "Cupid? What's wrong?"

His face is panicked and wet. "I should never have come here. Oh God, oh God." He puts his head back into his hands.

I pull his arms back from his face to look at him. "Cupid, what is it?" I ask just as the ground beneath my feet trembles. *An earthquake?*

"Stay away from me!" he shouts again.

The trembling increases and I stumble against him. He looks at me and his eyes are wild, angry. He grabs my arms, his fingers digging into my skin. His face is inches from mine.

"You seemed so sure. You said you wouldn't . . ." he murmurs. Rain runs down his face, flattening his hair and dripping into his mouth. He lets go of me and takes a step backward. "I thought I could stop myself," he says. "I thought I could stop myself from falling for you."

The shaking increases and I hear a clattering below as garden furniture falls over beside the pool.

"It's too late, it's too late."

"Cupid, what do you mean? What do you mean it's too late?" But I think I already know. Dread begins to grow inside of me. The floor beneath us shakes some more as a rumbling sound fills the air.

"I couldn't stop myself," he says. "I couldn't stop the feelings."

Then he looks up at me, the panicked expression replaced by something else—a hunger.

"It's too late," he whispers. "The match is made."

Suddenly he pulls me into him. He cups my face in his hand and leans forward. My heart pounds as I feel his breath on my face, then he brushes my lips with his—lightly at first, but then with growing ferocity.

My body sinks into his. Around us the ground is still churning but I can't hear it over the pounding of my heart. *I know I shouldn't be kissing him but I can't stop. I don't care. I don't care.*

As he runs his fingers through my rain-drenched hair, I vaguely register that the earthquake has stopped. But I feel the tremble in his chest as he parts my lips with his tongue. My stomach is somersaulting.

Then the door to the terrace bursts open and we spring apart. Cal stands in the doorway, a look of fury on his face. In one hand he holds his cell phone.

"Crystal's just called from the Matchmaking Service. I hope you're pleased with yourselves."

He looks at me coldly then slides his gaze over to Cupid. His voice is dripping with disdain.

"The match was made. Mom's home."

PART 4

CHIEF EXECUTIVE OFFICER

46

An extract from the Company Policy

1. Once hit by the Cupids' Arrow, you enter the service of the Founder indefinitely. On entering the service, you will make matches to serve the almighty power of the Founder and perform occasional additional duties as required. These may include sacrifice, arson, theft, battle, protection, guarding, cleaning, general maintenance, chauffeuring, and any other such tasks that may fall under the scope of serving the Founder.
2. Upon joining the service, you will have exactly one month to put your human affairs in order before surrendering your former identity indefinitely. This will include severing ties with family members, friends, and romantic partners in order to focus your attention solely on the tasks cited in Rule One.

*3. You may be required to relocate to one of the
many global Matchmaking branches to fulfill Rule
Two. On doing so, you will be eligible for our reloca-
tion package, including a new home and your own
personal cupid mentor.*

*4. You will master the art of the bow and arrow in
order to excel in the duties cited in Rule One.*

5. NO CUPID MUST EVER BE MATCHED.

*Upon adhering to the Rules, you shall be rewarded with
a benefits package including eternal youth, beauty,
strength, wealth, and a company carriage. Any breaking
of the Rules will result in the return of the Founder herself, whereupon she will take back her position as CEO
of the Cupids Matchmaking Service.*

*Any rule breakers will be put on trial and punished
most severely.*

Venus, Founder and Goddess

♥

Cal glares at us through the sheets of pounding rain. For a moment
no one speaks. My head is whirling from the kiss, Cupid's words,
and Cal's news.

Mom's home.

"Get inside," he snarls. "The pair of you." Then he spins on his
heel and goes back through the door.

Hesitantly, I pull my gaze up to Cupid. A mixture of longing
and regret swirls behind his eyes.

I touch my lips. I can feel the memory of his kiss bruised onto them. *What have we done?*

Cal is on the phone inside, his back to us both. As Cupid closes the terrace door, Cal turns, revealing two towels tucked under his arm. He throws one at Cupid, who catches it warily, then thrusts the other out to me. His silver eyes blaze with fury, but I can sense something else there too. Something that looks a lot like pain.

"Thank you," I mumble, taking the towel and looking down at my feet. I remember our dance, the way his arms closed around me. Maybe it had meant more to him than it had to me.

"What's going on there now, Crystal?" he asks, pushing the phone back to his ear and stalking off down the hallway.

I look up at Cupid, the towel hanging limply in my hand. He's used his to dry his hair, which now stands up in random spikes.

"Here," he says, gently taking my towel and looping it over my shoulders. As he brushes a strand of wet hair behind my ear, I shiver, unsure if it's related to the cold or the effect of Cupid standing so close.

I shake my head, panic growing inside me. "What have we done? Is Venus really back?"

"Afraid so, lovebug."

He lets me go and I take a step back, my stomach churning. "I should never have kissed you." The horror of what we've unleashed is slowly dawning on me.

"It was already too late," he says. "My feelings have been growing for a while. I let my guard down because I didn't think you liked me." He tilts his head a little. "But your feelings were growing too."

Despite the situation, he seems almost pleased. He touches my cheek, his thumb leaving a trail of energy against my skin. His mouth parts slightly and it takes everything in me not to grab his wet shirt and kiss him again.

"You're supposed to be a love god," I say, "and you couldn't tell I liked you?"

"I told you—subtlety isn't my strong suit," he says. "Next time get some flashing *I Like Cupid* badges and wave some flags."

"I would have but they were all out of them at the store."

He laughs. "You could have told me."

"I couldn't." I shake my head. "I was mad at you. I *am* mad at you."

"I know, lovebug, and I deserve it."

"Plus, I think I was lying to myself. Like, if I told myself I wasn't into you then maybe I could make myself believe it."

He shifts his gaze to the floor and the smile falls from his lips. "I should never have come here."

"No, you shouldn't have," snaps Cal, clanging back up the spiral staircase. He's carrying the black case for the Finis replica under his arm—I presume that this time it holds the real thing. "Venus is sending a team here to arrest us all," he says. "Now."

Then he races down the hallway and vanishes into a room across from Cupid's bedroom. I spin back toward Cupid, who looks resigned.

"We'll fight this, Lila," he says, then gestures that we should go after his brother.

We follow Cal into a large study with a prominent mahogany desk. Six monitors cover its surface, and the large tinted-glass wall behind gives a view of the approach to Juliet Hill. The sky is pink in the early dawn.

Cal places the Finis on the desk then leans over to switch on the screens. He looks at Cupid, oddly calm despite his fury. "I take it you still have all your security systems set up?"

Cupid nods and falls back into a leather recliner in the corner of the room.

"We're staying here, then?" I ask. "Shouldn't we be, I don't know . . . running away?"

Cal glares at me. "Don't you understand? They're on their way. *Now*. We'll never get away in time, and even if we could—*Venus* is after us. Venus with the full force of the Matchmaking Service behind her—the Matchmaking Service that, in case you've forgotten, has an extensive web of worldwide surveillance. There's nowhere to hide."

I stare at him defiantly. "But they know we're here, so we definitely won't get away if we stay, will we?"

"We'll keep them out," Cal says. "Or we'll try to, anyway."

He pushes another button on the computer. There is a whirring sound as metal bars slide down to cover the glass window.

"I have them over all my windows," says Cupid, noticing me staring. "Can't be too careful nowadays."

"What happens if they get in?" I ask.

"I don't know for sure," Cal says icily, "but I imagine we'll all die."

"All right, easy now, Brother . . ." Cupid says.

Suddenly, a shuffling noise comes from down the hallway. As the three of us look toward the door, Cal reaches for a letter opener that sits on the desk. My heartbeat quickens. Then Charlie walks in, rubbing her eyes.

She glances at Cupid and me, drenched with rain, and the small blade in Cal's hand. She wrinkles her nose.

"What's going on?"

"The match was made," says Cal coldly. "Venus is back, and her agents are coming to arrest us all."

"Oh," Charlie says. "Damn."

"Yes," Cal says, "damn indeed." He fires another look at Cupid. "Any idea how to get out of this mess you've got us into?"

Cupid sighs. "Perhaps." He pushes himself up out of the chair, shedding his towel, and comes to gently take my hands in his. "It'll be okay, we'll get out of this."

Charlie clears her throat.

"You, too, Charlie." He grins then turns to his brother. "Come to the combat room with me, we need to get set up with weapons."

For a moment the two brothers seem at an impasse, Cupid staring at Cal as though silently communicating something. Cal frowns. Then he nods sharply and the two of them walk toward the exit of the room.

"Lila, Charlie," Cal says at the door. "Keep an eye on the monitors. We have surveillance cameras all over the house and grounds. You see anyone approaching and you shout, okay?" He's gone before either of us can agree.

Charlie and I hurry around to the other side of the desk. Different parts of the house and grounds flicker in black and white across the screens.

"So, the match was made," Charlie says lightly.

I look down. "I'm so sorry, Charlie," I say. "You should never have been involved in any of this."

She shrugs and slides into the chair facing the monitors. "It's not so bad being a cupid. Forever young, powerful, weirdly good at archery. The resurrection of an ancient goddess who wants to kill us is a bit of a downer, though."

Although there's fear in her expression, she grins. I can't help but grin back.

"Did you kiss then?" she asks.

I roll my eyes and laugh. *The end of the world is coming and she still wants to gossip about boys.* I nod.

"Any good?"

I think back to Cupid's warm hands on my body, the taste of his kisses mixed with raindrops. "You could say that."

She leans her head against my arm and we fall into silence, staring at the grayscale monitors.

A few minutes later the brothers reappear. Between them, they carry bows and quivers for all of us, each quiver filled with all three different types of arrows. Cupid hands Charlie and me ours, then shares another odd look with his brother. Cal opens the case on the table and slips the Finis into his quiver, hiding it among the other arrows. I'm surprised—I thought that Cupid would have wanted to be the one to take it, given killing Venus was the original reason he came to Forever Falls.

A movement on one of the monitors stops the question in my throat. Tiny shapes are appearing on Juliet Hill. I grab the edge of the desk to prevent the tremble in my hand.

What I see is even worse than I'd imagined. This isn't a team of agents; it's an army.

"Oh my God," I say, my voice barely a whisper. "They're coming."

47

The screen shows a block of armed cupids marching across the grounds, their bows raised. My mouth dry, I spin around to study the barred window. As the steady mass of white suits gets closer, the stomping of feet begins to resound around the study.

"Oh my God," I repeat.

"Guys," says Charlie, still staring at the monitors. "There's more—they're surrounding the house."

The three of us crowd behind her. Similar blocks of agents have appeared on another two of the screens. As they reach the grounds they begin to disperse, forming a perfect circle around the building.

"Well, this is it," Cupid says.

He throws a sideways look at Cal, who is still staring at the screens as, outside, one of the cupids at the front of the ranks produces a megaphone from under his jacket.

"On the orders of Venus, you are under arrest! You are surrounded. Please exit the building with your hands raised above your heads."

I look at the two brothers. "Now what? They can't get in, can they?"

Cupid shakes his head and falls back into the leather recliner.

"Now we wait"—he looks at me darkly—"for as long as we can."

Around an hour passes. It's excruciating. The agents from the Matchmaking Service still surround the building, and at regular intervals the booming voice calls for us to go outside. Each time it does, my whole being fills with dread. Cupid, however, seems unperturbed. He continues to lean back in the recliner, his eyes closed.

Charlie and I have found a way to share the office chair, and stare at the screens. My stomach is turning anxiously. Across the study, Cal paces back and forth with his bow slung over his shoulder.

"Will you desist, Brother," Cupid says after a while, his eyes still closed. "You're making me nervous."

After a few more laps of the room Cal walks to the exit.

"Where are you going?" I ask.

Cal looks at me. "None of your concern."

As he disappears into the hallway, I share a look with Charlie, who shrugs.

"The longer you take the worse it will be for you!" booms the voice from outside.

I study the monitors. I don't see how we can get out of this.

After a few minutes Cupid sighs and gets up out of the chair. "Come on, let's go make a coffee or something. This is just depressing."

I hesitate, reluctant to go downstairs.

"It's safe," he says. "They can't get in unless the bars are lifted. And the only place that the bars can be controlled from is in here."

I share another look with Charlie, who shrugs again. "I wouldn't say no to a coffee," she says.

The three of us head down to the kitchen, where I see Cupid wasn't lying—large bars cover the glass entryway. Cal is peering out through them, his phone pressed to his ear. On hearing us enter, he hurriedly stuffs it into his pocket.

Cupid frowns. "Calling someone?"

Cal turns around slowly to face his brother. "Crystal." He looks uncomfortable for a moment, his eyes not quite meeting Cupid's. Then he stalks past us.

"You don't want to stay down here for a coffee, Cal?" Cupid says, his tone challenging—cold. I look between the pair of them, wondering if I'm missing something.

"Someone needs to watch what's going on outside," Cal says, his voice flat.

Cupid watches his brother leave with reproach. Then he wanders over to fiddle with the coffee machine.

"What's up with him?" I ask after a few moments of tense silence.

Cupid hands us two coffees. "I think my brother is about to betray us."

"*What*? What do you mean?"

He looks at me steadily. "I don't think he was on the phone to Crystal. I think he's just negotiated himself a deal."

"No," I say. "No. No way."

Cupid takes a sip of the dark liquid and leans back against the counter. "Wait for it."

A whirring sound kicks up a few seconds later. I spin around to see the bars over the windows slowly rising. The coffee mug falls from my hand and shatters, the black liquid splattering the white floor. I feel sick.

Cupid looks at us. "Upstairs, now."

When we reach the study, Cal is standing in front of the window, backlit by the warming light from outside. The bottoms of the bars disappear upward.

There's no doubt about it.

He did it. He betrayed us.

"How could you?" I screech as the sound of marching intensifies; they're coming. I run forward to hit Cal but Cupid grasps my arm firmly and holds me back.

"I bet you've been waiting for this moment, haven't you?" he says coldly. "The moment when you could turn me in and return to *Her* good graces."

Cal glares back at him. "I *tried* to help you. I *tried* to get you to leave town. I tried to protect *your Match.*"

"Look at her!" roars Cupid. "Say her name!"

Cal doesn't look at me. "You broke the law and you need to be punished," he says, dispassionate.

"Does Lila need to be punished?" asks Cupid. "Does Charlie?"

"There will be a fair trial."

"Like *hell* there will be a fair trial."

I've never seen Cupid look this angry before. He lets me go and races toward Cal, grabbing him and slamming him into the opposite wall. They face each other—almost nose to nose—anger burning on both of their faces.

Then the door to the study bursts open.

Cupid throws a punch at Cal's face, connecting hard and knocking Cal to the floor just as the agents begin to spill into the room. Although Cupid grabs his bow and begins shooting arrows, the agents are too fast and too close. Five of them grab his arms and thrust him to his knees, then flat on the ground. One grabs him by the hair and forces his gaze to me.

"Commander," shouts one gruffly, "we've got them."

The agents by the doorway part as someone walks through. He is tall and slender with dark hair and cold eyes. His black bow is larger and more elaborate than those of the other agents, and I notice a *V* broach pinned to his white jacket.

"Cal," he says, "take the girl."

Cal has regained his feet and now looks at me for the first time since his betrayal.

"Cal," I whisper, "please."

"Take the girl," repeats the Commander coldly. "If you want to come back to the service, if you want your crimes to be excused, *take the girl.*"

After only a brief pause, Cal moves toward me. Hands shaking, I grab an arrow from my quiver and hold it in front of me, my back still pressed against the window. I note the arrow's pink tip: the Capax, the truth arrow. I curse myself. It's not the one I need.

"Cal," Cupid warns, his neck still arched back. He's struggling against the agents holding him but they force him to watch as Cal gets closer. "Get away from her! Get away from her!" he says, starting to thrash.

"Cal," I say, "please don't do this."

Cal ignores us, his face full of disdain. I keep the arrow extended, and then, slowly he walks right into it—letting it pierce his stomach. His eyes widen as it does. Pain covers his face as it crumbles to ash in my shaking fingers.

"Did you ever care for me?" I ask. *He's been hit by the Capax. He has to tell the truth.*

He stares at me, uncertainty flashing across his expression before his face hardens once more.

"No."

He twists my arms roughly behind my back then pushes me forward, toward the throng of agents in the doorway.

"What about the others?"

"Leave the others," says the Commander. "Venus just wants the girl."

Cupid manages to throw off one of the agents, then another. "LILA!" he roars, meeting my horrified gaze as he tries to rise from the floor. But the agents keep coming back.

The Commander surveys the scene coldly. "Knock him out."

One of the agents raises her bow and thrusts it into the side of his head.

"*Cupid*!" I scream as he slumps to the ground, unconscious.

Cal just holds me in place, awaiting instruction from the agent in charge. I struggle against his grip. I want his hands off me.

"Take her to the cars," says the Commander. "We're driving back to the Matchmaking Service."

Then he turns to me and smiles thinly.

"Time to find out what Venus makes of Cupid's Match."

48

Cal marches me outside. The storm from earlier has passed, leaving puddles of water on the ground. The army of Venus's agents have begun to march back up Juliet Hill and their boots squelch in the mud. Cal and I follow, his hand tightly curled around my arm.

"How could you do this?" I seethe, craning my neck to try and look at his face.

Cal ignores me, continuing to push me along from behind. I think of Cupid, unconscious on the floor, and the steely gaze of the Commander as he instructed Cal to take me. I have to get away from these people.

With all the force I can muster I pull my arm away. It slips out of Cal's hand and I feel a moment of brief elation before he grabs me again and whirls me around to face him.

"Where are you going to go, Lila? Look around you. They'd catch you in an instant. Would you really rather someone *else* take you in?"

"Yes," I hiss at him. "I'd rather be taken in by anyone other than *you.*"

For a moment I think I detect a flash of hurt, which gives me a harsh satisfaction.

"Believe me, Lila, no, you wouldn't."

He pushes me ahead of him and we continue walking up the hill. As we do, one of the passing agents—dark haired and tanned—looks at me and smirks. He looks familiar and I realize with a jolt where I've seen him before.

"He's one of the Arrows. I shot him when we rescued Crystal. This is who you've chosen over your own brother?"

"The Arrows have always been an extension of the Cupids Matchmaking Service, if a little extreme," he says. "But we're all united under *Her* now."

After a push, we start walking once more. When we reach the top of the hill, I halt. Hundreds of expensive-looking cars line the summit. *Being a cupid has its perks*, Cal had said to me when he trained me for the first time.

I attempt to throw another angry look over my shoulder at him. *How could he do this? To me? To Cupid?* He stops moving. Our eyes catch—and for just a moment the angles in his face seem to soften. His mouth parts.

It gives me hope.

Maybe he hasn't betrayed us.

Maybe this is all an act.

Maybe he'll just take me in a car and drive me away from all this.

Maybe . . .

"You're traveling with us," says the cold-faced Commander, marching up beside Cal. "Need to keep an eye on you both."

He heads to a red Ferrari parked at the very front of the lot, where a stern blond awaits. She points a key at the car and two side doors slide upward. They climb inside. Cal marches me toward it.

"Get in."

His face is hard and, in an instant, the hope is gone. I look around frantically, trying to determine if there's any way to escape. Cupids are still making their way up the hill and climbing into cars. There are too many of them. There's no way out of this.

I have to turn around to get in the seat, and when I do, I meet Cal's eyes again. The angles of his face are sharp.

"Please, Lila," he says. "Just get in the car."

I stare at him for another moment and then do as he says. I have no choice: where else can I go? Cal gets in beside me. The doors close and the female agent starts the engine. It's then that if finally hits me.

This is it.

They're taking me to Venus.

♥

No one speaks on the journey. Cal stares down at his hands as he twists them in his lap, and doesn't look at me once. Turning in my seat, I glance out of the rear window, squinting against the early morning light. We're riding down a wide L.A. freeway with tall palm trees standing at attention on either side. The stream of the cupids' expensive cars surrounds us.

We must be heading to the Matchmaking Service. If Venus is the founder, then surely that's where she'll be. I try to cling to the hope that, while Cal might have betrayed us, Crystal could still be on side; maybe she will help me make my escape.

Soon we reach the boulevard where the Cupids Matchmaking Service stands. The driver presses a button on the dashboard and the pavement ahead slides open. She maneuvers the car through the opening and we drive down a ramp into a large underground garage. The girl parks the Ferrari in a space marked *Priority Parking*. Then she opens the car doors and my body turns cold.

"Thank you, Claire," says the Commander before looking over his seat at Cal and me. "Time to meet the boss," he says before climbing out.

"Get out," Cal says, still not looking at me.

I ignore him, my mind struggling to process what is happening. I was matched with Cupid. Cal betrayed us. They're taking me to meet an ancient goddess. She wants to kill me. *This can't be real. It can't be.*

Cal grabs his bow and quiver, climbs out of the car, and then purposefully makes his way over to my side. He opens the door and stands there stiffly for a moment, waiting for me to move. I don't. He sighs and leans across me—so close that I can smell his cologne. As he does so, I catch a hint of gold among the arrows in his quiver—the Finis.

As he unbuckles my seat belt, he turns to look at me, something in his expression that I can't read. For a moment I think he's going to say something.

But he doesn't.

Grabbing my arm, he pulls me up out of the car as the other agents' cars veer into the garage. The air smells like petrol and exhaust fumes. The Commander and Claire are both watching us.

"Come on," says Cal.

I wrestle my arm out of his grip. "Don't touch me."

A thin smile crosses the Commander's face, and he shrugs.

"She can walk on her own. This way please." He gestures toward a plain door in the corner of the garage, then walks ahead.

Neither Cal nor I move. I stare at him, breathing hard, and his pale eyebrows furrow.

"Lila. Don't." His voice is weary.

I turn and run. I sprint past the cars still flooding into the garage; the sound of their horns and the skidding of their brakes as they swerve to avoid me creates an unpleasant chaotic symphony. I leap away from a white suit who tries to stop my escape, eyes fixed on the ramp leading to the street, before two hands grab my arms and pull me back into a hard chest.

I spin around, almost nose to nose with Cal.

"I thought you were my friend," I say.

"And I thought you weren't stupid enough to fall for Cupid and bring back Venus."

Anger burns through my veins. I think about the dance, and the pain behind his eyes when he saw me out on the terrace.

"Is that what this is all about?" I say. "Is that why you're doing this? Because I kissed Cupid? This is what I deserve? I kissed your brother and so you want to hand me over to an ancient goddess who wants to kill me? Way to overreact, Cal."

His features harden and he looks like he's about to retort, but I don't give him chance. I spin on my heel—feeling the eyes of the other agents getting out of their cars—and storm after the Commander. He is watching us curiously as we reach the door.

We enter a nondescript stairwell and Claire leads us into an elevator. Inside, the mirrored walls reflect my messy hair and clothes, still slightly damp from the rain. My face is paler than usual, and I note the dark smudges underneath my eyes.

"Which floor?" asks Claire.

"*Her* floor," says the Commander. "She'll want to see the Match right away."

My knees feel a little weak at that, so I lean against the elevator wall for support as we begin to ascend. My three captors ignore me, all staring directly ahead at the sliding doors. When they open, I'm marched into a clinical-looking waiting room whose glass coffee table is surrounded by the same neon-colored armchairs that sit in the reception.

"Take a seat," says Cal.

As I do so, Claire and the Commander speak to a slender, red-haired young man at the reception booth.

"Venus's PA," Cal murmurs from across the table.

I shoot him a withering look. "I didn't ask."

After a few moments the Commander and Claire come back. "Charles will let you know when the boss is ready," says the Commander, then gives a gruff nod to Cal before he and Claire head back into the elevator, leaving us alone.

Cal sits in the luminous green armchair beside me. We wait in silence for what seems like forever. Then there is a beep and Charles the PA moves from behind his white booth. His gaze brushes over Cal then focuses on me.

"She is ready," he says. "Venus will see you now."

49

"So this is it, is it?" I say quietly. "Venus will see me now?"

This is where following a boy out onto the terrace at his party has led—to a reception with the goddess of love. I feel a pang and wonder if I will ever see Cupid again.

"Will she kill me?" I ask Cal as he rises to stand stiffly beside me.

Cal averts his eyes. "Get up."

I look at Venus's PA, who is tapping his fingers against the reception booth impatiently. "She hasn't got all day," he says testily.

I turn my eyes to Cal again. I wish I could read his expression. I wish I could understand why he betrayed us. As I stand, an unusual calm washes over me. Whatever happens, I will face it; there is no other choice.

Cal grabs my arm and marches me forward, his fingers digging into my skin. Despite his cool demeanor, I can tell he is nervous. I cast my gaze to the quiver still on his back. The Finis is still there.

"Let go of me," I say, my voice steady. *Maybe if I can get hold of the Finis I could . . .*

Cal follows my gaze and gives a subtle shake of his head. Then he pushes me ahead of him toward Charles.

"Don't do anything stupid, Lila," he whispers in my ear through gritted teeth.

"This way, please," says Charles.

Side by side, we follow him down a long, arched corridor whose walls are a blinding white. Our footsteps echo off the black and white checkered floor. While the décor is similar to the rest of the Cupids Matchmaking Service, the air smells strange and sickly sweet.

As we move on, I wonder if Cal is going to deliver the Finis directly to Venus. If he does, then she can use it to kill Cupid.

I glare at Cal again. "How could you do this?"

He says nothing, only gestures to the black door at the end of the corridor, where two armed cupids stand guard—one male and one female. As we get closer, I notice a white plaque with *Venus, CEO* in elegant pink calligraphy, nailed to the dark wood.

Charles stops in front of the two agents guarding the door and spins around to face us. His eyes are a dull green.

"Leave your weapons outside the door, please," he says. "You can collect them once She is finished with you."

My eyes flicker to Cal's face. If he's going to give the Finis to the Matchmaking Service then surely this is the moment to reveal its presence. But he makes no movement to give in his bow or arrows.

"No weapon can harm Venus," he says.

Charles shrugs disinterestedly. "I didn't make the rules. Leave your weapons with one of the agents, please."

When Cal only stares at Charles coldly, the agents by the door reach for their own weapons, suddenly alert. Then Cal gives a thin smile.

"Of course," he says. "As She wishes."

He passes the bow to the male then shrugs the bundle of arrows off his shoulder. The female agent takes it and balances it against the wall.

Charles nods, then raps lightly against the black door.

"Come iii-nnn," sings a high-pitched voice on the other side. *This is it.*

Without thinking, I look to Cal for some form of comfort, but of course, he doesn't give it. He stares straight ahead as Charles pushes open the door and walks through.

The first thing that hits me is the smell. It's even stronger than in the hallway; sweet, yes, with an undercurrent of something else—something nasty. Bile makes its way up my throat, but I swallow it down as Cal pulls me inside.

We've entered a narrow room with a black wood floor and dark-pink walls. Where we stand is lit by a cold, artificial light, but the end of the room is shrouded in darkness. I can't see Venus, but there are bouquets of flowers everywhere—blood-red roses and white myrtle burst out of vases and wrap up the walls to twine around ceiling beams. I can hear the trickling of water but I can't work out where it is coming from.

"Here they are, ma'am," says Charles. "Cal. And Cupid's Match."

After a low bow, he dismisses himself, closing the door behind him. There is silence for a moment. Then a shuffle from the dark end of the room.

"Come forward, plee-aaassee."

The voice is the embodiment of the smell—sickly sweet with something nasty roiling beneath the surface. Cal lets go of my arm and slowly walks toward the darkness. I look longingly at the door we've just come through. *But what's the point in running? They'll only bring me back again.*

Filled with dread, I inch forward, my breathing quickening with each step that I take.

"That's right," says the voice. "Come here."

As we get closer, I see the shape of a large desk and the silhouette of a figure sitting behind it.

Venus.

The sound of water is stronger here, and for a moment I think I hear the sound of something thudding against glass.

"That's quii-tte close enough," sings the voice. "Now—let me have a look at you."

Slowly and fluidly, the shadowed figure rises from the chair and stands to her full height. She is bigger than a human woman, in both height and breadth. Her body is exaggeratedly curved but, through the darkness, I can't determine whether it is due to clothing or her actual shape.

And then suddenly she is just inches in front of us.

At first glimpse, she is beautiful. Her hair, a fiery red, is braided around her head and entwined with white flowers. Her pale skin accentuates her clear blue eyes, and she's wearing a ball gown that looks to be made entirely of crimson roses. Strapless and cinched at the waist, it boasts a billowing skirt that seems to sway in a breeze that isn't there.

No one speaks. Venus continues to look at me, and as I stare back, my skin starts to crawl. There's something behind the beauty; something not quite right.

Her skin is too pale—almost translucent—and completely without pores or blemishes or marks of any kind. It looks slippery, like an imitation of skin. The pupils in her eyes are too small, and she doesn't blink often enough. They make me think of the eyes of a doll. And although she is smiling at me with full, red lips, there's a menacing twist to it.

Suddenly, in a movement too fast for me to follow, her fingers caress the side of my face. They are long and cold—corpse-like—and my skin crawls.

"So this is her, *Cupid's Match*," she says, tilting her head to the side. "The reason I've been called *back in to work*."

Her voice is like a little girl's, but she prods me in the chest with each word—the last push so forceful that I lose my footing, landing hard on my back. I blink and she is towering over me. Fear fills my body. I inhale sharply, taking in a sickeningly large gulp of the overpowering scent.

"You know—that's not very nice, being called into work on your millennium off," she says as she stoops down, picks me up like a rag doll, and plants me back on my feet. "There are a lot of things I could do to you if I wanted to. And you must be punished, of course. You have been a *very naughty little Match*."

"Mother," Cal warns.

She turns her head to focus on Cal. "I've heard you've been a naughty little boy too," she says, picking up her skirts and running with tiny steps over to her son. "*Again*."

There'd be something comical about her movements if she weren't so terrifying.

"Do you like my new hair?" she asks, beaming. "It's red. Like Charles's. We're matching."

Cal ignores her words and looks her straight in the eye. "If you don't hurt Lila now—if you give her a trial—you can make an example out of her," he says slowly.

She sticks out her bottom lip. "But I want to hurt her *now*."

Cal just looks at her sternly.

Venus sighs. "But of course you're right. We'll keep her for the trial. She'll be our little human pet." She looks back at me with those unblinking eyes and smiles a smile that makes my skin crawl. Then she claps her hands together. "Anyway—I've got you both presents! Come! Come!"

Dread fills me. *What present could the goddess of love possibly have for me?*

Suddenly, she's at the other end of the room, back in the darkness. She claps her hands again and the lights spring on. This time bile forces its way to the top of my throat. She stands between two glass doors, behind which two figures float in water.

Inside one—unconscious and ethereal—floats Crystal.

Inside the other—thumping the glass wildly with his fists—is Cupid.

Venus looks at us and smiles sweetly, but there is malice in her eyes. "Do you want to open them?"

50

Venus places her hand on tank where Crystal floats, ghostlike, in the water. Wisps of the cupid's blond hair twist and twirl in slow motion around her pale face.

My heart sinks. She looks like she is dead.

Venus looks at Cal. "This one is for you!" Then she runs over to the second door and brings her doll-like gaze to my face. "And *this* one . . . this one is for you!"

Cupid's thumps against the glass are becoming weaker. I can see his mouth moving, but the words are lost behind the window. Every inch of me starts to tremble. I'm dangerously close to throwing up.

I need to get him out of there.

She claps her hands together impatiently. "Well? Come on then. Are you going to open your presents or not?"

For a moment I stay rooted to the spot. *Is this a trick?*

Then I don't care anymore—I don't care if it's a trick, or if Venus is going to kill me, or that I'm going to be put on trial. I don't care that Cal has betrayed me, or that I'm terrified, or that I may never get to see my dad again.

All I care about is Cupid—his life slowly trickling away into that container of water.

I bolt forward, past the desk, and past Venus, until my body slams into the glass of Cupid's prison. I place my palms all over it, trying to find out how to get it open. There's no handle.

How can I get him out?

Cupid taps against the glass to get my attention then gestures behind him. I follow his gaze. Venus still stands between the two doors. She dangles two keys delicately from her fingers.

"*Silly little Match*," she says. "You'll need a key to open that door."

I snatch the one for Cupid's door from her, not looking at her face for a reaction; I just race back, my eyes searching for a keyhole.

I can't find it.

Cupid taps against the glass again and points to my left. There's a small hole in the glass. I jam in the key, turn, and pull backward. The door bursts open, ice-cold water knocking me to my back before Cupid crashes down on top of me. His skin is cold and wet and he burrows his head down by my shoulder as he splutters and gulps in the room's scented air.

I lay there in cold relief before I remember the other container.

Crystal.

I roll Cupid off me, frantically looking to see if Venus's other victim is all right. Cal is striding toward the second door, his expression unreadable. He snatches the other key off Venus and glares at her. Then he slips the key into the lock and turns it, standing to the side as Crystal's fragile body comes crashing out onto the floor.

"*Crystal*," I whisper urgently, "is she . . .?"

Cupid is now on his hands and knees—retching water. He coughs a few more times and then looks at me. "Our kind can't drown. Not fully," he says, his voice wheezy and tired. "She'll be all right, lovebug, eventually."

With that he collapses back to the ground and rolls onto his back, stretching out wearily in the shallow puddle of water.

I look up at Venus. There's a thunderous expression on her face and the air around her suddenly feels static and charged. The hairs on my arms prickle and stand on end.

"Look at the mess you've made on my floor. *Water. EVERYWHERE.*"

Although I flinch, Cal merely stares at her.

"Mother, what is the meaning of this? I understand Cupid—but why is Crystal here?" he asks, looking down at Crystal's collapsed body with distaste.

She finally moves—a weak gasp escapes from her lips. I feel a small moment of relief.

"I mean, I couldn't care less whether she lives or dies," Cal continues.

Suddenly Venus is standing in front of Cal.

"You couldn't care less?" Her lips are twisted into a smile but there is no kindness in her unblinking eyes.

"Of course not," he snaps. "She's one of *your* agents. She's nothing to me."

Venus steps away, her skirt of roses rustling as she moves. "Yes," she says thoughtfully as Crystal begins to retch on the floor. "She *is* mine, isn't she?"

She picks Crystal up by the neck of her drenched white jacket and throws her into the wall as though she weighs nothing. Crystal bounces off and thuds hard onto the ground.

"Mine to do whatever I please with." Venus smiles that twisted smile again and advances slowly toward Crystal's crumpled form. "She has been a very naughty agent, gallivanting around with Cupid and his Match. I think I will kill her."

"Mother, if you hurt her now, you can't make an example of her—like Lila, remember?" he says slowly. "You can put her on trial, too, so everyone will see what you do to people who betray you."

Venus blinks then gives a disjointed kind of nod. Her movements make me think of a character in a creepy stop-motion film. "Yes. I'll put her on trial with the others." She looks at Cal and smiles sweetly. "At least I have one good son."

She moves beside him and strokes his face with her white, slippery-looking fingers. Then she sighs.

"I'm bored of you all now. GUUAARRDDSS!"

The two agents from outside burst back inside.

"Help Cal transport these three downstairs. Put them with my other pets," she says. "Come on. Hurry."

The male agent scoops Crystal up over his shoulder while the woman pulls Cupid to his feet. Cal strides over to me and offers me his hand.

"Get up."

I glare at him but allow him to pull me to my feet. I don't know where we're being taken, but it has to be better than being in here with Her.

"GO ON. GET THEM OUT OF MY SIGHT!" Venus screams as we all scramble toward the door. "I DON'T WANT TO LOOK AT THEM ANYMORE. GO! GO! GO!"

I don't dare look back as the door closes behind us. Once outside, Cal lets go of my arm to pick up his bow and quiver from by the wall.

"This way," he says, striding down the corridor toward the elevator.

I look behind me. Crystal is still wet and unconscious, draped over the male guard's shoulder, while Cupid trudges beside the other guard, seemingly accepting his fate. I'm not sure if his calmness is terrifying or reassuring.

Does he have a plan? Or is he just too tired to fight?

As Cal and the agents usher us into the elevator, Cupid reaches for my hand and squeezes it. *It'll be okay*, he mouths.

I wish I could believe that.

Back on the ground floor, we are marched to the indoor courtyard, where the male agent brings Crystal to the statue of Venus. I notice Crystal's eyes blink open as the agent produces a key card and scans it across the face of the statue. Then he takes a step backward as the statue's circular pool rises a couple of inches and slides across the cobbled stones. In its place is a gaping hole through which I can see the top of a twisted stairway.

"Let me go," Crystal mumbles.

The agent places her back on her feet. He looks a bit embarrassed and I wonder if they know each other.

"Venus's orders," he mutters.

She gives him an icy look then surveys the rest of us. For a moment, she looks as though she's going to make some kind of cutting remark, before seemingly deciding we're not worth the energy. She shakes her head and heads down the stairway into the darkness beyond.

"I can take it from here," Cal informs the two guards. When they just look at him hesitantly, he frowns. "Need I remind you that I am your superior? Go back to your post. I can handle a few prisoners."

"You sure you can get their Sims fired up on your own?" the male guard asks.

I feel a cold dread as I remember what Cal had said about the Sims used for punishment. That is what is in store for us.

"Of course," Cal says scornfully.

"Very well, sir," the guard replies, and the two of them head back to their posts.

Cal leads us to the hole, waiting for Cupid and me to descend before he follows behind us. It's dark at the bottom, dimly lit by flickering artificial lights attached to the low ceiling.

As we walk along the narrow hallway, my stomach begins to turn. Doors with barred windows line the walls, each one with a chair behind it. On each chair is a person—a person with no space to move—staring blankly into the darkness.

I peer into one cell as we pass by. A petite girl with creamy brown skin and jet-black hair has her eyes closed as though asleep. She must be around my age. When I look at her more closely, what I see makes me stagger backward. Her hair looks like it is moving, and I notice a small black snake entwining itself around her neck. A scribbled placard above the door reads *Medusa*.

We pass another door behind which a tall, scarred black man sits, his brown eyes staring out at nothing. I don't catch the writing signaling his name, but I notice Crystal looking in at him and shaking her head sadly. I think back to *The Records of the Finis*.

Is he the Minotaur?

The lines of doors stretch onward and I see other names as we pass. Pandora. Romulus. Remus. Selena. And several I don't recognize at all. And then my heart stutters when I see Charlie's face peering lifelessly out of one of the barred windows.

Cal comes to a halt beside three empty cells. I'm filled with horror. I look up at Cupid for support, but to my surprise he is grinning. He walks past me and pats his brother on the back.

"Do you think Venus bought it?"

"I should think so," says Cal.

"You got the Finis?"

Cal nods again.

"Good work, Brother."

I'm confused, but Crystal just rolls her eyes. "You could have told me, you know," she says to Cal. "Jerk." With that she walks haughtily through the door nearest to her and sits down on the chair.

I stare at them, completely bewildered. "What's going on?"

Cal turns to me, looking bashful. "I'm sorry, Lila," he says. "It was the only way to get the Finis back in the building. You had to believe I'd betrayed you. Venus would have known if you didn't."

I think back to the house, remembering the long look that passed between Cal and Cupid before they went down to gather up the weapons. "You mean . . . this was the plan all along?"

Cupid nods. "A bit of a last-minute plan, but yes."

For a moment I don't know whether to feel relieved or annoyed. I decide to settle on relieved. Things definitely aren't perfect, but they aren't looking as bad as they did five minutes ago. "Does there happen to be a part two of your secret master plan?"

Cal gestures at the rows of barred doors.

"Behind each one is a powerful enemy of Venus, an enemy who would like nothing better than to take her down. She keeps them all here in their own individual Sims. They're tormented inside, their power used against them."

He passes me, Cupid, and Crystal each a small microchip. Cupid slips his into his ear.

"That's where we come in. We're going to go into their Sims." He flashes me a bright smile. "And we're going to wake up some Myths."

51

I look at the two brothers: Cupid, tall and happy-go-lucky; Cal, slender and serious, jaw set with determination.

"We're going to do what now?" I ask.

Cupid takes a step toward me, and although I can feel his body heat, I shiver. My clothes are still wet from the glass case that exploded water all over me when I opened it.

"It won't be easy," he says, "but an army of Myths will be the last thing Venus is expecting. And I want her *gone.*"

I think of her clammy poreless skin and those blue, unblinking eyes. I think of the way that she pushed me across the room without straining a muscle, and of Crystal and Cupid floating in those tanks. If we don't destroy her, she will kill us all.

"I want her gone too."

Cupid's face cracks into a grin. "I knew you'd come around to my way of thinking eventually."

"Well, to be honest, I'd prefer it if we hadn't brought her back in the first place." I bring my eyes up to his. "She's really your mother?"

He nods grimly. "Not the best meet-the-boyfriend's-parents situation, eh?"

"I'm not your girlfriend."

His grin widens. "Give me time . . ." Then he takes a step backward toward one of the tiny barred rooms. "See you in there, lovebug." He winks then goes in, closing his door behind him.

I look up at Cal—his expression is still stony but there's a softness in his eyes. "You're wet," he says. "Here."

He takes off his hooded sweater and thrusts it at me.

"I, uh, thanks," I say, taking it.

I pull on the hoodie, wrapping it around my body. It's warm from Cal's body and smells like fruity shampoo. He looks at me a moment, as though wanting to say something, then shuts his mouth.

"What is it?" I ask.

He sighs heavily, regret flashing behind his silver eyes. "I should have done more to keep this all from happening," he says. "When I had to act like I was betraying you, well . . . it was one of the two hardest things I've ever had to do."

"What was the other?"

He shakes his head.

"Amena?" I ask.

He looks up at me and, after a pause, nods.

"It'll be okay," I promise. "We'll get through this."

The ghost of a smile crosses his face. "I believe you," he says. Then he takes a step away from me and turns to the empty cells. "It's time."

I peer inside with trepidation. "You say we have to wake the Myths up. Can't we just pull their chips out? Like when we did the training Sim? Do we really need to go in there?"

"It doesn't work that way," says Cal. "These Sims are made specifically for containment. They have a much harsher psychological effect than the training simulations. You pull one of these out before the prisoner is ready, and their brain won't be able to cope. They'll die."

I walk into the small cell. There is a wooden chair inside, and as I sit down, Cal closes the door behind me, sealing me in with the darkness. I take a deep breath. The air feels heavy on my tongue and seems to push down on my chest. I fight the wave of panic, of claustrophobia. Cal looks at my face through the barred window.

"Put the chip in your ear."

I do so, feeling its alien coldness. Cal takes a step back and looks at the three of us.

"I'm going to establish a link between the Sims," he says, "so you should be able to navigate from one to the next. From what I know of the Minotaur, he'll have managed to create the most complex one. I should be able to fit the others inside of it. I expect his will be—"

"A labyrinth," Crystal's voice calls.

Cal's gaze lingers on her cell. Then he nods solemnly from in front of the bars.

"I suggest you split up and make your way through the maze, collecting the others on your way. The exit will be at the center— that's your way out." He looks at his brother's cell. "Stay away from the ferry port. And, well, you could be facing some pretty bad stuff in there. So don't die."

He turns on his heel and makes his way back up the corridor, leaving the three of us sitting uncomfortably in the small, damp cells. I pull Cal's hoodie closer around me.

"What happens if we die in this Sim?" I ask.

Suddenly, a loud, screeching sound of stone on stone resounds around the room. Cal must have gone back to the indoor court-yard and sealed us in. The lights in the corridor suddenly switch off and we are left in complete darkness.

"We die," says Cupid.

I nod.

"Figures." I'm about to ask him how likely it is that we will be killed when a wave of nausea overcomes me. I hear a faint buzz-ing noise and the room feels like it is moving.

"Close your eyes," says Cupid. "We're going in."

♥

When I open my eyes again we're still in darkness, but it feels more open, as though we're outside. In front of us is a massive arched door with brass handles.

Cupid and Crystal stand on either side of me. Crystal is wear-ing a clean version of her white combat suit, free of signs that just ten minutes ago she was trapped in a case filled with water. I look down at my body and see that I'm wearing a white combat suit too.

As I look at Cupid my breath catches in my throat. He's now dressed all in black: black jeans and a black top underneath a worn leather jacket. On his feet are heavy army boots. His stormy eyes seem to pierce the door straight ahead.

He looks both scary and dreamy: a perfect nightmare. Whatever is on the other side of that door, he seems ready for it. He takes a step forward and puts a hand on the brass handle. But instead of opening it, he pauses.

"I don't know what we're going to be faced with in here," he says, and the uncharacteristic seriousness of his face unnerves me.

Crystal arches an eyebrow. "Got to be better than what's out there," she says gesturing upward.

Tension bristles between the two of them, and I think back to the moment when I first met Crystal behind the reception desk— there was fear in her eyes when she realized I was Cupid's Match.

She knew what it would mean. She knew that Venus would return.

Cupid looks at her. "Come on, don't tell me you're not excited that we finally get to use your golden arrow. You've been sitting under it for over a hundred years! You wouldn't have taken it if you hadn't the same ambitions as me . . . at least on some level."

"Same ambitions? I would *never* have brought *Her* back— risking war, millions of lives, the fate of the world . . ."

Cupid raises his hands in surrender. "I said on some level." Then he grasps the handle again. "Well, here we go," he says, and pushes open the heavy, wooden door. It makes a loud screeching sound as it scrapes against the rocky ground.

And then everything is different.

We're standing atop a steep staircase leading down to a vast maze stretching for what seems like miles. I can't work out whether its high walls are made of many different colors, or whether they are all the same slate gray. Eerie landmarks are silhouetted against the sky —in one spot I notice a group of tall, derelict skyscrapers; in another I can see some form of carnival lighting. The maze looks like a collection of abandoned cities, filled with dead ends and decay.

Somewhere nearby I hear the crackle of fire and I spin around. A ladder now climbs the wall behind us, leading to another level. The enormity of the task before us hits me; I can't fathom how we will find anything in here.

Cupid takes a step forward, to the edge of the staircase, and then turns around to face us, grinning. "Ah look—my brother's left us some weapons."

Propped on the wall behind us are three bows and quivers. Crystal scoops them up and distributes them between us, thrusting Cupid's into his arms so forcefully that he stumbles back a few inches. He teeters on the edge of the stairs before regaining his balance.

"I'm getting a very subtle hint that you're mad at me."

She scowls. "Damn right I'm mad at you. We were all doing fine without you and *your mother.*"

Cupid looks like he's about to retort when I step between them.

"Guys," I say, "can we just put all this behind us until we get out of here?"

They both look at me, then Crystal shrugs.

"Fine," she says, swinging her arrows onto her back. "We should split up anyway." She turns to Cupid. "We're on a pretrial Sim. We don't know how much time we have in here before we're brought back to the real world," she says. "The quickest way to do this will be to send each of the Myths we free off to find the next Myth, agreed?"

He nods and she turns toward the ladder in the wall and begins to climb.

"How will we find you again?" I call.

"We meet in the center," she says, looking down at me before disappearing over the top and out of sight.

Cupid looks at me and wiggles his eyebrows suggestively. "Alone at last."

"Yes, and it's superromantic here, trapped in the dungeon of an ancient goddess who wants to kill us, having to battle our way through a ginormous labyrinth to recruit her other prisoners . . ."

Cupid laughs. "I guess that just about sums up the situation. I'll take you on a real date when we get of here."

"Yeah, well, we should probably go through your family tree before we do that, in case we bring back any more murderous supervillains. Who's your dad, by the way?"

He looks at me, his eyes twinkling, but says nothing. Then he turns his sights ahead. For a moment we both stare into the gloom. Then I take a deep breath and walk to the edge of the stone staircase.

I look behind me at Cupid. "Come on, then. Let's get this over with."

Then I step down onto the first step, beginning my descent into the labyrinth.

52

As I walk I sense Cupid starting to descend the uneven steps behind me. I glance over my shoulder.

"Something amusing you?"

He lets out a light chuckle. "I've never seen someone so eager to descend a dark staircase into a mysterious labyrinth full of unknown peril before."

The high walls on either side of the stairway are sending thick shadows across our path. As we continue, they seem to be closing in.

"Have you ever seen *anyone* descend a dark staircase into a mysterious labyrinth before?" I ask.

There's a pause behind me.

"I suppose not. But it *is* dangerous, you know?"

I don't reply for a moment, concentrating on a particularly deep step. I look up at him once I have lowered myself down, my palms still flat on the stone stair above.

"I know that," I say, "but I assume we're on a deadline

here—what with our *actual* selves awaiting trial back in the Matchmaking Service."

The corner of Cupid's mouth quirks upward. "Time in the Sim passes differently. Hardly any time will have passed in the real world . . . which is a good thing, too, because I don't know if you've noticed, but this labyrinth is pretty huge."

He trails off and I resume my journey downward, suppressing a smile despite the grim circumstances. There must be a thousand steps or more, some so thin and steep that I stumble on a number of occasions.

When I finally stagger onto flat ground I feel a small wave of relief. The muscles in my legs are aching and I feel slightly breathless, even though rationally I know that this is all just a simulation. I remind myself that it's not real, but then I remember Cupid's warning: if we die in here, we die in real life.

Cupid startles me by jumping down from the last step, his face half hidden by shadow. I look around, wondering if the path to the center will be obvious. We're at a corner point in the maze, with two wide paths extending in different directions. The ivy-covered stone walls are so high that I can't see their tops. The air is stagnant, lightly scented with must and damp.

"Which way do we go?"

Cupid frowns as he moves beside me. "The Sims of the different Myths won't have been merged seamlessly—there'll be discrepancies, clues. We need to look for anything that seems out of place."

"How will we know if it's out of place? I've not exactly seen the labyrinth blueprints."

Cupid laughs and looks around. "Hmm. I guess anything that isn't gray or . . . wall-y. I'll go left, you go right. But make sure I'm always in your vision. If you stray from my sight I may never find you again."

I nod, swallowing my alarm, and head along the path to the right. I scan my eyes over the gray walls and the cracked concrete. I wish I knew what I was looking for. As I walk onward, I don't think I have ever experienced such an overwhelming lack of sound. It's dark, too, and I keep glancing over my shoulder to make sure Cupid is still there. When he starts to look small in the distance I stop.

There's nothing here.

I decide to head back. As I do, something catches my eye—a shape carved into the ground. I crouch down, brushing aside some rubble.

"Cupid?"

The silence of the maze swallows my voice and he doesn't look up from the stretch of wall he's studying.

"Cupid!" I shout. "Does this mean anything to you?"

This time he hears me. As he jogs toward me I turn my attention back to the carving. It's so small I almost missed it—a cube carved into the stone.

"Looks like . . ." I begin.

"A box."

There's a triumphant note in his voice. He steps over the carving and heads down the shadowed path behind it. I push myself to my feet and fall into step beside him.

"I found a clue?"

"Yup, you found a clue. This path will lead to the Sim of one of the Myths, and if I'm right, I'm guessing it's Pandora."

"Pandora as in Pandora's box? The Myth who opened a box that let out all the evil in the world?"

Cupid laughs. "According to you humans. Come on—we must be close now."

A few minutes later we reach a large black door covered with carvings that curl around the frame. Some are cubes like the one that marked the entrance to our path, others depict monsters and beasts.

"The Sim of each Myth has been created to torture them," he says. "They're designed to turn their own power against them." He caresses one of the arrows in the quiver over his shoulder, and I wonder if he knows he's doing it. "Pandora is very powerful. She found a way to control the sins her box was said to contain." A dark look passes across his face. "She's been in here a long time," he says, "and whatever her power has conjured up for her, I don't think it will be pleasant."

He looks at me and all of the lightness and amusement I'm used to seeing in his expression is gone.

"Stay close and don't lose sight of me. And do as I tell you, whatever that may be. I'm a trained cupid, and though you showed promise in the training Sim, you are not. Do you understand?"

There's a new ferocity in his eyes, so I nod. Then he pushes open the door. It screeches against the stone floor—if there is anything there, I'm now sure it's heard us.

We enter a long tunnel, dark except for a small square of light far at the other end. Where there was sky above us before, there is now a ceiling low enough that the top of Cupid's hair brushes against it as we walk. The walls are closer together here, and if I stretch my arms I can touch both at once. The walls are damp and cold.

As we get close to the middle of the tunnel, Cupid suddenly stops and shushes me.

"Listen," he whispers, carefully pulling one of the black arrows from its case.

For a moment I hear nothing. Then my body tenses as a faint scream sounds from faraway. I'm about to ask Cupid about it when I hear something worse; something that sends a chill down my spine.

Coming from the end of the tunnel is a low rasping noise, followed by a grotesque squelching. It sounds inhuman. Whatever lays at the end of this path, I'm pretty sure I don't want to encounter it.

"What *is* that?"

Before Cupid can reply I notice another noise, this time coming from all around us. It's a loud screeching—like the tunnel door scraping against the stone, but worse. Cupid's gaze flicks up over my shoulder, his face confused. Then his eyes widen.

"The walls," he whispers in horror.

Tentatively, I reach out to touch them again, finding I don't have to stretch my arms so far. Then I feel the vibrations emanating from inside and the full force of our situation hits me.

The walls are moving.

Slowly, the walls on either side of the tunnel are closing in on us. I zero in on the small space of light where the horrible, rasping noise came from—it must be about two hundred feet away. A cold panic fills my body.

Get crushed to death or face whatever lays at the end of this passageway?

"What are you waiting for?" Cupid bellows, grabbing my arm. "*Run!*"

53

I sprint down the tunnel after Cupid, my heart pounding against my chest. The screech of the walls fills my ears, so close to me now that my sides ram against them as I stumble forward. My leg muscles are screaming with the effort and my breathing is hard and fast.

We're getting closer to the opening at the end, but it's still a good fifty feet away. Panic fills me. I'm not sure I can make it.

Twenty feet to go.

Cupid glances over his shoulder as he reaches the end of the tunnel. The walls are now almost touching me.

"Lila!"

I'm almost there.

With a spurt of strength I thrust myself forward. I can hardly breathe—the air is close and I have a stitch in my side.

Five feet to go.

The tunnel walls have almost closed in on Cupid's broad frame. With a screaming effort he twists his body to the side and grabs my arm so hard that I feel my shoulder wrench in its socket. He pulls me forward and together we burst into the light, our sides scraping against the narrow edges of the walls as the passage clamps shut behind us.

For a moment we find ourselves falling through the air. Then pain explodes through my body as we hit the floor hard, in a crumpled heap of arms and legs.

Cupid groans as I disentangle myself from him, then rolls onto his back and pushes himself up so he's leaning on his elbows. I kneel on the floor beside him, trying to catch my breath.

"Pandora's box," he says. "I should have guessed there would be some claustrophobic element to her Sim. Are you okay?"

I nod, glancing down at my body; my once-white suit is covered with a thick layer of dust and rubble. I brush off my arms and look around us.

We're in a small, square room filled with flickering torch-light—it makes the eerie carvings in the stone walls seem like they're moving. I try to make them out; there's a strange horned goatlike creature on one side and what looks like a human heart carved on the other.

Across the room is a metal door, a letter *L* imprinted on it in ancient-looking calligraphy. Around the frame the numbers one to seven are repeated in flourished carvings. I remember Cupid saying something earlier about Pandora keeping sins in her box.

Seven sins?

I turn back to Cupid, who is still reclining, propped up on his elbows. I wonder why he hasn't got up yet. His gaze catches mine and he holds it. The black top beneath his leather jacket is damp with sweat, and it clings to his body. Even though I know we should move through the marked door, I feel strangely reluctant to go. I kneel beside Cupid. I can feel heat radiating from him.

"What is this place?" My voice comes out croaky and breathless. I'm hot, and I feel different.

Cupid doesn't answer me. His eyes burn into mine, almost feverish, and his breathing intensifies. Though I am close enough to touch his skin, he is not close enough.

Suddenly he grabs the back of my head with a large hand and pulls. I fall into him and he kisses me; the movements of his mouth are hot and heavy as his arms encase me, pulling me closer as he parts my lips with his tongue. I run my fingers along the back of his neck then grab at his hair. A small groan escapes him. With a sudden movement he seizes me and flips me over onto my back, pressing his body against mine, thigh to thigh.

Then, just as suddenly, he propels himself away from me. Looking astonished, he leaps to his feet and plasters himself against the far wall. His breathing is heavy and his eyes wide.

I scramble to a sitting position, trying to control my racing pulse. His skin is flushed and I don't feel right. What's wrong with us?

"We need to get out of here," says Cupid.

His voice sounds different; lower and rougher.

"What's going on?"

"I told you that Pandora could control the sins," he says between hard and heavy breaths. "There are seven in total. Lust is one of them." He gestures to the door. "L for lust—it's controlling us. We need to get out of here."

I lurch to my feet and try to walk toward the door, but somehow find myself approaching Cupid instead.

"Lila," he says, his breathing still heavy, "you need to stay away from me. It'll work on us like the Ardor. Drive us mad. We'll never get out."

When I try to move away, I somehow end up touching his arm. There is an ache inside of me that only he can ease.

"Lila," he warns, alarm in his eyes. His jaw is clenched, like he's waging some kind of internal battle. Then suddenly the resolve dissolves. He grins, but it's wider than usual, and there's a flash of white teeth.

"Could have been a worse sin to be stuck with, I suppose," he says mischievously as he steps toward me. He loops an arm around my waist and I stagger forward, bracing my palms on his chest, my fingers curling around the fabric of his top.

He tilts his head to me, leaning in for another kiss.

His words repeat in my head.

The lust will drive us mad. We'll never get out.

I wrench myself away and bolt toward the door, ramming my shoulder against the metal. It gives way, screeching against the floor, and the spell is broken. I lean my back against the carved metal and, panting, catch Cupid's gaze.

"Well, that was interesting," he says, striding toward the exit. "Though as I said, it could have been worse. Sloth, wrath, greed . . ."

"Gluttony might not have been so bad," I say, my voice still a little croaky. "Maybe we'd have just got to eat a load of pies."

"You're thinking about pie at a time like this?" He chuckles. "Come on," he says, and we walk through the door together.

Almost instantly I feel the wind get knocked out of my lungs as something hits me, throwing me to the hard ground. I hear a woman's voice raised in a war cry, and the sudden clash of metal against metal.

Cupid is fighting an athletic-looking female.

Her hair is long and black, and whips ferociously around her face. She wears a light dress, which moves and flows with her quick, fluid movements. She's wielding what looks like a samurai sword, which Cupid deflects with an arrow he's brandishing with both hands, like a shield.

I glance around hurriedly. We're in a vast arena. There are seven doors around the circle, including the one Cupid and I just came through. In the center of the arena is a hatch in the floor.

My body tenses. Behind the sound of fighting, I hear something worse; something that makes the hairs on my arms stand on end. It's the weird squelching sound I heard earlier in the tunnel.

What is that?

The girl has pushed Cupid up against the wall, his arrow at their feet.

"Pandora," he says, raising his hands in defeat. "Hey, Pandora, it's me."

She stares at him for a moment with ferocious, catlike eyes. Then she furrows her eyebrows.

"Cupid?" she says as the noise sounds again—closer this time.

"Yes, we've come to get you out of here."

She looks at him suspiciously. "There's no way out of here."

The noise is loud now, coming from the hatch at the center of the arena. I stare as the doors begin to move; something is pushing against them. *There's something in there.*

Pandora finally notices me on the ground, and then turns her gaze coldly back to Cupid.

"Every hour," she says, "every hour for as long as I can remember, a sin comes out of that box, and I have to kill it or be killed myself. Next one is Gluttony."

She strides toward the hatch which is now rattling, and brandishes her sword.

"If you really are here to help me, then get ready to fight," she says. "I've been here a long time, and I'm tired."

My heart races as the hatch suddenly bursts open.

"Oh," she adds, "and don't get eaten."

54

Gluttony looks like a huge worm. Its bulbous, swollen flesh drips with a sticky fatlike substance that shudders as it lurches forward. With each movement, the squelching sound I heard earlier reverberates about the room. The worm gives off a pungent odor: the smell of old sweat, rotting garbage, and death.

Pandora stands before it, swishing her sword through the air. Her words repeat themselves over and over in my mind.

Don't get eaten.

Suddenly, Gluttony lifts its entire top half into the air, exposing an underside completely covered in sharp, needlelike teeth. It stays there a moment, reared back, its body pulsing, before suddenly turning and lurching in my direction.

"Lila!" shouts Cupid. "Get out of the way!"

I scramble to my feet and instinctively pull out an arrow. I thrust it upward as the monstrous creature strikes, the black weapon sinking into the rolls of fat on the side of its body. I try to pull away, but find half of my arm sucked into its flesh; it's moist and hot and feels like jelly. The stench is unbearable and the intense pressure against my arm makes me feel light-headed with pain.

With a heave, Cupid hauls me away from the beast, creating a suctioning noise as my arm is released from its flabby prison. We both fall to the floor and Pandora leaps before us—slashing at the monster with her sword and scattering lumps of flesh about the arena.

"Eeeww," says Cupid.

The monster, however, does not slow down. It advances again and again, forcing Pandora to move backward until she is fighting with her back to the far wall. Every time a part of it is cut off, its body pulses a new roll of slippery fat into place. It moves with an extraordinary speed, its teeth gnashing and gnawing.

"A little help," she calls between heavy breaths, "would be *nice*."

Cupid gets back onto his feet and grabs his black bow. He looks at the creature distastefully. "It's just so . . . gross."

The beast hits Pandora with the side of its body, throwing her across the floor.

"Okay, I'm coming," Cupid says. "As long as I don't have to touch it."

He fires a rain of arrows into its swollen body. It rears up again, away from Pandora, and for a moment it looks like it's sniffing the air. Then it turns toward Cupid and me.

"Fire into its mouth," Pandora shouts, springing back to her feet, "between its teeth. That's the only place where it's vulnerable."

Cupid does so—firing arrow after arrow as it bears down on him. As the arrows find their mark, one after the other, the monster begins to thrash about in the air. Then, suddenly, it falls to the floor, its flesh exploding on impact and spurting a sticky, gelatinous substance across the entire arena. Cupid gets the full brunt of it, the dripping fat coating his body. He turns around and looks at me, a pained expression on his face.

"So. Disgusting," he says as translucent goo drips down his face.

He strips off his leather jacket, wipes his face and hair with it, then casts it to the ground. My eyes linger on his muscular arms. He somehow manages to look hot even while covered in goo.

He catches me staring. "See something you like?"

Pandora walks forward and stands beside him, surveying him with dark eyes. "Of course she doesn't. You look disgusting and you smell like a trash can."

She smirks, the smile lighting up her otherwise serious face. I laugh, instantly liking her refreshing bluntness.

Cupid's eyes glint with amusement. "Pandora, this is Lila," he says. "She's my Match."

Pandora purses her lips. "I assume Venus is back then?"

"You assume correctly. We've come to ask for your help. You and all the others trapped in Sims."

A dark look passes across her face. "Sure, you want to break us out now that you need something." She wipes her sword against her sleeve. "Where have you been for the past . . . however many centuries?"

Cupid shrugs. "Hey, I've been banished. You can take that up with my brother when we get you out."

Her eyes flash. "Cal."

"You know Cal?" I ask.

"He was the one who put me here."

I'm not sure how to react. In the silence, Cupid looks between the two of us.

"Well, granted, this could cause some awkward reunions when we get out of here," he says, "but be that as it may, Cal has connected all the Sims, we have the Finis, and we're breaking out all *Her* prisoners. We're going after Venus." He pauses, then adds, "Will you help us?"

Her steely gaze passes over Cupid then me.

"Fine. But only because I'd be happy to watch her die."

"Excellent," he says. "Now . . . how exactly do we get out of here?"

She gives Cupid a look. "Well I *obviously* don't know. I've tried all the doors—they're all dead ends leading to the sin rooms. The hatch that spat out our friend Gluttony is home to all the monsters." She shakes her head. "You seriously came in here not knowing how to get out?"

Cupid shrugs. "Not really thinking that far ahead. However, when the Sims were merged they created links between themselves. We just need to find the link—something out of place."

Pandora raises an eyebrow. "Well, we better be quick—the next sin will arrive soon."

◊

The three of us search the vast arena for what feels like an age. I keep firing glances at the hatch in the floor. Pandora says the next monster will appear in the next five minutes.

I force myself to look away and my eyes settle on the carvings of the nearest door. A *W* is embossed into the metal along with the picture of a fierce lionlike creature. I walk to the next door. This one is marked *E* for Envy. An image of a snake curls its way around the letters.

I'm about to move on when something glinting on the ground catches my eye. I crouch down and brush away the rubble to expose a dirty mirror. There's an *M* engraved in the center.

"Cupid," I call. "The girl in the Venus's prison—Medusa. I saw a snake in her cell."

He looks up from the door he's examining and nods. "Yes, she always has snakes. They're kind of her trademark."

Pandora looks my way as Cupid comes over. "What is it?" she asks.

Cupid inspects the mirror on the ground, then the snakes on the door. He grins. "Medusa's Sim must be close. The way out of here will be through this door."

Pandora looks unconvinced. "If you're wrong, we'll be faced with Envy in there. We'll kill each other." She pauses. "Well . . . I'll kill you."

A hissing sound suddenly echoes from the hatch behind us, which has started to move once again.

"Shall we take our chances?" Cupid suggests.

She sighs then nods, resigned. Cupid opens the door and we hurry through, slamming it shut behind us just as something large and horrible—with the head of a lion and scaly skin—bursts into the arena. With a wave of relief I look around. We're back in the labyrinth, its high concrete walls leading to a junction just ahead. The faint sound of carnival music hums in the air. I hear Pandora's intake of breath beside me.

"It really was the exit."

"Good to be out of there?"

"You have no idea," she says, her eyes drinking in the black sky above us.

We walk to the junction, where, to the right, the labyrinth

walls have been replaced by a network of abandoned carts, tents, and fairground rides. Far in the distance are eerie red and white lights. Along the path to the left, the labyrinth darkens ominously. I shudder as I notice a substance on the wall that looks suspiciously like blood, dark and shiny.

"You see that building glinting in the distance? Through the carnival?" Cupid says, pointing right. "That's a house of mirrors. Medusa has the power to turn people to stone at will with just a glance. She won't be able to control her powers in here. One look in a mirror and she'll turn herself into stone." He looks meaningfully at Pandora. "She'll be there."

"I agree. You want me to retrieve her?"

Cupid nods. "Then tell her to find the next Sim and get to the center of the labyrinth—that's where the exit lays."

Pandora turns without another word and makes her way through the desolate carnival. I look up at Cupid. "What now?"

"While the others recruit the rest of the Myths, we're going to get to the center of the labyrinth and face the worst Myth of them all," he says. "We're going to face the Minotaur."

55

We walk down the left-hand path, away from the eerie sound of carnival music and into the darkness. The air is cold and silent, and as we progress, a thin layer of fog begins to conceal the landscape. I squint as I try to pick out the distorted shapes of derelict buildings. A large, domed cathedral looms beside us, and somewhere in the distance I hear the hollow chimes of a clock tower. An industrial scent lurks within the icy breeze: like smoke and blood and iron.

Something about the place seems both familiar and wrong, but I can't figure out what it is. I shiver and rub my arms to fight against the cold.

"How do you know the center of the maze is this way?" I ask.

"The blood."

I follow Cupid's gaze and notice rivulets of deep crimson running through the cobbled stones.

He smiles grimly. "Where the blood runs, the Minotaur will be."

I suppress a shudder as we follow a red stain along the side of an old, abandoned pub. Somewhere above us, a weird mechanical sound is jarring against the silence. Although I search, I can see nothing through the layer of thick mist.

"What *is* this place?"

Cupid looks at me. The mist clings to his face and gives him an almost ethereal look.

"I'd say we're in the Minotaur's version of Victorian London. Things are in the wrong place, and he's not quite remembered it right—but it fits. He spent some time in London before he was captured."

I nod as I recall Crystal's account in *The Records of the Finis*. He was in London when she retrieved the golden arrow from him.

"I thought she let him go," I say. "Crystal, I mean. Why did the Matchmaking Service capture him? That would have been after Venus's time."

Cupid's hands go to the arrows hung over his bare shoulder. "Did I mention the Minotaur might not be too pleased to see us?"

"*No*. You must have forgotten to mention that."

He gives a half smile then shrugs. "It was after my time at the Matchmaking Service. We need him on our side to take down Venus, but he's a killer, Lila. A lot of the Myths are. A lot of them were put in here because they were too dangerous to be a part of the outside world."

As we follow the trail of blood down a dark alleyway, I hear that mechanical sound again coming from somewhere ahead. Cupid apparently hears it, too, and stops still in his tracks.

"That and the fact that the Minotaur had a surveillance system to rival ours."

He suddenly pushes me against the wall, his tensed body pressed against mine. He places a large hand over my mouth then gestures that I look up. Slowly, I do so.

Above us, jutting out from the wall, is a small camera. I hear the mechanical sound again as it moves, its lens surveying the surroundings.

"He's watching," I whisper. "Does he know we're here?"

Cupid looks up at the camera again, and then down into my eyes. "Most certainly. Come on."

He pushes away from the wall and continues to walk onward. I fall into step beside him as we navigate the labyrinth of narrow, bloodstained streets. As we progress, the mechanical sounds follow us. There can be no doubt about it: he's watching us.

Soon we reach a vast iron bridge, on the other side of which rests a crumbling palace. Dull white, it has rows of blackened windows that peer out like hollowed eyes. On the roof, rippling in the icy breeze, is a red flag with the letter *M* in its center.

"Welcome to the Minotaur's Buckingham Palace," says Cupid.

"I'm guessing the queen isn't home."

The air around us smells metallic. I warily approach the railings of the bridge only to find myself awash in nausea; below, in place of the Thames, is a rushing river of blood. Cupid pulls me away and steadies me.

"I thought the Myths were in here to be tormented," I say. "Pandora was stuck fighting the sins, Medusa trapped in a house of mirrors—this is different." I stare at the palace ahead. "It's like he can control the simulation. Like he's made it how he wants it to be."

Cupid nods. "Everywhere the Minotaur went, humans would begin to build his labyrinth. He has more than just physical power—his mind is strong too. The Sim wouldn't have been able to fool him, which is why we are faced with a difficult task. And why he concerns me the most." He looks at me through the fog. "If he could have escaped at any time, why didn't he? What is he waiting for?"

Together we walk over the bridge. Slumped by the tall, iron gates to the palace are two dead soldiers in red uniforms and tall, black bearskin hats. Arrows jut from their chests. Cupid examines one of the bodies.

"Crystal's been here."

He pushes against the gates, and the rusty metal screeches against the cobbled ground of the courtyard. We walk purposefully toward the grand entrance, where the heavy door gives way to a musty entrance hall. A stone staircase covered in rich red carpet leads to a mezzanine, and around us the walls are covered with monitors. They each depict areas of the labyrinth we've just wandered through.

Some show the distorted London streets, but some show other areas. My eyes wander toward one, and I see Pandora and a dark-haired European girl in a blindfold making their way through the carnival.

Suddenly all the monitors flicker off. When they click back on, the image on each is identical; it's Cupid kissing me on the floor of the Lust room in Pandora's Sim. Heat rushes to my face as I see myself passionately kissing him back while he runs his hands through my hair.

"Yes, you've made your point," Cupid calls out to the grand room. "You've been watching us."

The moving image loops around once more, and I feel momentarily grateful that Cupid avoids commenting on our performance.

Then the screens flicker off and a tinny crackle comes from above.

"Please, come through to the great hall," a deep British voice says from a speaker in the corner of the space. "Head down the corridor on the right. We'd be delighted for you to join us."

I share a look with Cupid as we make our way down the decaying corridor.

"Am I a good kisser?" he asks. "It looks like I'm a good kisser—from the film, I mean."

So much for not commenting. "Now is not the time, Cupid."

He smirks as we enter a grandly decorated hall. It has been set up like a ballroom, with circular tables arranged so as to leave space for dancing in the center. Stone steps lead to an arched front entrance. On it, in unnerving contrast to the gold-plated candelabras and old-fashioned tapestries, is a modern exit sign in luminescent green.

The way out.

In the center of the hall, Crystal is locked in silent battle with a tall man, an arrow gripped in her hand. Her face is set with resolve and her eyes gleam furiously. The male is grinning wickedly. He's wearing a white shirt, rolled up at the sleeves with the top buttons undone; it exposes a sleeve of tattoos on one of his arms—an assortment of black lines and shapes that create their own labyrinth of ink. There's a vicious scar over his left eye.

The Minotaur.

"Cupid, Lila," he says, his voice silky smooth as he slides his gaze toward us. "Welcome."

Cupid walks forward. "Hope we're not interrupting anything."

The Minotaur shakes his head. "Not at all, not at all. Crystal and I are just resolving a bit of unfinished business."

He looks at us, a charming smile on his face.

"You asked out there what I was waiting for. It's true I can leave whenever I wish, but you see, I've grown to quite like it in here—it keeps me out of trouble. And you're right, I *have* been waiting. I've been waiting for Crystal."

56

"He wants me to come live with him in his little fantasy world," Crystal says, rolling her eyes. "But it's not happening." She turns back to the Minotaur. "Sorry, love, but there are things up there in the real world that require my immediate attention. Things that we could use your help addressing."

With that, she grabs my arm and leads me up the steps to stand by the exit.

"Now, are you two coming or what?"

Before either of the men can reply, Crystal pulls me through the doorway.

My eyes fly open.

I'm back in the claustrophobic cell, my knees touching the rotting wooden door. I feel dizzy. My skin is damp and Cal's hooded sweater is still wrapped around my body. There's a cold buzzing in my ear, and I hurriedly pull out the small microchip that sent me into the Sim.

I'd expected Venus's dungeons to be alive with the sounds of Myths waking up, but it is as silent as before. I look through the small barred window to find Cal sitting rigidly on a wooden stool, watching me.

Then the door to my right bursts open and Crystal walks out of her cell. Her hair is matted and her white suit is stained a murky brown.

Cupid's face appears at the other side of the barred window next. He opens my cell door, and when he holds his hand out for me, I take it, letting him pull me to my feet. As we stand almost nose to nose, his eyes blaze into mine. For a moment we are caught in each other's gaze, somewhere far away from the murky dungeon and impending danger.

"Have any of the Myths woken up yet?" Crystal asks, jolting me back to reality.

"Charlie and Selena are awake. The others are starting to show signs. It may take them a little longer. They've been in their Sims for years."

I feel a wave of relief that Charlie is okay.

"Listen," Cal says, looking worried. "Cupids have started to arrive from the other branches. Venus has called them all here for the big trial. There'll be more to fight than I had hoped."

Cupid frowns. "Have you managed to get any on our side?"

"A few but not many. They're too afraid to go against Venus." Nervousness flickers across his pale face. "Look, that's not the worst thing," he says. "The trial . . . *She* wanted to get to it right away. The Commander will be coming for you any minute now."

I feel my stomach plummet. I thought we'd have more time to prepare.

"The Myths aren't even awake yet," Cupid groans.

Crystal looks concerned too. "I thought we'd have more time. Listen, Cal, there's something I should tell you."

Suddenly Cal shushes us. We stand in silence a moment, and then I understand. All around us come the sounds of rustling and murmuring—quietly at first but then with increasing vigor. Down the dark corridors, doors creak open. There is laughter close by. I hear the breaking of rotting wood and footsteps against the muddy ground.

Cupid's face suddenly brightens.

"Looks like our army is arriving."

57

Shadowy figures emerge from their small cells on both sides. In a few moments' time the group of prisoners have surrounded us.

Charlie is near the front, and I catch her eye. She looks exhausted but grins when she sees me. I can't help but wonder what she would have experienced in her version of the Sim.

Selena stands beside her, looking irritable, and I notice Medusa among the group as well. She is no longer blindfolded—she must be able to control her power outside of the Sim—and I see that her eyes are an unnatural glassy blue that stands out against her tanned complexion. A black snake curls around her right arm.

Others in the crowd greet each other like old friends. A blond guy is chatting animatedly with a group of disheveled gladiators, and Pandora talks warily to a pair of wolfish teenagers. Leaning against the wall by the back, the Minotaur watches Crystal, a half smile playing about his lips.

Cupid looks around. "I guess you are all now aware of our . . . little predicament."

The Minotaur's gaze slides to Cupid. "Your mother is back in town and you're inviting us to the reunion," he drawls. "How kind. Do you have any plan beyond that?"

Cupid shoots Cal a sideways look. "Er, Brother?"

"The trial is due to start any minute now," Cal says. "We allow it to proceed as planned."

"Are you kidding me?" Crystal exclaims. "I'm not—"

Cal fires her a cold look. "Do you think I want to put you all in danger? It's the only way to get the Finis close enough to Venus. I need to get into the courtroom with it, and I can't if we've already gone into battle."

My stomach turns. Cupid frowns and I feel a shift in his mood. It seems he wasn't expecting this.

"So where exactly do we fit in to all this, then?" asks the Minotaur. "You know, I was perfectly happy where I was before." His dark eyes find Crystal in the odd group. "Well . . . almost."

"You're here to serve as a distraction," Cal says. "When Venus officially starts the trial, you'll break into the courtroom and the battle will start. When Venus's attention is on you, I'll fire the arrow."

"What about our weapons?" asks Pandora. There's a murmur of agreement among the others.

"I managed to recruit a couple of agents," Cal says. "When the four of us are up in the trial room, they'll bring down your weapons." He turns to Crystal. "You said you wanted to tell me something?"

Before she can respond, the sound of marching footsteps vibrates through the dungeon ceiling and makes the artificial lights jitter.

"Everyone back in their cells!" Cal says. "The matchmaking

agents are making their way to the courtroom. I need to get back upstairs to avoid suspicion."

He looks at Cupid and Crystal, then his silver eyes settle on me. There's a pained expression on his usually stern face. "Good luck," he says. Then turning on his heel, he heads off through the group of Myths.

"Brother?" Cupid calls, making Cal glance back. "When you fire the arrow . . . don't miss."

The two brothers share a look and Cal nods.

When Cal is gone, everyone stands in silence for a moment, as though contemplating the enormity of the battle ahead. Cupid finally steps forward.

"Better get back to the cells," he says. "Someone'll be down for us any minute."

A few groans resound before the beings skulk back to their tiny barred rooms. Charlie touches my arm as she passes by me.

"You okay?"

I nod. "Yeah. You? What happened in the Sim?"

"Oh, it was awful," she says lightly. "I was trapped in an eternal history lesson, and there weren't even any boys."

Something in her eyes tells me she's lying, but I humor her anyway.

"Sounds terrible."

She grins then makes her way to her cell, turning around for a last look at me before entering. "Be careful, Lila," she says, closing the door.

Minutes later the corridor is clear, leaving just Cupid and me. He moves in front of me, looking into my eyes with uncharacteristic seriousness.

"I'm sorry, Lila. I've put you in so much danger."

"Yes, you have."

"I should never have come here."

"No, you shouldn't have."

His face is so crestfallen that I reach out to touch his arm.

"But I'm glad you did. You were right before," I say. "I *had* given up on love. On everything, I think. But then you came here. You turned my life upside down. You've put me in danger, you've put my friends in danger, you've been selfish, and reckless, and *insanely* annoying—but whatever happens, I can't regret that you came. Because I think you helped me find that spark inside of me again. And . . . well . . . I kinda like you."

He reaches for my cheek and brushes it with his thumb. "I won't let Venus hurt you. I'd sooner impale myself with the final arrow than have anything happen to you."

I give him a half smile. "Well, let's not do anything too drastic . . ."

He smiles back, resting his forehead on mine. I feel the comforting tickle of his eyelashes against my skin. I wish we could stay this way forever. I wish we didn't have to risk our lives in a battle that he'd started.

"We'll be okay," he says. "My brother won't miss."

"I know."

Suddenly a screech of stone fills the corridor.

Cupid pulls his head away from mine. "It's time."

We look at one another for what seems like an eternity. Then I turn and head back to my cell.

"Lila."

Cupid grabs my arm just as I'm pushing the door open and spins me around. He loops his other arm around the back of my waist and pulls me into him.

"I could never regret coming here either. I know I should, but I don't. No matter what happens to me in there, I could never regret meeting you. You've changed everything."

"Cupid—"

Before I can finish he presses his lips to mine. I grab the back of his shirt, bunching the material in my fingers, and kiss him back until he pulls away. I look up at him, breathless, blood pounding in my ears. There are voices coming from down the corridor.

"Go back into the cell. Put the microchip back in your ear and act as though you've just come out of the Sim," he says. "It's what the agents will be expecting. They're programmed to stop at the time of a prisoner's trial."

I nod and open the door. "See you on the other side."

I throw myself back down on the seat and slip the chip back in my ear. Cupid looks at me one last time then closes the door and disappears out of view. My heart thumps hard against my rib cage as I hear the approaching sound of heavy boots.

A few moments later the sharp face of the Commander appears through the bars of my door. Six armed guards are at attention behind him. I feel a wave of nausea. I want to be brave but I can't steady the slight tremble in my legs.

"Wakey, wakey, rise and shine," says the Commander. "Venus and her army are waiting."

He smiles coldly.

"It's time for your trial."

58

The Commander pulls me out of my seat, his fingers curling tightly around my arm as he drags me into the dungeon corridor.

This is really happening. There is no turning back now.

Cupid and Crystal are also being dragged out of their cells, shouting insults and threats at their captors all the while.

Cupid catches my eye as four of the white-suited agents surround him. They seem to be taking no chances when it comes to risking his escape, and I watch in horror as they tear at his clothes and punch him in the stomach. I rip my arm away from the Commander's grip, wanting to rush to Cupid's aid, but I'm grabbed again and pulled roughly back.

Cupid doesn't react to the beating—he merely holds my gaze. Crystal just looks irritated. I watch as she shrugs off the male agent who is attempting to hold her still.

The Commander releases me and stands back from the group of us, watching the scene dispassionately. "Christian, handcuff the prisoners," he says once everyone has quieted down.

The agent I presume is Christian slips a thick black cable around my wrists. The material is ice cold and pinches my skin. As he moves over to do the same to Crystal and Cupid, the Commander gives a thin smile.

"Time to go, Venus is waiting."

The Commander strides down the damp corridor ahead of us, and I am pushed forward. I can hear the sounds of Cupid and Crystal being marched along behind me.

I glance through the bars of the dark cells as we walk by, catching glimpses of the Myths sitting inside. The Minotaur winks at me as we pass, a dangerous smile playing about his lips. I remember what Cupid said in the labyrinth.

The Minotaur is a killer.

We could use a killer around about now. But when I think of Pandora's reaction to Cal back in the Sim, and Cupid's revelation that the Matchmaking Service had put a lot of the Myths in there, I find myself wondering if they'll really come to our aid.

We are forced up the stone steps and into the indoor courtyard. As we pass the stone statue, I think of the real version of Venus: her corpse-like touch, her unblinking eyes, her impossible strength. With every part of my being I will Cupid and Cal's plan to work, but I can't help but doubt it. Are we really going to win against a goddess?

We're taken down a long, wide corridor that's new to me. The walls, floor, and ceiling are all checkered black and white. At the end is an archway through which I can hear the slow, rhythmic pounding of a large drum.

It's here that the Commander stops for a moment and turns to check that everyone is in position. Then he nods at the agents and steps through. I take a deep breath, mentally preparing myself.

Christian marches me through the arch as blood pounds in my ears. We enter a vast room that looks like a mixture between a temple and a courtroom. Ahead of us, stretching past a high podium all the way to the other side of the room, is a sea of white suits and glinting arrows: rows and rows of seated cupids. They all stare at us as Christian grabs my arm and pulls me forward.

As we pass the tall, wooden judge's bench, Venus's sickly sweet scent almost overpowers me. I glance up and see she's decorated the bench with bouquets of myrtles and roses. They look wilted and sad, like flowers at a funeral.

When we're marched onto a raised stone platform, I gasp despite myself. In the center are three black metal poles, a length of cable hanging from each. Around the outside are ten agents, each with a large drum that they bang rhythmically.

The stern Italian Arrow who kidnapped Crystal stands at the ready. His bow is much larger and more elaborate than the ones I've seen Cupid or Cal use, and in his quiver are three black arrows and one gold: the replica of the Finis.

As the agents force me, Cupid, and Crystal toward the poles, I realize that if Cal doesn't act soon, this is where we will be executed. Christian roughly pulls my bound hands above my head and attaches them to the cable hanging from the top of the pole. I let him, because it is part of the plan, but a wave of panic consumes me as soon as I am trapped in place. When I pull against the restraints, the bindings dig into my flesh. There is no escape.

"I don't like this," I hear Crystal hiss at Cupid as she is bound to the pole to my left. "I need to tell you—"

One of the agents slaps her across the face, silencing her.

"Crystal!" I say.

She looks up at me, her cheek an angry pink. Before she can

say anything else the same agent looks into my eyes. "Shut it."

Moments later Cupid is bound to the pole on my other side. Although his hands are bound above his head, too, he turns to give me a weak, worn-down smile. There are rips in his black cotton T-shirt and tired smudges below his eyes. I wish I could reach out to touch him.

"You okay, lovebug?"

I can hardly hear him over the pounding of the drums. I nod but I'm not; if I wasn't tied to this pole, my legs would be buckling. My mind reels over images of my life, my friends, my dad. He must be so worried.

I don't want to die.

Frantically, I search the crowd for Cal. Finally, I spot him standing at the end of the front row. His face is a mask again, his silver eyes cold.

Then suddenly the pounding of the drums stops, leaving the vast space in deathly silence.

Venus is standing behind the floral bench.

Her red hair is newly braided with white flowers and her glassy eyes look straight ahead. She is now wearing a revealing white strappy dress that is almost the same color as her pale skin.

Her gaze falls to Crystal and Cupid, then slides to me. I feel my skin crawl as her lips twist into a cruel smile.

"Well, shall we begin?"

59

The courtroom is completely silent.

Cal said that the Myths would arrive as soon as the trial started. Where are they?

I twist against my bindings to scan the vast room. Crystal's face has drained of color, but Cupid wears a defiant smile, his gaze never leaving his mother's face. She stares at him for a moment, her doll-like eyes unblinking, before looking past us to the rows of matchmaking agents sitting behind.

"We are here today to witness the trial of Cupid, my son; Crystal, the traitor; and Lila"—she slides her gaze back to me, her full red lips contorting into a grin—"*the Match.*"

As her childish voice echoes around the chamber, the cupids begin to stamp their feet against the ground—quietly at first, but then with increasing vigor. I feel a chill creep down my spine.

When the noise has faded, Venus picks up a white myrtle from the high desk in front of her. "Should they be found guilty," she says, violently plucking off the flower's petals, "they will be punished by *death*."

She opens her hand and the flower stem falls to the ground.

"Charles, read out the charges."

The redheaded PA scuttles forward and stands by her side. In his hand he clutches an electronic tablet. I notice a slight tremble in his hands.

"Cupid. Charged with breaking the company policy."

The Italian Arrow with the elaborate bow turns toward Cupid and points his weapon. He is clearly to be our executioner.

"Lila," says Charles, and my heart jumps into my throat as the executioner turns his bow toward me. "Charged with being *the Match*."

"Hardly her fault," says Cupid, "but rationality was never your strong suit, was it, Mother?"

Outrage flickers across Venus's face. "SOMEONE DEAL WITH THIS INSOLENCE. CAL?"

A red-tipped arrow sinks into Cupid's shoulder and he cries out. I twist against the post, the bindings pinching my skin, as his cries fill the air. Cal's expression is blank. A flicker of anger ignites in my heart, but I snuff it out. Venus has to think he's still on her side.

Venus sighs, as though in relief, and she turns to look at Charles. "Well? Carry on."

Charles coughs nervously as Cupid's cries turn to soft grunts. His face is pale and clammy, but the pain seems to have lessened. He is back to staring at Venus, a forced smile on his face.

"Crystal. Charged with conspiring against Venus and the Matchmaking Service."

I frown. Something about the wording of the charges stirs something inside of me. Before, in her office, Venus had said that Crystal was being put on trial for *gallivanting about with Cupid and his Match*. There was no mention of conspiring. Venus doesn't know we are conspiring to kill her. Does she?

I turn my head toward Crystal, whose face is panic stricken. She looks past me at Cupid, as though trying to tell him something. He stares straight ahead at his mother but he is no longer smiling.

Crystal's eyes focus on me. *The Finis,* she mouths, *it's not—*

Before Charles can finish reading the charges, and before Crystal can finish whatever she is trying to communicate, the doors to the room burst open. A red-tipped arrow flies straight past me and embeds itself in Charles's chest. He crumples to the ground screaming.

Venus's eyes flash with rage as a humorless laugh bubbles out of Cupid's mouth.

"What is it, Mother?" he says. "Surprised to see your old friends?"

The Myths are here. I spot Charlie among them, her bow still raised and pointed at Venus's PA. There are two agents on either side of her; the one who took us to the dungeons, and Curtis, who Cal must have talked around to our side. They raise their bows and shoot silver-and-pink arrows at Cupid and Crystal.

I feel a momentary flash of panic as I watch the arrows fly through the air, then relief as they hit the cables binding my two fellow captives. They burst free, stumbling forward onto the platform.

As soon as he's regained his balance, Cupid darts forward. He grabs the head of our executioner, and in a sudden movement, breaks his neck. The executioner's face looks momentarily surprised before he thuds to the ground.

The action jolts Venus's army out of their stupor and behind me I hear the sounds of chairs crashing to the ground and arrows slicing through the air. Screams and shouts echo around the courtroom. Cupid, crouching by the dead executioner, catches my gaze.

Then he swipes a black arrow from the quiver and runs toward me. Reaching for my wrists, he stabs the cable with the arrowhead. The cable bursts apart, and I fall into his arms. For a split moment I bask in the feeling of safety, before he grabs my shoulders and brings my gaze to his face.

"Lila," he says, his voice breathless, "come on."

Holding my wrist he pulls me forward and we race off the platform. On the way one of the drum-bearing agents hurls himself toward us, but Cupid knocks him out with a hard blow to the face.

We leap over his body and dart past Pandora. She's pointing a strange sort of gun at a female agent running toward her. A ball of energy bursts out of it, hitting her would-be attacker in the chest. The agent crumples to the floor, unconscious. Pandora grins.

"Sloth, sends them straight to sleep." Then she bounds off, smacking another agent across the jaw with her weapon.

Cupid's grip tightens around my wrist. "Come on."

He pulls me past Medusa and a stone statue of an agent, his face contorted in pain, and toward an upturned jury bench, throwing me down behind it just as an arrow shoots past my cheek. He cups my face in his hand.

"Are you okay?" he whispers, his voice raw with emotion.

"I think so. Are you? What do we do now?"

Peering over the upturned bench, I see a blur of color as the Myths fight the army of cupids. Arrows fly through the air, and bodies and blood cover the mosaicked floor. I gasp as an agent points a black arrow at Crystal's back. I'm about to shout to her but the Minotaur gets there first, picking up the archer and hurling him through the air. Then he turns and leaps on top of another agent, biting her neck until she crumples to the floor. He notices me looking and grins, red blood seeping from his mouth. I duck back out of sight, my stomach turning.

"I need to find my brother," says Cupid. He leans forward and lightly brushes my lips with his. "I'll be right back."

He starts to get up but I pull him back down. "Venus said that Crystal was on trial for conspiring against her," I say, my voice almost drowned out by the sounds of the battle. "What if she knows what we're doing?"

Cupid grabs my hand and squeezes. "Something's not right," he agrees. "That's why I need to go and help my brother. Just stay here—out of sight."

"Let me help."

He looks at me intensely for a moment.

"Please, Lila," he says. "Original cupid here. I can handle this."

I see the pleading behind his eyes and, reluctantly, I nod. He gives me a weak smile then darts back into the battle. I peer back over the top of the wooden bench as he goes, trying to find Cal. For a moment, I can't see him among the chaos, then I catch sight of him disappearing behind a group of gladiators.

He's making his way toward Venus, who, to my surprise, is still standing behind the flower-covered desk, a bored smile across her red lips.

Why isn't she doing anything? Why is she just standing there?

Dread fills me. Something isn't right.

I watch Cal as he reaches the edge of the stage. He pulls out the golden arrow from his quiver and raises it to his bow just as

Cupid reaches the other side of the platform. It looks like Cal is about to shoot when Venus's laugh suddenly booms about the courtroom, unnaturally amplified.

I throw my hands to my ears, and see Myths in the battle falling to their feet and doing the same.

In a disjointed movement she turns her head toward Cal. "Do you really think you could fool *me*?!"

Cal's face whitens but he holds the bow steadily.

"I'll admit, breaking my *pets* from the dungeons was a surprise, but did you really think I didn't *know* that you had the Finis?" An incredulous expression flashes across her face. "I mean, helloo, I *am* a goddess, you know?"

Cal stares at her, determination etched on his angular face. "Then you know that when I shoot you with it, you will die."

Venus giggles. "Oh, foolish boy. Even if you could hit me— don't you *know*? Don't you know *anything* about the Finis?"

Cal looks at her blankly and she shakes her head.

"Allow me to clear something up for you," she says, her voice sickly sweet. "The Finis was forged by my *tedious* husband— the blacksmith of the gods. It was a weapon forged in secrecy, intended to destroy my illegitimate offspring and me. But here's the catch: he didn't want *me* to be able to harness its power, and so its power cannot be wielded by gods, or Myths, or cupids; I couldn't destroy you with it any more than you could destroy me. It was created for the humans."

She looks at Cal, a twisted smile on her face. A flash of understanding flickers across his eyes. "It will only work if shot by a mortal."

She grins and gazes around the room, taking in the bodies scattered on the floor, and the Myths still crouched with their hands over their ears.

"But I believe we have one of those here, don't we?" Venus says.

I clench my fists. Adrenaline surges through my body.

I am the only one who can save us.

"Guards, seize Cal."

Cal frantically looks about the courtroom as agents swarm him. They grab his arms and the Finis clatters to the ground. He struggles but there are too many, and they drag him over to one of the black poles and bind him. One of the agents picks up the golden arrow and hands it to Venus. On the other side of the stage Cupid makes a move forward, but Venus glares at him and he stops in his tracks.

"Lila," Venus says, her voice ringing in my ears, "I speak to you now. As the only mortal in the room, I have a decision for you to make. You see, you have been a *very naughty little Match.* And not just for matching with my son Cupid, but for feeling something for my *other* son too."

My heart does a strange leap. What is she talking about? I don't feel for Cal—not in that way.

"Oh, I know all about that. I *am* the goddess of love after all. You can't hide it from me, even if you can hide it from yourself." She laughs. "But I digress. I can't kill Cal, but I *am* going to torture him. I'm going to torture him in every way imaginable. He will beg for death by the time I'm done with him—but I won't stop."

Cal begins to struggle against the pole, his eyes wide with panic. At the side of the stage Cupid's face drains of color.

"But *you* can make it stop, Lila," she says. "You just have to do one little thing for me: you need to make a decision. You need to choose a brother."

She holds out the Finis in her pale hands, and her eyes fix on mine as I stare with horror over the top of the upturned bench.

"To save Cal, you have to kill Cupid."

60

I duck back down behind the bench, pressing my back against the hard wood. My heart is racing and my skin cold.

To save Cal I have to kill Cupid.

"Come on, little Match, we haven't got all day."

There's silence. I don't move.

"Very well. We'll start with the Ardor."

There's a pause and a whooshing sound, and then the air is filled with Cal's contorted screams. My heart tightens.

I can't let them torture Cal.

But I can't shoot Cupid either.

My mind feels dizzy, unfocused. Cal's shrieks stall any train of thought and make my stomach turn. I peer over the top of the bench again. Venus still stands there, her hands extended; offering the golden arrow to me.

I can shoot Venus. I'm the only person in the room who can.

I can almost sense Cupid willing me to hide, to find a way out. But I have to do something. I take a deep breath, then resolutely stand up.

"That's right, little Match," says Venus, "come to me."

I begin to walk toward the stage. Apart from Cal's screams, the courtroom is silent. I can feel everyone's eyes on me.

"Lila," Cupid says as I pass, "don't do anything stupid. Do what you have to do."

I look away. I'm not going to kill him. I won't.

I'll kill her.

"That's close enough," Venus barks.

She's stopped me next to Cal. He is writhing in pain, his wrists bleeding where the cables are too tight.

"Cal," I whisper.

He looks up at me, his silver eyes weary and unfocused. A drop of blood has congealed at the corner of his mouth. I want to reach out and help him. I've never felt so powerless.

"Lila, I—"

Suddenly another red-tipped arrow plunges into his stomach. He screams and I rip my gaze to where the Commander stands beside Venus, a quiver of arrows slung over his shoulder. Venus nods at him and he takes another and shoots it into Cal's thigh. Cal cries out again, his body convulsing.

"Stop it!" I shriek. "Stop it! Leave him alone."

Venus smiles. "You can stop it," she says. "Kill Cupid." She turns to a tall female agent standing nearby whose scowling face is bloody from the battle. "Carla, take the Finis to our naughty little Match and give her your bow," Venus orders. "Guards—bring Cupid onto the stage."

As Carla walks forward with the golden arrow, five agents surround Cupid. His eyes flash dangerously. He throws one of them to the floor and punches another across the jaw before grabbing an arrow from Carla's quiver and impaling the next agent with

it. The remaining two agents take a tentative step back as Cupid
raises his arms.

"Don't touch me," he snarls. "I'm coming on my own."

He walks past them to stand a few feet away from me. I take
the bow and arrow from Carla, the bloody-faced agent, my hands
shaking. The Finis is cool between my fingers.

"And before you get any ideas," says Venus, "I am quicker and
more powerful than you could ever imagine." She looks at me
coldly. "If you shoot the Finis at me, I will catch it, and then I
will kill you. But first, I will kill your family, and I will kill your
friends." Her voice is suddenly laced with venom. "And as for
your two lover boys, I will have them tortured until they forget
who they are."

Her lips twist into a contorted smile. I think back to how fast
she was when we were brought into her office and I know she's
right; I'll never manage it.

"Kill him, little Match. Kill him and I'll let you, and Cal, and
your family go free."

I look at Cupid. He's planted his feet firmly, proudly, on the
stage, acting as though his clothing isn't ripped from where the
agents grabbed at him in the dungeons. He holds my gaze. His
ocean-like eyes are calm.

Behind me comes another whoosh of an arrow and Cal's ele-
vated shrieks. I flinch. Cupid nods.

"It's okay, Lila. Do it."

My eyes sting. "I can't," I say, the bow and arrow trembling in
my hands.

He takes a step closer. "I've lived a long life," he says. "You have
to do it. You have to save my brother. *You have to save yourself.*"

I feel a tear slip down my cheek and rub it away, not wanting to give Venus and all of the other cupids the satisfaction of seeing me cry. Behind me, Cal's screaming doesn't stop as more Ardors plunge into his flesh.

"You can stop this," Cupid says, taking another step closer. "Look at my brother. *Look at him.*"

Hesitantly, I turn to Cal. His face is red from screaming. The drop of blood on his mouth has turned into rivulets. My heart clenches. I force myself to look away, back at Cupid.

"Only you can stop this. She'll kill you if you don't." He shakes his head, his eyes filled with urgency. "And I can't live with that."

"I don't want you to die," I say, my voice quivering.

He smiles at me and takes another step forward until we're an arm's length apart.

"That's *quite* close enough," chimes Venus.

Cupid stops in his tracks and I find my eyes drinking in every part of him. I want to reach out. I want him to hold me and tell me everything will be okay.

"It's okay, Lila," he says. "I'm ready. After all these years of being alone, after all these years of thinking love was futile, I finally met you." He smiles. "I finally found my Match."

His eyes shine with raw emotion. Behind me I hear Cal wheezing, coughing up blood.

"*Don't!*" he cries out through rasping breaths. "*Don't . . . kill . . . my . . . brother.*"

I look at Cupid and raise the bow. He nods reassuringly, his eyes unmoving from mine. My arm shakes. Tears spill down my cheeks—I can't help it.

"*Do it,*" urges Cupid as Cal is struck again.

I take a deep breath.

"No regrets," he says, smiling weakly.

I steady my grip on the bow. "No regrets," I whisper.

I lock my gaze with Cupid's.

His eyes widen with panic; he can see what I'm about to do. He shakes his head but it's too late. With a sudden movement I turn my bow toward Venus. I release the golden arrow.

"*No!*" Cupid shrieks.

I see it in slow motion: the blur of gold, the whoosh of air, and Cupid suddenly hurling himself into the path of the Finis. His eyes, still locked on mine, show only surprise. He opens his mouth as though he wants to say something.

And the final arrow sinks into his heart.

There's a deafening thumping sound as his body hits the ground. I scream and the bow clatters out of my hands.

"He's dead!" booms Venus, clapping her hands together with glee. "She did it! She really did it! She killed Cupid! CUPID IS DEAD!"

The courtroom is suddenly filled with noise but I can't hear any of it. I fall forward toward his body, crumpling to my knees beside him. I throw my head onto his unmoving chest.

"Cupid!" I scream. "You can't be dead, you can't be. I didn't mean to, I . . ."

Dimly, I feel a hand on my shoulder. Crystal has grabbed me and is pulling me around to look at her. I push her away and she slaps me across the face. I look up, startled.

Venus is laughing. Behind us the battle between the Myths and the army has restarted, but I don't care about any of that. I pull away from Crystal and grab Cupid's hand. Whatever she wants, it doesn't matter. Nothing matters anymore.

Cupid is dead. Cal is still shrieking with gut-wrenching grief behind me.

"He's gone. I killed him."

Crystal leans close to me and whispers, "He's not dead."

"I killed him. I . . ." My gaze snaps to her face. "What?"

"He's alive. But we haven't much time," she whispers urgently. "I lied before, back at Cupid's flat. I didn't bring the replica of the Finis to the Matchmaking Service—I brought the real thing. I wanted to tell Cal, before, in the dungeons, but we were interrupted. I knew Venus would find out—she's too smart."

"So Cal had the replica?" I look down at Cupid's body. His hand twitches in mine. *He's not dead.*

"Stay dead, Cupid," Crystal snarls through gritted teeth.

"Aye-aye, Captain," he croaks, his eyes still closed.

He squeezes my hand, and for a brief moment I see a small half smile on his face before he wipes it of expression once more. Relief floods me.

I look at Crystal, then at the dead body of the executioner just a few feet away. I catch a glint of gold in his quiver.

"That means the real Finis is . . ."

She nods, holding my gaze. "You're the only one who can do it, you're the only one who can kill her."

Venus is no longer surrounded by agents; they are all fighting. The goddess catches my eye and grins. Moving with exaggerated slowness, she gets down from the stand and makes her way toward me. My eyes dart to the body of the executioner. *Can I make it in time?*

I scramble toward it, my heart racing in my chest.

"You killed my son," says Venus, her voice quiet and childlike. "You thought it would save you . . . but I lied."

I reach the cold body as she looms closer. *I can see it. I can see the Finis.*

She advances toward me, her movements quick. Her sickly scent washes over me and makes me gag, but I clutch the quiver to my chest.

"You must be punished, little Match."

Her hand bears down on my throat and my feet are wrenched from the ground. Dots begin to form in front of my eyes. I can't breathe. One hand scrabbles against her slippery skin while the other feels for my weapon.

"Let her go!" Cal screams from behind me. "You promised you'd let her go. Let her go."

Venus's lips convulse into a cruel smile. She laughs as darkness begins to creep over me. *This can't be it. This can't be the last thing I ever see.* My fingers fumble over the ends of arrows. I pluck out an arrow, praying it's the right one. I struggle to stay conscious as I feel my final breath escape from my lungs.

With the last ounce of strength I have left, I plunge the arrow into her heart.

Then darkness.

61

When I open my eyes again, a white ceiling floats above me and my ears are filled with a steady beeping sound. I swallow. My throat feels like it's on fire and as I try to raise my head, it feels like it's going to explode.

I squeeze my eyes shut again, staying still so as not to cause more pain.

What is going on?

Then it all comes flooding back to me. I remember thinking that Cupid was dead. I remember Venus's face inches from mine. And I remember plunging an arrow into her heart.

Was it the Finis?

Suddenly, I scramble into a sitting position, ignoring the pain. My eyes widen. I look around. I'm in a hospital ward. On the chair next to me is my dad, his eyes closed and his chest softly rising and falling. As though sensing me regaining consciousness his eyes flicker open.

"Lila," he says in relief. "I was so worried."

I look around through bleary eyes. Two figures stand outside the door, facing away from me.

"Dad?" I say through sudden tears.

He reaches forward and pulls me into a hug. On hearing our voices, the two figures in the doorway turn around. I am overcome with relief.

Cupid and Cal. They're okay.

As they enter the room, I notice Cal's subtle limp and the bruising around his wrists where the cables bound him to the metal pole.

My dad pulls away. "I should get a doctor, tell them you're awake. You gave us quite a scare. It's a good job these two young gentlemen were around to get you to a hospital. They've watched over you this entire time."

He looks approvingly at Cupid.

"Some scaffolding fell on you, Lila," my dad says, seeing my confusion. "The doctors said you might forget. I'll go and get someone now."

Behind him, Cupid grins as my dad kisses me on the forehead and hurries out of the room. He throws himself into the chair beside me while Cal lingers by the door.

"Got to be careful of that scaffolding, lovebug," Cupid says, winking. He's wearing gray sweatpants and a white cotton T-shirt. He looks tired, but unharmed.

"What"—I cough, my voice a croak—"what happened?"

I rub my throat. Cupid picks up a jug on the side table, pours a glass of water, then hands it to me. I take a gulp. It cools the fire in my throat and I attempt to speak again.

"What happened?" I ask again "Is *She* dead?!"

Cupid nods, his face suddenly serious. "She nearly killed you.

You managed to grab the Finis as she was choking you, and you stabbed her in the heart with it. After that she kind of imploded." He shakes his head. "You were thrown back with the force of it, and you knocked your head pretty hard against the wall. For a moment we thought . . . we thought—"

"We thought we had lost you," Cal finishes quietly from the doorway.

I'm surprised by the intensity of his tone. But when I glance over at him, he looks away.

"What about Venus's army?" I ask.

Cupid shrugs, taking a glass of water for himself.

"They were never truly behind her. Once you destroyed her, a few of the more extreme agents tried to fight us —the Commander, members of the Arrows—but they were outnumbered. It wasn't hard to beat them. There's a lot of work to be done to bring order back to the Matchmaking Service. They'll be holding an election at the end of the week to nominate a new leader." Cupid looks at Cal, still standing rigidly in the doorway. "It won't surprise you that my rule-abiding brother over there is one of the forerunners for president."

Cal gives Cupid a reproachful look, but I notice that he seems to be fighting a smile.

"What about the others? Charlie, Crystal?"

Cupid nods. "All fine."

I sigh with relief and take another sip of water. "Sorry I shot you."

Cupid's face cracks into a grin and he waves a dismissive hand. "Nah, don't worry about it," he says. "It was quite invigorating. I saw my whole life flash before my eyes, and I'm quite an interesting guy. It was like watching a movie."

"Plus you *did* jump out in front of me."

He laughs. "True. Anyway, we have something to show you."

I look at him curiously and he gestures to the hospital corridor, where my dad is talking to a doctor. I can tell from his expression he is telling one of his dorky dad jokes. She laughs and his face lights up.

Is he flirting?!

I look at Cupid, suddenly catching on. "Are they . . . *are they matched*?"

I can barely hope to believe it. He's been so down and alone for so long. Cupid nods. I look at the two brothers, and then back at my dad. He gives me a small wave from outside.

"I thought everyone only had one match," I protest. "You said so yourself. That once a person's match was gone, they would be alone forever."

Cupid shakes his head. "Not anymore," he says. "Now that Venus is gone, the rules are gone too." He grins. "We're free," he says, squeezing my hand. "You freed us all. And not only does that mean that your dad is free to love again, it also means that us cupids are too."

His eyes twinkle mischievously. "I hope that doesn't ruin the whole *forbidden love* thing I've got working for me."

"So you're sticking around then?" I ask, serious.

He nods. "I'm staying right here with you. You saved me. You saved all of us. Everything is different now."

I sense Cal watching me from the doorway, something new, something almost like passion, burning in his silver eyes. The corner of his lip quirks up into a half smile.

"Everything is different now," he agrees softly.

ACKNOWLEDGMENTS

I want to thank everyone who read *Cupid's Match* in its early draft stages. As any writer knows, the world of publishing is incredibly competitive, and when I wrote and posted the first draft of *Cupid's Match* on Wattpad, it was purely for fun; I'd all but given up on the idea of ever seeing one of my books on a shelf. The support, kindness, jokes, endless arguments about which couples to ship, marriage proposals to Cal, urges to update quicker, and general feedback from fellow Wattpadders kept me writing, smiling, and helped me to believe again in a dream that had started to fade. I don't think I would have written this book without you.

I'd like to thank all the wonderful people at Wattpad HQ for seeing the potential in *Cupid's Match*—even in its messy early stages. There have been so many people from Wattpad involved in this cupid journey, but the people I've worked with most closely on the book have been my talent manager, Monica Pacheco, and Ashleigh Gardner and Deanna McFadden from the publishing team. Thank you for answering all my questions, and for believing in me and the cupids.

I'd like to extend a huge thank you to my editor, Andrea Robinson, who completely got my sense of humor, understood what I was trying to do with *Cupid's Match*, and really helped me to take the story to the next level. It was a joy working with you. Thank you also to my copy editor, Rebecca Mills. I'm not a very detail orientated person and there were a lot of strange things (not including the general cupid-y strangeness!) going on within the pages of *Cupid's Match* that I would not have picked up on without your help! And thank you to the *Cupid's Match* cover designer, Greg Tabor, for his work and vision.

Lastly, thank you to my family and friends. A huge thank you to my partner, Jamie. He has been my rock throughout writing—always happy to chat cupids with me late into the night, make me laugh when I need to be distracted, calm me down when I'm stressed, dance goofily with me in the kitchen when I'm excited, and bring me endless tubs of ice cream! Thank you also to my dad and sister for never doubting that one day I would write something that people would want to read. And thank you to my mom, Debbie, for being my (and Cal's!) biggest cheerleader. When she found out I was writing on Wattpad, she signed up for an account and read *Cupid's Match* as it was being written. I will always appreciate the unwavering support.

About the Author

Lauren Palphreyman's supernatural teen romance series, Cupid's Match, has accumulated over fifty million reads online and has been developed into a pilot for CW Seed. As part of Wattpad's social influencer program, Wattpad Stars, she has written for brand campaigns, spoken on a panel at London Wattcon, and completed a chapter for Writer's Digest's *The Writer's Guide to Wattpad*. When she's not writing, drinking coffee, or plotting for cupid world domination, you can find her posting first drafts of her fantasy romances on Wattpad @LEPalphreyman or sharing her current reads on Instagram @LaurenPalphreyman. She lives and writes in London, England.

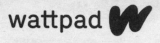

Buy the stories already loved
by millions on Wattpad

Collect the #OriginalSix Wattpad Books.
Now available everywhere books are sold.